NIBBLETS

tasty verbal tidbits
hand-picked
ripe for nibbling

marc frederic

marc frederic

NIBBLETS

tasty verbal tidbits

hand-picked

ripe for nibbling

Published in the United States of America

© 2024 Marc Frederic

All rights reserved

No part of this publication may be reproduced, stored in a retrieval system or transmitted in any form or by any means, electronic, mechanical, photocopying, recording or otherwise without written permission of the publisher or Marc Frederic, except by reviewers who may quote brief passages in a review.

Permission requests
should be emailed to:
mrwhimsy@worldofwhimsy.com

ISBN: 9798335308878

FIRST U.S. EDITION
August 2024

Other Books by
marc frederic (aka *Mr. Whimsy*)

Benny's Pets
Jenny's Pets
Denny's Pets
Timbo's Tale of transition
Beyond the Great Oak Doors
AbsurDitties/Trivia Chucklettes
Son of Trivia Chucklettes
Jasmine and the Snowman
Looking at Life Through My Left Ear
Who Put the "P" in Pneumonia?
Touch of Class

(out of print)
Rainbows, Butterflies and Other Assorted Edibles
Life Inside an Apostrophe
Strawberry Glue
The Enticing Wonder of Gaylan

Enjoy the following website for book descriptions and information on Marc Frederic and World of Whimsy Productions   www.worldofwhimsy.com

contact Marc Frederic at
mrwhimsy@worldofwhimsy.com

marc frederic

ACKNOWLEDGMENTS

To Betsi Newbury, bouquets of appreciation
for your editing and formatting skills.
Equally notable, your enthusiasm and sense of humor
have stimulated a professional relationship
to bloom in delightful friendship.
What productive joy!

Thanks also
to you two handfuls of people who have not only acted as sounding
boards but proactively contributed specific thoughts about my
writing. You've been a valuable part of this book's creation.

And lastly,
to life, which keeps things coming my way
that amaze, bedazzle, and offer so much to contemplate.

WELCOME FROM MARC

Welcome to *NIBBLETS*, a smorgasbord of verbal hors d'oeuvres, desserts, and meaty delights in the form of short stories, essays, vignettes, and verse.

Its content is presented in three sections. All are creative in nature and meant to be thought-provoking, enjoyable, or both.

The first is a GENERAL section that includes spontaneous pieces based on figments of my imagination, reflections of my experience, and expressions of deep inner knowledge seemly garnered from other realms.

The second section is a selection of pieces I have written for CREATIVE WRITING ASSIGNMENTS. The assignments we received varied. We were to write 250 – 300 words incorporating a given subject matter, five specified words, or a predetermined *prompt* (phrase).

In addition, there is a small grouping some readers may consider to be "extraordinary". It is labeled STRONG TASTE.

Feel free to graze, lick, nibble, or even devour whatever you find desirable.

> Bon appetit,
> marc frederic

marc frederic

"HELLO from Nibs ...
this book you're holding"

"My formal name is Nibblets, but you can call me 'Nibs'.
I welcome you to read me. Just open up my ribs.
I've tasty verbal tidbits—stories, vignettes, verse,
fictitious/true to show to you that range from fun to terse.
They might address a subject that somewhat overwhelms
or use imagination to visit other realms.
This invitation is from me. I hope you can't resist,
but there's another reason that I, my friend, exist—
marc frederic, my dear inner elf, requested me to share myself
and that I'm truly pleased to do. My flavors vary through & through.
I'll leave you with fine memories too. But tasting me is up to you."

"Bon appetit",
Nibs

NIBS INTRO TO
GENERAL PIECES

Figments of imagination.
Actual experience too.
Some deep-seated inner knowledge.
Hoping they appeal to you.

Nibs

THE IDEA

Smoothly entering his left ear, the idea
slowly sails tipsily through the man's mind.
It hesitates on the opposite side before exiting;
then, clears his right ear.
Outside the man's head,
the idea grows dramatically,
shimmering pink and blue,
filling space just long enough
for the man to walk right into it
and disappear.
Where has the man gone?
How do we explain such an occurrence?
Some may simply say he's lost in thought.
But is he lost? Or actually living
what someone else
could only dream?

5/11/2007

DREAM TIME

On a sunny Sunday morning at 7:25, I had just awakened. I turned to see my black and white tuxedo cat stretched out next to me, still asleep.

Softly, I asked him if it's true cats sleep 70 percent of the time. Without budging, he meowed a simple yes.

I was pleased to hear that because I'm regularly gone from the house for five, six, or seven hours at a time and felt guilty about leaving him alone.

I asked him if he dreams. He was quiet. Surprised I could remember it, I told him a vivid dream I'd just had about paddling around in a plastic canoe.

He didn't respond immediately. But after he absorbed the scene, he sat up and expounded on dreaming. Amazed by what he shared, I rose from bed and came to my computer to type up the experience.

I'm stopping temporarily. Louie, my cat, has just come in to tell me he's hungry. After his dissertation, I can believe it. I'm going to feed him.

***

I'm back. Took time to text my daughter that I'm up and well. Which is part of my daily routine. And darn it, I've forgotten most of what Louie had to say. Maybe I wasn't quite awake when he shared his expertise. I certainly remember the feeling he imparted and the ambiance he described. It was magnificent. Similar to, but better than, some of the places I go when I sleep.

Louie just returned to my home office to thank me for breakfast. I petted him and gave him a quick "You're welcome", then asked if he would reiterate what he had told me about cat dreams. I suppose he was too awake for that conversation. He simply said, "They're great." And sauntered away.

6/4/2023

90 MINUTES

90 minutes it will take
to service my fine car.
That is plenty long to wait,
unless you're in a bar,
or have a book that's good to read,
or people whom you like, indeed,
to join you in conversation
or to give you inspiration.
But now, I have not one of these
things that help time pass with ease.
Yet, I am sure that I can find
some vivid thoughts within my mind,
which either make the time go fast,
or thrill me deeply as it's passed—
first, I'll soar through golden clouds;
then, quote my verse to cheering crowds;
next, sample many tastes galore;
then, hold the woman I adore.
You see, I'm lucky as can be.
Imagination sets me free.
And so, it is my great delight
not to simply wait, but write.

6/17/2024

BRICKLE

Brickle. I have no idea what it is. But the word has a familiarity to it, making it readily acceptable. I think it would easily get along just about anywhere.

Domestically, it could grow in a well-trimmed garden as a sturdy border for a stone path. Wild brickle would enhance a desert scape.

Then again, it could be a currency of sorts—a pocket full of golden coins, round, rectangular, oval, even star-shaped, displaying marvelous characters on either side and tiny notches that define their perimeters.

What would brickle smell like? Careful…it's too similar to prickle to put close to your nose.

Brickle. Such a lovely-sounding word—tasty, fun, concise, like a short dessert in a colored, frilly glass.

It could be feed for cattle or a pattern in the sky. It could easily be a flavor, a sound, or even a confusion like a kerfuffle.

Brickle can be whatever I wish, because I don't know what it is. I just like the word.

Now, I'm going to take a chance—to risk ruining the frivolous nature I've bestowed upon the word. I'm going to google it. I sincerely hope the internet also is baffled and brickle remains free to be whatever anyone wishes.

On second, thought, I'm not going to look it up. I did that once with Zamboanga and was sorely disappointed.

But, if your curiosity is more powerful than your imagination, you go right ahead.

1/13/2021

General Pieces NIBBLETS

bored

It's not easy to be bored. Something exciting is always moving, vibrating, flowing through my mind, my body, the universe. I'm typically observing or moving along with it, even when I first awaken.

But one Saturday morning I wake up bored. I'm not tired. Not rested. I'm listless. I lie here, as if encased in cotton. Totally insensitive. I don't care. I don't care that I don't care.

I lie here.

What finally snaps me out of stagnation is realizing boredom is a rarity for me. It seems to be an absence of emotion. But like joy, sadness, peace, fear, pride or love, boredom can be felt. I'll capture the feeling. On paper.

The difficulty in depicting *boredom* is not becoming too excited about doing so. Keeping that in mind, I mentally sink back into the cotton. I blindly stare at the ceiling, fog over and fool myself into believing I'm not going to write anything about boredom. Ever. I lie to myself. My self knows it, but chooses to believe.

I lie a little longer. Right here. For a few minutes. And a few more. Feeling hardly anything.

Eventually, I return to the state in which I awoke.

Then, beforemybraincanadjusttothefact, I shift into "creation mode" to write:

I'm so bored I can't even pick up a pen. I feel like a single curd in a carton of plain cottage cheese on a back-office lunch table with only one secretary sitting at it. And she has nothing to read.

1/18/2003
(first published in LOOKING AT Life through My Life Ear)

DOOR DASH DUMMY

Two days ago, an elderly fella shared some philosophy with me: "Skin is a good thing to have covering your body. When it goes missing, that hurts.

"Never race a descending garage door. Especially in your eighties. You tend to leave skin in the game.

"I'd rather be stupid and lucky than smart and unlucky. I'm lucky my stupidity didn't lead to breaking anything. Smart and lucky's now the goal.

"That pretty much sums up the situation," he said. Then added, "I was a dope."

I followed his glance at his scabbing knees. He turned over his hands to show me his palms. It hurt to look at them.

Realizing his advice was good, I thought back to when I was in my sixties. A friend, then in his eighties, had broken his leg racing a garage door. He was a sensible man who held a responsible position as minister of a church. I visited him in the hospital. Didn't mention the cause of the break. Too embarrassing. We both understood his act had been foolish. Strangely, it made him more human. I didn't lose respect for him. It seemed like something anyone might try.

Remembering my friend, I stare more closely at the man who has just given me his advice. He, like the minister, is a good man. He's a thinker as well as a doer. He knew the minister and what happened to him. Because of that, I thought he was wise enough not to subject himself to such risk. Why in the world did he do it? What makes him tick? Who is he?

He's the man in my mirror.

7/15/2023

SOMEHOW IN HER MISTY MIND

Her home's assisted living. She doesn't know or care.
She says she lives "where birds and butters fly."
Her moods are mostly mellow as she wanders through her mind,
so no one ever sees her pout or cry.

Her daughters come to visit with hope they're recognized.
It doesn't happen often, but at times they are surprised.
It's then that hugs are traded. And with glimmer in her eye
she asks her constant question, "When's your daddy coming by?"

Somewhere in her memory is a man who cooks for her,
who loves his country music and his friends.
Somehow in her misty mind, his image doesn't blur.
Her patient waiting for him never ends.

They smile and say he's busy while holding back a tear.
They've never ever told her. He's been gone now 'bout a year.
To think he's running errands or cooking keeps her bright.
Tomorrow she may greet him; she'll dream of him tonight.

Her girls just keep on caring, 'cause that's what women do.
Most give and share and say a prayer to help their loved ones through.
For them that's what it's all about. With aid from up above
they'll pad her soul protectively and stock her heart with love.

1/28/2019

marc frederic   General Pieces

REMINDER

Rolling, writhing, cresting, diving, the sea unfurls its persistent power.
Completely devoid of boats and birds from horizon to shore, its muscles ripple with frothy whitecaps.

A large double-pane bay window separates me from the wind, the sound, the smell of saltwater, and any telltale spray flung four stories in height. That sturdy glass prohibits almost everything from entering, except the view. And what a view it is!

I have turned a plush living room chair toward the window and now sit passively absorbing an awesome display—bright sunlight illuminates distant folding, sliding waves, transforming them into advancing ranks of a sizzling metallic army. Racing the wind, they continue to roll closer, endlessly pressing onward, becoming animalistic, clawing their way to shore.

The scene is unusual, magnificent; somehow made surreal by the glass window that separates me from it, robbing me of its raw intensity; allowing me to feel only the sun which bathes me in its warmth.

One further incompatible feature completes this powerful vision—a lone female sunbather clad in black bikini rests comfortably on a small patch of pink-toweled beach. Occasionally, she turns over, seemingly oblivious to the white frothy foam lurking, reaching and retreating, stretching and recoiling, within yards of her calm-weather, tropical dreams.

As I finish compiling my observations, the young lady rises from her towel, saunters slowly toward the large expanse of glowing foam, and seems to stroll on top of, rather than into it. Am I dreaming? Is this an apparition? The foam finally envelopes her thighs. She then calmly returns to her towel.

It cannot be as cold outside as it appears. I rise to visit our balcony and find the wind, although extremely strong, is relatively warm. It's a strange, but fitting, reminder not all things are as they seem, and by making assumptions, we, at times, miss the full experience.

I must vividly imagine I am visiting from another planet and not take anything for granted.

5/29/2011

I'VE MELDED WITH THE UNIVERSE

I have no cares. I'm joyous, whole.
I'm here. I'm everywhere—
a carefree, weightless, happy soul
that now needs no repair.
I've melded with the universe
in tune, in harmony.
And all there is
is all I am
as far as I would be.

Rediscovering the above words, the conclusion of a poem I wrote long ago, affords me such peace and freedom, I have decided to put them to memory.

They allow me to bring the future into the present—to enjoy my essence and how it connects with, becomes immersed in the universal energy many people refer to as God.

Rereading them, I realize that in this world we unconsciously contend with gravity. A toddler learning to walk, an elder trying not to fall. How wonderful to imagine being weightless! Free to float and glide at will. To live the stuff of dreams.

Many wonders we take for granted—our breathing and heartbeat. Our ability to see, hear, feel, taste and smell. When mentioned, those gifts are easily recognized. But what of other senses that allow us to appreciate, love, telepathically send and receive messages, shift dimensions.

Being open and receptive frees us to meld with marvels, dance with destiny, eliminate time and space by utterly embracing both. The result is endless joy.

How can I feel this way when we are constantly being reminded of Earth's problems? My answer is, "Sauerkraut, chocolate cake, country music, aquavit, a clap of thunder, a baby's gurgle, the glint of a sword, a cat's fur, a skunk's squirt, a flower's fragrance, vivid reality, pastel dreams, physical exercise, warm cuddling."

oh, oh, OH! As my delightful companion, Betty, would say, "Life is TOO-LICIOUS!"

12/14/2023

FILLING OUT FORMS

Central Celestial Station is a flurry of activity. Not having traveled recently makes me feel like a tiny lost soul.

"What must I do to enter *that* world in human form?" I ask The Conductor, pointing at the third planet from the sun in a small eight-planet solar system approximately two light weeks to the South.

"Simply take one of those forms and fill it out," He replies.

A long line of newly-conceived embryos waits in the direction of his nod. They aren't yet fully formed. I hop into the one at the head of the line to fill it out… take off…and here I am…growing at the end of a flexible cord in warm, dark, thumping wetness… just like millions of other Earthlings waiting to be born.

8/25/2002

General Pieces   marc frederic

ROSEBUSH

You reached right out and grabbed me.
And now won't let me go.
You seem to like my sport shirt.
How much is hard to know.
You felt me lean in deeply
to attach a brand-new hose—
a simple, nonaggressive act
most people would suppose.
You, rosebush, are quite thorny.
You could be called reactive;
or maybe you're just horny
and find that I'm attractive.
Your grip is fast. I can't stand up.
Your prickly thorns do hurt.
I'm tiring and now must act.
I'll have to doff my shirt…
I'm almost free. Let go of me.
I am no kind of stud.
I'll soon retrieve my clippers though
to nip you in the bud!

5/25/2024

BUSH CAVE

"Why sure, Sam," I cheerfully answer my black Labrador retriever when she asks if the sun-drenched afternoon is good for walking. With that, she shows me a neighborhood venue I never knew existed.

I'm intrigued by the bush cave inhabited by a pack of tame six and seven-year-old boys counting snails they've stuffed into a washed-out mayonnaise jar. The boys have lost the knees of their jeans, but don't seem to notice. They do notice me. I'm blocking their light.

I'm invited in. I kneel, my hands on the ground, my head inside, but my shoulders won't fit through the entrance. Sam alternates running around the bush and nosing under and over me in a futile attempt to join us.

The cave smells of dust and honeysuckle. Like the boys, it has lost something…its echo. An echoless cave can be very cozy—a nice place to talk about snails. I learn the indefinite plans the boys have for the snails, and listen intently while John Paul explains how he acquired his interest and expertise in the hunt…

"My pet chameleon, the circus-bought one with the string around his neck and the safety pin to keep him on my shirt, escaped from his shoebox one day. Since then, I've taken to following snail trails.

"It's exciting!" he beams. "They go everywhere! 'Long the sidewalk, 'cross the grass, over rocks, up walls, even sideways on windows and hard things like that. I'm the second-best snail tracker on our block. The only one better is Howard Smythe. And he's three weeks older than me. These guys," John Paul proudly points, "are my assistant trackers and bearers."

I congratulate the boys on their successful hunt and promise to keep my eyes peeled for snail spoor. The boys then interrogate me about my snail-hunting skills.

General Pieces   marc frederic

I let it be known, as a lad, I studied snails and came to understand their habits. That the prehistoric snails I tracked were similar to the species of today. "But," with wrinkled brow, I add, "there is one question that still bothers me: *Do escargot inside your tummy chew on your innards, like snails outside chew on leaves? Or is it just the garlic?*" The boys laugh, not really knowing why.

Winking goodbye, I back out and dust off. Sam whines and prances in anticipation of continuing our walk. Her excitement is infectious. We're off to enjoy whatever other delights she discovers at the end of her poke-into-everything nose.

1974

SUMMER CAMP

"What would you like, Hunk?"

"Some more gravity please."

"You've already had three bowls!"

"But, Mom, it's only five weeks till I go to summer camp on Uranus. And remember last year how my cord broke and they couldn't get me down for so long? Besides, I'm trying out for The Boulders this year."

"Oh, Hunk. I thought we decided that you are too young for that. Wait till your cover grows tougher. The rock storms will shred you at your age. You were so good at avalanche dodging last year. You're agile and still young enough to jump them."

"But, Mom, indoor sports are a drag. And they're lowering the ceiling this year. I'd have to have all new equipment—graphite helmet, neck brace with firmer springs; and even my dust mask wouldn't fit. That'd be expensive. Besides, it's boring."

"You know, Hunk, maybe your father's right. Maybe you shouldn't go to Uranus this year. Perhaps a different planet is better.

"So, if you don't get rounded off in a hurry and make do with what we think is best for you, maybe we'll just buy you a one-way ticket to a place where the sun knifes through the atmosphere and stings your eyes. Where the planet's pull is so great that it takes a whole gort to move ten fleebs. Where the sand eventually ends and you sink in thin goo. And where creatures make sounds to communicate. Certainly, you could eat yourself sick on gravity there, but I don't think you'd have much other fun!"

"Aw, Mom. Come on."

"There really is such a place, you know. Ask your astrophysics teacher. It's called Earth."

1975

General Pieces   marc frederic

COFFEE MATING

The little female coffee bean
enticed her mate one day…
The smile she flashed was sensual
as they began to play.
She batted her long, dark lashes;
she wiggled her tan behind;
sighed, "I can be made in an instant, but
prefer the regular grind!"

1979

SOMETHING REALLY IMPORTANT

It wasn't early. It wasn't late. It was 10:45 on Friday evening at my house, in my bed, with my wife. My eyelids were very heavy. The T.V. became a radio…then a T.V.…then a radio…then a dream.

The phone suddenly made the dream a T.V. again. It then did a perfect imitation of a close friend from whom I hadn't heard in a long time. I was instantly and pleasantly awake.

"I've got a problem," my friend said, "and I knew if I heard your voice, everything would be all right."

My friend hadn't heard my voice for over a year, and maybe two to three years prior to that, but last night he listened to it off and on for over an hour.

My friend is self-dependent, deep, and solid. He's also a bit of a magician. Whenever we talk, time disappears; not just minutes or hours, but years.

It was either last night or twenty-five years ago the two of us left our college campus on the spur of the moment and drove two hours to the mountains. It was dark when we left. Come to think of it, it was about 10:45 p.m. On the way to the mountains, we stopped only once, to eat tacos and hamburgers. We both ate five of each. They were little and cheap. We were hungry.

The night was coal black when we arrived at the deserted Boy Scout Camp. My friend knew the place. We "pitched" our sleeping bags. We didn't have a tent to pitch. We hadn't made tent plans. We hadn't made any elaborate plans. This was a spur-of-the-moment, informal trip. It's a good thing we had eaten a lot of hamburgers and tacos. Food was no exception to our lack of planning.

We pitched our bags on a soft bed of needles under a huge pine. The darkness hid the size of the tree. We didn't know it was huge until the next morning. The only thing we knew was huge that night was the thick, black, pine-scented air which hovered over us. We liked it. It served as the tent for which we didn't make plans.

General Pieces   marc frederic

Waking outdoors in the sun-drenched pine forest was exhilarating. With the warmth came a melange of soft aromas and flickering sounds. We hiked several miles along a nearby stream until it suddenly tumbled into a deep pool ringed by gigantic polar bear rocks. Many trout lived in the pool. My friend and I shed our clothes and dove in. The water was clear and cold.

The trout must have thought it strange we didn't like being buried in liquid ice. After we scrambled out, they continued to enjoy it. They transformed themselves from silver darts into motionless underlines. They became the kind of lines you find under written words, which people want to emphasize. All the trout were now underlines. Emphasis hung in that pool as if something really important had been said there.

We had no towels. We slowly baked dry on the smooth polar bear rocks. I'd never before been nude in the wilderness. As I put my clothes back on, I could feel myself being separated from our surroundings. It was like trying to eat an ice cream bar through its wrapper. We hiked back. And drove back. We had thoroughly enjoyed a special experience.

Last night, this man, my friend, the one with whom I had swum through trout, hurt. He called because his daughter's one-month marriage had just failed. It started to fail two weeks ago but had completely run out of steam night before last.

Yes, my friend hurt. Not for himself, but his daughter. You see, my friend is a very warm man with a very warm family. His very warm and steady wife was with him when he called. But last night he needed someone outside his family—someone with distant perspective, a loving sounding board.

I know his wife but not his children. I've read about them for years in Christmas letters. They're all good people.

Their problems will pass.

2/1/1986

TAKE A BITE

You may like me for what I've written
but you're reading yesterday's me.
And you always will be unless
you're right there when
I put down my pen and excitedly
offer the paper.
Even then, at that very moment,
I'm feeling the fulfillment of having
expressed myself.
You are still feeling what I have just been.
No, you can't read this moment's me,
you have to taste it.
And I don't mean "fresh-out-of-the-oven"
or "just-picked."
Take a bite while I'm still growing!
Of course, I won't be writing about it
when that happens. I'll be feeling your
teeth & tongue and lips & gums (and maybe
even your throat, if you swallow.)
I'll be bitten.
But it won't hurt. I'll love it.
Devour me.

8/22/1987

MY BED MISSES YOU

On occasion, my bed talks to me about you. It was a virgin before you and I met. And, like any recently satisfied virgin, it's enthralled with its first sexual experience. I agree with my bed it is fortunate to have held you in its palm. However, it gets a little carried away.

It has loved you in the afternoon but longs for you at night. At times, I wake up wondering why I'm not sleepy, what's going on, who's trying to get into my head by dreaming about me?

Then, slowly, I realize that it's not someone else at all. It's my bed that's remembering and sighing in its sleep. I talk to it gently, soothing its loneliness, assuring it you will return. It appreciates my assuaging manner and usually drifts off in a mellow state.

But at other times it will let me neither read nor sleep; not until I've bounced around on it in a very sexy manner or stretched languidly, emitting tiny sounds. This action undoubtedly reminds it of you and provides temporary satisfaction.

I can't fool my bed for long. It misses you and knows the real thing when it holds it. The next time it has an attack I'll call.

Thank God you're a certified parabedic.

3/7/1988

NIBBLETS   General Pieces

A MATTER OF TIMING

I'm in deep trouble.

It's February 14th, Valentine's Day.

Not feeling well, I came home early to take a nap before my dinner date at 7 p.m.

Waking, I see it's already dark outside. I look down through the glass wall of my oceanside condo. In constant rhythm, the surf is pounding the beach. But the pounding in my head has stopped. I feel good.

Now time is the threatening factor. Reservations for two await at Babouche, a romantic Moroccan restaurant where people sit or recline on colorful floor pillows to dine.

I intended to have live orchids delivered to my lady's home before I picked her up but, feeling ill, had forgotten to order them. Now, after calling three florists, I find it's too late even to have them dropped off at the restaurant.

The situation is serious. I understand how this lady likes to be treated, and know well the effect she has on me. From the day we met, I've stood taller. She brings words to the tip of my pen. Though approaching middle age, she's taken magnificent care of herself. And she cares about others. She's a lady who makes plans and executes them with ease. Besides, she loves my white hair.

I want our relationship to be mutually satisfying and permanent. I want what's right for her.
Following my instinct and expecting the best, I call the restaurant to explore further options. And find the perfect solution.

Will it work? Can I pull it off? Will she be surprised?
On the phone, I quickly devise and coordinate the special delivery, then jot down the following poem:

General Pieces   marc frederic

>The mellow moon on an indigo sea;
>the balmy breeze, as it sighs to me.
>Life holds many a marvelous thing,
>but the greatest of these is Gaylan King.
>
>I think how heavenly angels are.
>I'm awed by a brilliant shooting star.
>I'm thrilled by sounds the songbirds sing.
>Yet, these all pale near Gaylan King.
>
>The unicorn is quite a beast;
>the cornucopia, a feast.
>The velvet pansies highlight Spring.
>Yet none can rival Gaylan King.
>
>The pink of a flamingo's wing.
>The dreams that gods to lovers bring.
>The world presented on a string.
>No, none compares with Gaylan King.
>
>What can I give this wonder girl
>to set her head and heart awhirl?
>Although she likes most everything,
>I keep on thoughts soliciting…

I title the poem *FOR THE LADY* and, to end it, add two lines that will hopefully be the highlight of the evening.

Everything depends on timing—first, getting to the restaurant by seven o'clock, which will be difficult due to my oversleeping, and the holiday traffic. Then there's the other matter.

As we drive through the dark, I glance at Gaylan's gorgeous profile illuminated by neon signs of businesses we're passing, then concentrate on the traffic ahead. I mentally cross my fingers and give thanks in advance to the powers that be for getting us to our destination on time.

During our drive, Gaylan expresses how much she looks forward to the food and belly-dancing entertainment. Then, sensing my concern, she alleviates it somewhat by telling me, "I'm sure everything will work out beautifully, darling. But, if we aren't able to dine there, just know I'm glad you're feeling better and we're together."

Suddenly, it's cozy in the car. I'm in seventh heaven, enveloped in gentle warmth.

"Thanks, sweetheart," I reply. "It'll work out." Now timing is even more important.

Miss Gaylan King and I arrive at the restaurant and are shown to the room in which we'll dine. After ordering drinks, I excuse myself to quickly confirm my plan with Kashim, the maître d' with whom I had spoken earlier.

Returning to Gaylan's classic beauty lounging amid red and gold silk pillows, I barely notice the ceiling and walls draped in brocade fabric. The Arabian music caressing our ears blends wonderfully with exotic aromas of cinnamon, cardamom, roasted lamb, and chicken.

Our beverages arrive and the waiter bathes our hands in warm rose water poured from a large, brass urn. We feel thoroughly pampered.

Half lying on the pillows while facing Gaylan and away from the room full of diners, I smile at her, pull a paper from my sport coat, and lovingly recite my poem.

Just prior to delivering the last two lines, I slowly raise my arm high, tilt my palm backward, and quote, *"Aha, now this may curl her toes—"*

Recognizing my signal, Kashim, complete in turban and genie shoes, scurries across the dining room floor with his hand extended. In it is a long-stemmed chocolate rose covered with red foil. He lays the rose in my open palm. His timing is perfect.

Without turning to acknowledge his presence, I swoop the rose, seemingly out of thin air, in a downward arc, presenting it to Gaylan as *"Babouche's famous chocolate rose."*

General Pieces   marc frederic

I'm told the room broke out in applause. I couldn't hear them. My ears were filled with heart-pounding love.
1989

SWITZER LEARNING CENTER

Just what is Switzer Center?
And why do we purport
that this organization
deserves your strong support?

Come with me now, as we explore a world you may find strange—
a world that Switzer Center can often rearrange.
What if two plus two were five, instead of good old four,
and You were asked to total up a snail, a pail, and door?
And what you thought you knew as blue, others all called red?
And letters became numbers or strange symbols as you read?
And everyone misunderstood most everything you said!
And you reached out, but no one tried to get inside your head!
And you got MAD, or maybe sad, and wished that you were dead!
And any shred of hope you had just shriveled into dread.

But now, somebody comes along with patience, love and care,
who understands and takes the time to teach you how to share
your thoughts and feelings, hopes and dreams, and all for which
you yearn
by working with and teaching you a different way to learn!
And, Life becomes a pleasure! In fact, it's downright great!
Yes, you've become a part of it. You can communicate!
Your disability's not *cured;* you've *learned* to fill the gap.
No longer are you hostage to your hidden handicap.
You now can grow and fly. You're free! New worlds you now can
enter!
Miraculous? It's what takes place in Switzer Learning Center.
But, friend, this couldn't happen were it not for folks like you.
So, Thank You for supporting us in any way you do.

April 1995

With this poem, I was privileged to raise over $1 million for the Center

General Pieces   marc frederic

HANGERVILLE

Sliding down the back side of the afternoon, my eyes come to rest on a yellow woven plastic basket full of hangers.

The bottom hangers are nearly dead. Having hung long ago, they now smother in a wire, wood, and velvet-padded tangle.

A neck or elbow occasionally pokes through the open spaces in the sides of the container, as if protruding out the window of a crowded school bus.

Silent, still chaos reigns in Hangerville.

Here these vagrant, scarecrowish derelicts wait. Starved for affection and purpose, they twist a skinny, static orgy in their plastic yellow grave.

Whatever happened to the orderly manners of hangers on a rack, suitably dressed, performing their duty, taking pride in their closets?

Rise above it, hangers! All is not lost. I'm buying a colorful new wardrobe for your Spring reincarnation.

1977

THE SEA

The water beckons.
How clear the sea…
She takes me to her breast.
I swim and skim her surface
on a smooth, refreshing quest.
She gladly shares her secrets—her grasses, fish, and rays.
I glide ahead, exploring with a flying wonder gaze.
I'm welcome and protected, yet also quite in awe.
Such power's unexpected; so gentle, yet so raw.
I'm buoyed like an eagle as currents it does soar,
but know the sea is fickle. I've courted her before.
The lady can change quickly; this sea of many moods.
In minutes she'll turn murky, as solemnly she broods.
Yet, she can be hypnotic in feathering, rhythmic ways
or even quite exotic with curls deserving praise.
And now one foggy winter day I've come to find her ailing --
quite calm she is and mostly gray, with scumminess prevailing.
Yes, she is reddish/brown, I'd say, for thirty yards from shore.
She smells quite putrid, like decay, and beckons me no more.
The sewer drains run through her veins. They've emptied in her smile.
While some complain, most folks just feign an innocence that's vile;
for even though you're not the one who's causing the pollution,
we all who live beneath the sun are charged with the solution.
So please, my friend, do give a care 'bout what goes down the drain.
And if you should become aware of oil and sludge -- Complain!
We must do all we can, you see, in treating waste above her
to bring our sweet sea back to me and all of us who love her.

2/1996

General Pieces marc frederic

SCUBA DIVING IN COZUMEL

Today I'm SCUBA diving for the first time in my Life.
Will Gaylan be a widow or continue as my wife?
Well, if a fellow's got to go, this way is sort of nice;
a bit anticlimactic though, 'cause I'm IN paradise!

11/5/96

THIS TIME AROUND

This time around my appendages are thicker. I have only four of them. I receive visual stimuli through two orbs in the upper extremity of my casing. It's a casing which contains systems for automatically moving gaseous, solid, and liquid sustenance to its various parts while at the same time eliminating waste. It's quite different from my last shell and those before it. I especially like how the sensitive organ between my lower appendages responds to friction.

This casing or "body," as it's referred to by my current species, can experience just seven senses. Most always it limits itself to five. They can be pleasant or horrid. Much depends on the environment to which they are exposed. The five most frequently used senses are dimensionally tangential, thus, often quite distracting. But then, that's part of the challenge.

Of my various life forms to date, it's the ethereal existence, which I've enjoyed the most. So simple, so pure—the ability to be everywhere at once in a world in which time does not exist. There are no physical distractions, nor parts to be maintained.

But gaining perspective and growing oneness over the millennia is the goal— understanding axioms of different worlds and how they do or do not merge is fascinating. Here, for instance, time and space are deemed to be an integral part of existence. They lack importance for this "human" species only when it dreams. Otherwise, both seem to act as constraints in the form of constant measurement.

I vibrate in tune with most others of my kind, yet physically remain an individual. I am unable to participate in the "community" movement found in this planet's flocks of birds and schools of fish.

I use only two small openings in my entire body to hear, have no innate connection with magnetic north, cannot change my shape to flow around or through physical impediments, nor can I vaporize at will.

General Pieces   marc frederic

But with patience I am gaining perspective and possibly a whisper of wisdom. I'm warmly amazed to realize unconditional love is a constant that flows throughout and transcends the many worlds I've had the pleasure of exploring. Yes, even in the galaxy of !@*(0)^ the Pygrods comprehended that.

How thrilling the process is! What joy—first experiencing; then, when I'm ripe, transitioning onward with such ease from one world to the next! It's exciting. Exhilarating! How best to describe it? Normally I'd say, "Melding with the IS." But from my present form and smiling mind, I might emit explanations such as *"Consciously tasting life wherever I choose to be born"* or *"Dancing with discovery through a vast bouquet of dreams."*

2000

CONFUSION IN PARADISE

Here I sit at 4 a.m. wanting to produce something... needing to feel productive.

Two things render me sleepless. The upper half of my left arm is working its way through the dire itch of a week-old sunburn. And, my wife banged hard around the kitchen before coming to bed tonight. I was three-quarters of the way into Dreamland when I sensed tension...

"Are you upset about something, Sweetheart?" I asked. Fire fumed intensely within her. As she opened her beautiful mouth to answer my inquiry, imaginary flames shot out, singeing the unsuspecting bed sheets, startling me into an upright position.

Throughout the heated discussion that followed, she could not let go of the feeling I had made light of her serious comments during the dinner we earlier shared with another couple. She rode that feeling as if it were a bucking bronco, continuing to spur it long after she received the third apology for my unintentional behavior. She hung on to that idea as if she couldn't let go. By then I was feeding the idea crisp apples and sugar lumps, but a spurred idea has a tough time settling down for good.

Never go to sleep on an argument is advice we've always lived by. I suppose that's why my wife is upstairs while I'm still awake, sitting in the living room of a condo we have rented on a small, lush island in the Caribbean. My lone companion, the sunburn, was conceived at Lake Arrowhead, California. Neither it nor I are quite sure what we are doing awake in the middle of the night.

Two things are certain—my peeling is ruining a dark tan and, more importantly, my concern about my wife's and my relationship has put a cramp in our vacation. There is also a third factor—two vacations too close together. I don't feel I should be here. I thoroughly enjoyed the longed-for rest at Arrowhead a week ago. And the three days

General Pieces	marc frederic

here have been splendid. I am now rejuvenated and ready to go back to work, but still have five days of vacation remaining ahead of a heavy work schedule when we return home.

In addition, we have two months of pre-planned, jam-packed weekends that seem to have grown like party mushrooms on our social calendar. I feel compelled to begin working through these things now. More vacation I don't need. The timing is all off.

Somewhere out of sight, the sun is stirring. A lizard just scrambled into the middle of our terra cotta living room floor. I didn't know they got up this early. I hope it's a lizard and not a scorpion. I cannot see as well through my glasses as I can through my contact lenses.

All's okay. It just scurried farther. It is a lizard.

Bird chirps punctuate the dawn. My arm has stopped itching. The islands in the distance curiously poke their heads past the palm trees, peeking in to see if I'm going upstairs to snuggle next to my wife, to bestow soft shoulder kisses of love and respect. They will not be disappointed.

Partially awakened by my tenderness, she places her cheek close to mine. "Thank you, Honey," she whispers, "We must be kind to one another."

Little do we realize her thyroid gland output has for the first time fallen through the floor; that her lovely mind and body are in a state of heavy turmoil. We simply blame it on the mosquitoes.

6/4/2000

THE VIEW

AAAARGH! Jagged shards of SOUND ADRENALINE!

Ripping the silence, a radio loudly comes to life. Without even a head fake it pierces my dream! Then, like a hungry ghost preparing breakfast, it bangs metallically through my mental fog, yanking me into a strange new day.

I hadn't set an alarm. I hadn't flicked a switch or turned a knob. Though I don't know this radio personally, it evidently has slept next to me throughout the night and is now venting at will.

It takes me a short eternity to determine how, but I'm finally able to grope the radio's ghost back into the silence of its grave.

Sunlight presses hard on the back of rough, dark curtains mothering the window. I can feel its heat searching the room. Just where am I? I need to back up my mind. I'll reverse slowly into my dream…park for a while…then return to the room in a smooth state of being.

But as I start to back into it, I find that my firm, colorful dream has barred the door and taken a powder. Poof! It is now nothing more than a dried bubble—a vanishing act of which Houdini would have been proud. And here I am…alone in a vaguely familiar, slightly muggy room with the corpse of a radio buried on the nightstand next to me.

The radio! Of course! A live radio might help. Radio CPR! Now just how did I manage to turn it off after it scared the wits out of my dream? This is a strange contraption—smooth, flesh-like surface; pliable, with just two controls. It has no cord and, seemingly, no place to insert a battery. It's like a loaf of bread made out of skin. With sliding…

The window! I'll open the curtains and see where I am. Part them and…My God! Water! Falling water, blue-bright warm! I can touch

General Pieces   marc frederic

it! There's no glass in the window! But no noise either. The water's very clear. Within it, swim miniature mermaids dodging the slow descent of gently blooming tropical flowers. Somehow the mermaids maintain a calm, playful demeanor as well as their positions amidst this cascading water garden. I can't see through the liquid to anything else. Is it actually water? Where is it falling to? How high up am I?

A door! This room must have a door…but, no…there is no door in sight. The room is, in fact, curved. There are no straight edges to it. Hey, there's no symmetry to it either. What is this place?

There's air to breathe…it's comfortable…

The radio! How did I get it to work before? Hmm. Actually, I didn't get it to work. It came on by itself. I just turned it off. Let's see…Weird. It's like holding a live football…the pigskin…with a tiny headless, legless, tailless pig still in it.

What had it sounded like when it came on? It wasn't talk. I wasn't music. It was some kind of computer language—a cross between metal gadget jargon and electronic notes. That's it, they were individual tones which seemed to stagger out of the radio like a drunken string of clear, jewel-colored candy.

Yes, I remember…the string then became a long, ribbon-like procession of candy cane question marks…red wax lips…M&M's chasing one another in single file, leading a trail of lemon drop tears…black licorice stars in creamy moonlight…a few nutty frowns and caramel doubts...and the hard, chewy memories of fruit-flavored jujubees.

They floated toward me in a squirming rush, jumbling and banging hard against invisible tin which turned out to be a wall of badges worn by the candy police. Then, I seem to remember a crystallized marzipan dimple twisting electronically into a pointed smile. At triple speed it slithered its way into my ear, permeating my dream, causing it to run in place so fast that I burst into another dimension! A truly rude awakening!

NIBBLETS   General Pieces

But…this radio has no speaker! No holes of any sort! How did the sound candy fly OUT? What IS this? Where AM I?

"Hello? HELLO? Is anyone there?
Can anyone hear me? Does anyone care?"

The walls weirdly wiggle, now shimmering bright. It's sort of a giggle. It starts to feel right. It's coming together; I'm feeling sublime. I now wonder whether it's due to the rhyme—a semblance of order; structured, yet free. The walls, now transparent, allow me to see a world which I'm used to. I'm now right on track. The view's so familiar. Indeed, I am back!

At times when this happens my mind takes the brunt…I peer through my eyeballs out back 'stead of front.

11/17/2001

RADIO WAVE

It's been said that Jack's facial complexion could be mistaken for the surface of Earth's moon.

And we all realize plans made for trajectory through space occasionally contain errors.

Therefore, it's understandable why a minuscule spaceship is firing its retrorockets in an attempt to slow its decent just prior to landing near a crater below Jack's right cheekbone.

As the heat from the rocket stings his face, Jack reflexively swats the life right out of that space ship. To him, it's an unrecognized, inconsequential event. To those tiny citizens waiting back at their home planet, following this intergalactic exploratory project from afar, Jack's slap contains the makings of a national tragedy.

Their hopes now ride a bleak, static-blitzed radio wave, an emotional tsunami, surging back at them, hissing its way through space, altering destiny across the cosmos.

11/25/2001

MASSAGE

Your warm touch pours forth from a cornucopia of whisper-like dreams, blond notes of music, jungle fruit aromas, gracefully erasing the blackboard of my mind. Smoothly, you bestow the gift of total relaxation.

Your "good-for-prone-dozing" massage table becomes a magic carpet on which I glide, through warm showers of sparkling gold and ruby stars.

Now, diving into the soft, pink cave of a blossoming rose, I drift deeper through darker shades until I'm surrounded by the future... I'm in my bed at home, having failed to make my next appointment with you before I left.

With calendar tucked gently in my mind, I float backward through the fourth dimension into the present, temporarily landing my flying carpet on your massage table beneath your hands. How readily I can travel time as well as distance in reverse.

Your miraculous fingers, forearms, elbows, and palms continue to melt my legs and back, releasing me to fly onward. A beautiful flight it is—a magnificent, five-dimensional swoooooooooooosh into worlds so worth the visit. I lick ice blue cream cones which, in response, produce soul-bathing rhapsodies... I play hide-and-seek 'midst vast, mellow folds of a tropical sky, as the close-of-day sun slowly sinks into bed, pulling bright coverlets over its head.

Then, having turned over some time ago, I feel your gentle touch do a slow-motion hop from my temples to my shoulders...to my forearms...to my knees...to my feet, which you temporarily hold, letting me know it's time to ground myself.

"Thank you, Margo."

General Pieces   marc frederic

Thank you for all you do. Much more than a kneader of living meat, you apply your talents to my soul…encouraging it to stretch and grow, fly and flow…to evaporate in ethereal bliss, while my body, leaving itself in your loving care, enjoys a dose of relaxing repair.

It's only when you reunite my body and soul, I realize a tiny miracle has occurred.

Your business card should read either *Heavenly Mechanic* or *"Hands On" Angel*.

1/22/2002

WHIZZING MY WAY THROUGH KOREA

Through the eye-level window above the urinal, I gaze out at a grass-covered extinct volcano. It is approximately three hundred yards away and maybe five hundred feet tall. It wears a pathway and stairs which are being climbed and descended by throngs of people imitating ants. Framed by brilliant blue air, the crater mothers a flock of stores nestled at its feet. More ants…shopping ants…mill the stores seeking souvenirs, while a herd of colored buses waits patiently for the hunt to be completed. Visually pleased and physically relieved, I'm off to join the hunt!

* * *

I stand, gazing down through the open window, watching my friend and his young son and daughter explore an isolated rock formation three hundred feet below me at the edge of the East Sea. Clear, cold water hugs the South Korean coast, lounging its way through and around the rock garden to lap the passive sand. Meanwhile, the other, rockless part of the beach lazily yawns, stretches for miles and, in the crystal-clear distance, turns a slow corner, completely ignoring the children's faint shouts of glee. Zipping up and stepping outside to a nearby rail, I look down, raise my arm, and move it side to side, creating the only wave in the entire scene.

* * *

Like the many meals we've enjoyed lately, this one was unusual, mind-broadening, and delicious. The fermented grain, milky-sweet, beer-like beverage with which I've washed it down has "filled up all the cracks" so to speak, and is now begging to be eliminated. I wander outside to find the men's room adjacent to the rural restaurant in which we've dined.

As I stand before a urinal, I realize that I am not actually in a "room," but rather an "L-shaped" structure with a roof on it. I've entered the structure by walking around the short side of the "L." Three urinals line its long side. Just behind me is a wall which belongs to another building, but the building doesn't extend far

General Pieces   marc frederic

enough to block the view (in or out). Some scant foliage is the only thing separating me from a country road along which cars are intermittently trundling. I feel as if I've stepped through a culture barrier into another world. I don't wish to be rude by keeping my back to it; but figure it would be ruder to do otherwise.

* * *

The urinals in one of the men's rooms at the Pusan Airport are all currently in use, so I enter a stall. Everything is extremely clean and modern. There is even a pastoral mountain scene affixed to the inside of the door…beauty to contemplate had I been seated. As I empty my bladder, I notice a button on the toilet tank. The toilet flushes automatically, so I decide to push the button to see what will happen. By doing so I am immediately serenaded by bird songs.

April 2002

PAINTING AT LAKE COMO

She wears Italy's Lake Como like a hula hoop. It hugs her tiny waist in a two-dimensional sort of way. Her slender arms and well-developed bust line are visible above Lake Como; her hips and long, blond legs can be seen below it.

It's as if she has twirled, making Lake Como stand out from her body. The lake is now an enormous clear tray of sapphire encircling her waist. At the edges of the tray are small mountains fronted by the colorful aroma of restaurant gardens.

The tray becomes a mirror on which puffy white clouds, the bluest of skies, and occasional birds in flight are being served.

I shrink Lake Como to fit her perfect body. Tiny fish shower out of what was water, landing around her bare feet. The lake maintains its horizontal hold.

On tiptoes she stands in smiling wonder…and a hot pink, one-piece bathing suit.

This early summer afternoon in the malleable liquid of Italy's Lake Como, she becomes a delectable version of a Salvadore Dali painting.

5/28/2002

CREATING A FLOWER

Seven decades ago, butterflies tickled the sky and gardens of our residential neighborhood. Small ones flitted, large ones fluttered. That fascinating memory wings its way through my mind as if it were taking place today…

The butterflies' colors and shapes vary greatly, as do their flight and landing patterns. One small, agile species known as a "skipper" is good for catching practice, but is not a keeper. We always let skippers go.

A tiger swallowtail is a different story. This grand, striking beauty catches one's eye from a distance. Its yellow wings are vertically striped and outlined in black; the lower portion elongated (like a swallow's tail), and covered with blue and scarlet scales.

My brother and I collect butterflies. We mount each species, then label it according to information we glean from a large, hard-covered book so stuffed with butterflies, it's a wonder it doesn't fly away on its own.

Occasionally, we mount a tiger swallowtail with its wings partially open, put a hairpin around its body, and present it to Mom on fluffy cotton in a small, white cardboard box. She graciously accepts our gift and proudly wears it either on a knit dress or in her hair. As she does so, Mom, herself, becomes a flower, restoring life to these wondrous creatures whose beauty is appreciated by folks who are otherwise too preoccupied to have noticed it.

Mom later hugs and tells us how the butcher was startled, then amazed; how her bridge club admired the glorious insects; how friends she and Dad had met for dinner thought her sons were both considerate and clever.

Whenever Mom shares these comments, my brother and I feel a bit taller. It makes us all proud of one another. It makes our insides smile.

1/1/2003

APPRECIATION

Ah…Thank you, Miss. I appreciate both your attention and intention.

You are more than attractive, you're intriguing. It would be a delight to do you justice in many, many ways.

Before I fell in love with the woman of my dreams, I was a player. I played frequently and with passion.

But I am now married to that woman. Together we have grown and groomed a storehouse of peace and happiness. I love and respect her. She trusts me. I honor that trust. In turn, it allows me a freedom greater than any I may have conjured up on my own. It allows me to appreciate *all* of Life. To live for more than just the moment. To enjoy, through imagination, the many short-term possibilities; yet thrive on living the long-term reality.

As a short-term possibility, you truly are more than attractive, you're extremely intriguing. I appreciate both your attention and intention.

And it is delightful doing you justice as opposed to simply "doing you" under false pretenses.

1/9/2003

I USED TO THINK I KNOW MYSELF

I thought I knew myself better. I thought I was a more "other-directed" person. I thought I genuinely appreciated my family and people in general. I thought I liked myself.

I learned something last night during an extemporaneous recap of what's happened to me since I graduated from High School. Over dinner, I audibly presented the synopsis to my fellow graduates, most of whom I hadn't seen in 45 years. In doing so I forgot to include my wife, kids, and grandchildren. My wife was in attendance.

I learned a dramatic lesson—the eyes through which I look at life are not "eyes." They're "I's."

Something will have to be done about that.

1/18/2004

FOCAL POINT

Having traveled boundless distance to feather on the shore, rolling waves deliver their salty message. Their bubbly white foam reminds my toes the ocean and I are one. Water within my body seemingly unites with the vast ocean's myriad wonders—colorful coral fans and reefs, starfish, dolphins, fish shapes, and scapes beyond imagination—Neptunian delight. I, too, am the ocean.

The warm breeze is a balm upon my shoulders. I calmly evaporate internally as the oxygen throughout my body recognizes the tender wind—the traces of mountain peaks, dry deserts and forested lands over which it has blown. I, too, am the air.

Soft sun whispers I am an integral part of everything on which it sheds light, not only here on Earth, but throughout the solar system, our galaxy, even the universe. I'm connected.

As windows of my soul, my eyes have surveyed an array of amazement—a marvelous collection of visual imprints—an additional celebration of connection.

But you, my love, are now the focal point of my world, for our laughter and your hand in mine fill my heart to overflowing. Thank you for being. Thank you for enhancing life with your wonder and making time stand still.

Yes, here we are, two of us in time, the marvelous intangible that need not be extended. Time—a measurement to be applied and appreciated not as a string of events, but simply now, this instant. With no past or future, no doubt exists, only enlightenment. In absolute present, we are completely at one with the IS. We are everything. Absolutely everything. And, understanding that, what more is there to do but love?

8/29/2004

SUNSATIONAL

The sun was at work well before me, as I drove eastward this morning toward my office building. With gusto, it splashed brilliant shades of delight on early clouds.

It most probably worked diligently throughout the day for, as I return home this evening, that same sun, with great flair, now glamorizes the western sky.

Soon afterward, exhausted yet proud, it gently places its tools on the undulating ocean, revels briefly in its colorful creation and puts itself to bed.

I can understand why the sun is weary. It has filled a long day with vivid effort.

It has earned its black and briny slumber. Within the dark, cool depths, it seems to find renewal…rejuvenation…the inspiration to paint another day.

The Sun must dream magnificence.

11/21/2005

TONI CANUCCI'S TIME MACHINE

Waking up dead didn't seem unusual. I felt frisky and light. I could see forever and was, in fact, everywhere at once. It seems I simply ran out of time in one dimension and just popped into another.

Who will run the time machine? I wondered when I realized I no longer had hands, or even a body for that matter, to operate the controls. I'm out of it. Loose and free! That machine is now on its own, hurtling on and on; disappearing and reappearing in one dimension, then the next. No matter to me. I'm thrilled with my new freedom. To someone else who vibrates at a higher frequency in another dimension, however, the machine may appear to be standing still. That someone or thing may enter it and take control, going faster or slower, further or back.

Back. That's what got me here. My dear inventor friend Toni Canucci had asked me last evening, "If you had the opportunity to take a ride in a time machine, would you visit your past?"

"My past is already a part of me," I replied. "It's the present that's exciting. And the future. But a time machine! It's an intriguing thought."

"It's more than a thought, "she smiled. "I have one."

"You've invented a time machine!" I blurted.

"I didn't exactly invent the thing," she said. "It just appeared. But I've been in it. It works!"

"You mean you've traveled through time?" I questioned.

"Yep. Not far. Just back to when I was a little girl. I was afraid to go further. What if I didn't exist and couldn't return to the present?"

"Come on. You're kidding. Right?"

General Pieces   marc frederic

"No, it's true. Want to see it?"

The interior of the barn she used as a laboratory was spic and span. The walls had been covered with soft white vinyl so that minimal lighting illuminated everything. Toni walked me past several lab tables, shelves lined with equipment, a desk, bookcases, and chairs to a spacious part of the building.

"Here it is," she offered. "What do you think?"

The time machine was not immediately evident. I'm not sure what I expected, but this wasn't it. At first, I could barely tell an object sat before us. It was a cross between a bubble and a spider web. Almost invisible. But, as I gazed at it, something adjusted—either my eyes or the object, itself, for it appeared to become more tangible and detailed.

"This is a time machine?" I asked. "Where did it come from?"

"God only knows," Toni shrugged. "It's only been here since yesterday. You're the first person I've told about it. I'm not sure what to do. But it's exciting. It will definitely take you through time. It works! Like a dream!"

Toni was relieved to share her find. It was phenomenal. Too big a responsibility to keep secret. Too dramatic a discovery to make public.

"Want to get in it?" she asked.

I was still a bit skeptical. Toni, a brilliant inventor and scientist, also enjoyed practical jokes.

I stepped in. I felt as though I were inside a jellyfish. The laboratory outside seemed to wobble. The gossamer net walls of the "time machine" shifted shape and began to glow.

"Want to take it for a spin?" Toni questioned with raised eyebrows, eyes wide with anticipation. She seemed to need someone to verify her experience. "I'll wait here until you return. You won't have to go far to be thrilled. Just don't let it overwhelm you. Retrace a few years. You won't believe it."

I scanned the interior. What appeared to be a hazy control panel became more distinct as I concentrated on it. PAST and PRESENT were obvious. There was also a meter which indicated the date.

The past? Friendly…familiar…might be amusing to revisit. But the future! *Now, that,* I thought, *is exciting!*

So that's the direction I took. That's how I wound up in the next dimension, a light, airy being with no need for an earthly body. I suppose I just outlived it. But the freedom I feel! It's glorious! I'm so at ease and peacefully in tune with all there is. All there is everywhere. Even within the "time machine," which moves on without me. I wish it well.

But what will Toni think, waiting anxiously in her laboratory for me to return? Oh! There she is now. I truly *can* see everything; be everywhere, even time-wise!

"It's O.K., Toni. Everything is right. All is well.

"You think you hear me talking? You're not imagining it. You do. You don't need a time machine. Come on along. That's it…be calm and listen. Be open and know. Here you come.
Love…Peace…Bliss… You're ready for the dimension shift. It's so smooth. It's…"

…ONE CAR OFF TO THE SIDE. TRAFFIC IS BACKED UP FOR A GOOD TWO MILES ON THE 110 NORTH OF MARTIN LUTHER KING BOULEVARD. THIS WILL DEFINITELY DELAY…

Thank God for the snooze button. I can't believe it's time to get up. The night passed in a flash. And, yet, I feel so rested.

General Pieces   marc frederic

Let's see, what have I got on today's agenda? Six or seven calls to make before the financial plan presentation this morning at 10:00; lunch with Tom (can't eat too much, I've got my swim workout at 2:00); then pick up some books at the warehouse; and a Switzer Learning Center board meeting at 5:30.

Now what was I dreaming about? A time machine?

7/5/2005

AMAZED

My wife's kiss and hug, accompanied by a scotch and water, were the perfect welcome. I'm pleased to be home from my office, now relaxing on our couch, allowing the T.V. to tell me what it thinks was important today.

The phone rings. My wife answers. It's someone checking to see how she feels, a member of a group she will be meeting with shortly. She's very upbeat, even melodious, assuring the caller she'll be "just fine."

Hanging up, she asks what I'd like for dinner. I tell her, "Mashed potatoes, corn, and something green. I'll make the potatoes." I'm not up for meat. I've recently consumed more of it than usual.

"I don't think we have any potatoes," she replies, "How about some bouillabaisse?"

"Great!" I answer, thrilled with the choice of food as well as not having to create it.

Soon, my dinner is lovingly set before me. Before tasting it, I wait for my wife to join me. After a few minutes, I call to her, questioning if she's going to dine.

She'll do so when she returns from her meeting. Right now, she's in her dressing area preparing to leave.

I love my scrumptious dinner and marvel at my wife's ability to create such a wonder with ease.

Enjoying her creation and thinking of her physical beauty, I walk into her dressing room to share my awareness…

"Do you realize there's a group of people who, right now, are very excited about seeing you? You, Sweetheart, have a charisma that

General Pieces   marc frederic

precedes you. You've developed it unconsciously. But others are extremely aware of it. They grow warm in anticipation of sharing your presence. Part .of it is your easy graciousness. Part is your stunning physical beauty. But mostly it's your genuine interest in and caring for others."

"Thanks for your kind words, Honey," she replies. But her mind is centered on preparing for the meeting she will chair.

My mind, however, is not finished defining the concept. So, I continue thinking it to her rather than audibly interrupting her train of thought...

You deserve every bit of love, praise, friendship, and admiration you attract. And, recognizing your wonder through the eyes of others, I fall even deeper in love with you.

know well not only the poised, genuinely warm woman, but also the little girl inside, who is sometimes confused and has doubts.

*Thank you, Darling, for grooming yourself to become all you are. You affect the lives of so many in such a positive, unforgettable manner. I'm proud **of** you. I'm happy **with** you. You amaze me."*

2/27/2006

CRASHED

A stranger's coming to perform an autopsy on my computer. He'll then transplant its heart and soul into a new computer and jump-start it.

My computer's heart and soul are reflections of mine—a lifetime of my thoughts and dreams in written form. If computers could chuckle, gasp in amazement, and revel in wonder, the new one would undoubtedly have an intense reaction when reflectionized. It would most probably turn outside - in with the joy of all it suddenly contains.

As long as it lives, stores, and shares these feelings with others, I'll be happy. My deceased computer did just that. It was loyal and responsive; never thought of itself as either a critic or promoter, and seemed to enjoy my input. It would giggle or sigh when it processed words and occasionally hum when I retrieved previously created works.

This new computer is smaller than my deceased one. I'm told it's faster too. Fast can be good. Possibly, it will have excess time. Maybe enough to create a garden in which the muses can play—a "muse garden" stocked with glowing pastels, soft moss, and gentle waterfalls.

Will the new computer make time to visit other dimensions, retrieve wonders with which to stir the imagination. Possibly, it can collect samples for an "emotion zoo" the muses will tend and nurture; and from which they can whimsically pick and choose. There may, indeed, be no end to what this new computer can accomplish in its spare time.

In the interim, a difficulty in transplanting the heart and soul of my old computer seems to have developed. It involves technical matters, those discussed and understood by technicians, not laymen or poets. I'm told there is hope…if this operation cannot be completed on an outpatient basis, the technician may have to "take the old hard drive home." How hard a drive can it be? I have no clue where the technician lives and very little knowledge of computer jargon.

5/27/2006

NOT ENOUGH TIME TO FORGET

It's been a week since I've shared his company. I miss him both terribly and joyously.

Sorry, no…I don't have a picture with me. But would you like to meet him? You're welcome to take a peek into either my heart or mind. I'll introduce him to you…

Trenton's unique. Not simply because he's my grandson; a lot of people say that about Trent. He has a special effect on people. People like Trent. He likes them back, drawing them even closer.

There's much more to Trent than simple friendliness. It's the way he processes and reacts to whatever he experiences. He's mature for his age. "Precocious" some folks call him. It's amazing, considering he's less than two and a half years old.

Physically he's perfectly proportioned, yet slightly smaller than average, which makes him even more attractive… like a human "pet," or a real, live toy…a "lovable, lap-sized doll," absorbing, understanding more each day.

See how he endearingly cocks his head. Notice his twinkling eyes smiling up at you from under arched eyebrows. See the slight upward tilt to the edges of his lips? It's as if he's both amazed and amused by what he observes. He's so interested in all things, yet at ease with letting their mysteries unfold; enjoying the moment, while awaiting whatever is about to take place.

Could it be that he has experienced these happenings long ago, but is now looking at them from a new perspective? Or maybe he's so comfortably at one, he welcomes it with love, even though he has no idea what's coming.

General Pieces   marc frederic

Trent seems to see everything at which he looks. My wife thinks he has a photographic memory. And, he most definitely has a "bit of the parrot" in him.

Whatever the case, I believe you'll find our grandson intriguing as well as adorable—a tiny being who can simultaneously inspire and calm others. He loves to hug and be held but is comfortable playing alone. He can be unobtrusive; yet, at times, he'll sure demand answers.

What astounds me is how he commands one's attention without trying to do so…even when he's not present! Just thinking about him makes me wish I could put him in my shirt pocket and have him with me all day long.

And look! Now, suddenly, Trent has a new little sister, Brooke! Cute as can be! An apple cart up setter? Not on your life! This apple cart is well-balanced and grounded. His sister is simply another joy this world has to offer, another wonderful being to love. See how Trent already holds Brooke while he, himself, is being held. It's a marvelous, natural, family oneness kind of thing. But even more than that, I think he truly understands the realm from which they both have come. It's not that he "remembers." It's just that he hasn't had enough time to forget.

Trent, say "Hi" to…

5/27/ 2006

THE EYES HAVE IT

Framed by fine hair and the smoothest of skin, God's eyes look at me through the face of a child.

I gaze deeply into them, amazed by the kaleidoscopic journey on which I have been so calmly invited. Deeper I venture…and deeper, until I am completely involved. Herein, I discover long-ago galaxies of light and color to which I most naturally respond. I belong here. My essence reaches out to greet and embrace my surroundings. All distraction has evaporated. There is no separation, only a marvelous, warm, gentle yet inspirational, reunion. I am totally in tune. Peacefully happy. At one with everything.

All is beautiful. Positive. Self-fulfilling. Self-generating. I'm reminded I am thoroughly loved, provided for, and free to develop in any direction. Everything will constantly improve. I revel in the freedom to appreciate every aspect of life as I experience it in this, all past, and future dimensions. What Joy!

It's a refresher course in why I am! Being reminded to…live the moment…reach out even further to assist people through my business acumen…give and take even more in my relationships with family and friends…look for all the good in everyone I meet, and let them know what I've found, be it through a smile, appreciative comment or an anonymous deed…create and share my writings…and, above all, enjoy the next dimension in this one.

Why not? We are totally taken care of and free to grow. What could be more natural than recognizing others and sharing love with them?

"I must say, your grandson is very special. He's so calm and attentive for a toddler. Just looking into his eyes is an experience in its own right. Thanks for bringing him into my office. It's going to be a pleasure designing a plan for not only his college fund but his financial freedom."

1/29/2006

General Pieces   marc frederic

FEELING DUSTY

Something's askew. I feel different physically. For the last few days, I've been dusty tired. Not exhausted. Not ill. Just slightly drained.

I don't hurt anywhere. I'm just generally fatigued. Sleep doesn't seem to help. I feel...*average*. I feel like I imagine many people feel most of the time...slightly dull.

This sensation is so unusual for me, I think I'll write about it. I did that one morning years ago when I woke up "bored." Imagine being bored first thing in the morning. It's freaky. But I managed to catch the feeling on paper...made something rather unique out of it. The description of that apathetic emotion now lies listlessly in the dark between closed pages; but twinkles to life whenever someone opens to and reads it.

I'm slightly amazed that simply writing about this current languor seems to have alleviated the feeling. It's akin to sweeping it into a small pile, gathering it up, and letting it funnel through my hands into a tiny, make-believe bottle, the neck of which I then plug with decisive vigor.

"So long, Lethargy. I'm up and at 'em!

  "What's that? I can't hear you.

     "And don't think I want to."

6/19/2006

NIBBLETS   General Pieces

SOFT SHOTS

My wife's upset. She's been putting up with the situation for months. It's getting worse…proliferating.

Having just hung up the phone, I sit on the edge of our bed, looking through the sliding glass doors onto a sparkling, endless ocean. Between me and the ocean are two pigeons sitting on our balcony bar.

Their nesting place behind the bar, which was cleaned out two days ago, is now blocked off by a large piece of cardboard. The pigeons are in a quandary about how to regain entrance. That doesn't stop them from leaving massive amounts of digested deposits on the bar, barstools, railing, table, and chairs. The constant deposits are upsetting my wife. This is the third season the pigeons have nested. We've tried various solutions. Something more drastic must be done.

I've been on the phone to solve the problem…waited thirty-three rings before the Sporting Goods department at Sears answered. They "are extremely busy and don't sell BB guns." K-Mart's Sporting Goods Department is one third faster (22 rings) and does sell BB guns—both pistols and rifles. Good. I'm an ace with a Daisy rifle. At least I was forty-five years ago.

I was twenty-one, had just completed my junior year of college, and flown to Florida where my brother, Freddy, had wrapped up his freshman year. Together we spent the first weeks of summer driving his car back to our parents' home in a suburb of Los Angeles. On route, we stopped at a distant relative's home outside of Nashville, Tennessee. Joel was in his early forties and apparently quite well-to-do. Among his hobbies were model train collecting and shooting skeet. His train collection was vast, intricate, and fascinating. But it was the shooting that directly affected our lives…

General Pieces   marc frederic

During the course of conversation on the evening we arrive, Joel mentions he has recently hired a "trick shot artist" to hone his skills. The trick shooter suggested that, in order to save shotgun ammunition, Joel practiced with a BB rifle, "It's all about hand/eye coordination. BB's will work fine."

We are told the trick shooter's tutelage has made Joel so proficient he can throw a BB into the air and hit it with another BB shot from a Daisy rifle. I suppose Freddy's and my faces express our doubt, for we are immediately invited to witness an exhibition. Outside, to our amazement, we see him do it. We're then invited to try it, ourselves, with a twenty-five-cent piece. But, first, we are instructed to toss the coin so that it presents its broad surface as parallel to the ground as possible. We are then told to aim slightly above it. (We learn that, conversely, when shooting at something on the ground, it is necessary to aim slightly below it.)

A*iming* is not done exactly as one might think. By example, Joel explains to us why the sights on the barrel of his rifle have been filed off, "Pick out an object, any object you wish, preferably a small one. Raise your arm and point your finger at it," he suggests. "Now, without moving your finger, look down your arm at that object. Is your aim accurate?"

We agree it is.

"That's how you use the rifle. Not by aiming along the sights, but pointing it at an object you wish to hit. Point it a bit higher above the coin than you think you need to."

After several attempts, we begin to dramatically deflect the quarter's flight pattern.

"Do you notice," Joel asks, "where you're hitting the coin?"

"On its rim!" we exclaim after examining it. "Always on the rim."

"It's because that's where the light hits it and directs your eye."

We are astounded we can hit the coin at all, especially at night. It's a test that expands both our physical ability and the limits of our imagination. Joel assures us with practice we can shoot a BB out of the air.

When we leave to continue our journey west, we immediately stop in town to purchase two Daisy BB guns and have the sights filed off in the shop. We practice regularly during our various stops. Behind country restaurants, we set up tin cans and do some distance shooting. We find we can make discarded cigarette butts jump along the ground with four or five consecutive shots.

But it is in Houston that the rifles come in especially handy when we stop to visit a girl with whom I went to college. On her folks' property rests a large pond. As we are pushing a rowboat off the bank, Diane jumps back screaming!

Coiled beneath the bow, is a fat, black cottonmouth snake. Right away, it shows us how it got its name. Rather than running or backing away, Diane grabs an oar and tries to beat the snake to death before it escapes and someday kills her or a loved one. The snake slowly retreats, attempting to get back under the boat. It isn't planning to go anywhere and I don't like the idea of getting close enough to beat it with an oar. Who knows how far a snake that large can strike.

"Hold up!" I yell at Diane who is unleashing controlled hysteria. "I'll get our rifles."

She backs off but makes sure that cottonmouth stays put. When I return, Freddy and I pump BB's into the eyes of that snake until it lies limp. At that point, Diane takes over. She wants all traces of future harm removed. Once again using the oar as her weapon, Diane soon has the snake's head staring blindly at its somewhat distant body.

Later that summer my brother and I occasionally roamed the hills near our home. We followed deer trails through pungent sagebrush, which covered the ground on which the Getty Museum now sits.

General Pieces   marc frederic

Back then, the artworks, which the museum now houses, would have been shocked to realize they would someday be hanging on the very spot where we were hunting lizards.

Now days, I have no shred of interest in hunting, let alone killing, any creature. I'm confident, however, I've retained enough shooting skill to avoid hitting our balcony pigeons in the neck or eye. I believe my "aim" is still accurate enough to simply startle them away with soft shots.

7/1/2006

PLENTY TO GO AROUND

The monologue sounds out of place. It's wafting in a clear voice through the lobby of the building I've just entered. I come here every two weeks for my massage. Today, a few tiles of the lobby floor are torn up.

The monologue is emanating from a workman standing with his back against the wall, taking a break from whatever it is he's repairing. He leans there, calmly explaining to his co-worker how he sells options on stocks he owns to enhance his income. He sells them three or four times a year regardless of whether his stocks rise or dip or simply lean lazily against the inner wall of his account.

As I walk down the hall and wait for the elevator to arrive, the workman continues to explain one can either sell or buy options, but that he only sells them. There he lounges in his coveralls, giving an explanation of a somewhat sophisticated financial ploy of which few business executives, let alone construction workers, are aware. He is avid in his commentary, yet quite casual in his stance.

His stance and incongruous dissertation combine to hurl my memory forty-five years into the past. I'm now a college student sitting in a Political Science class. The lecturing, middle-aged professor sports a rumpled sport coat, tie, and hairstyle. He's smoking a cigarette. Although the professor is quite adamant about the point he's making, he is casual in stance. He leans back against the blackboard, smudging the notes he has scrawled. His hand holding the cigarette, is raised and resting above his head.

The point he's making is stronger than the ever-lengthening ash. The ash can no longer hold on. The professor doesn't seem to notice. The students love him for it. No one ever questions how his barber and the cleaner of his coats react to ashes and chalk. The professor is eccentric. It is rumored his wife is independently wealthy, thus allowing the professor to teach for a salary of one dollar per year.

General Pieces   marc frederic

Things work out. My masseuse, who is hardly ever late, is this afternoon. Perfect! It's a small miracle in timing. Her lopsided schedule has given me minutes to plant the workman and professor on the surface of this paper. That done, my mind is free to go dimension skipping.

Now face down on the table, I try something new—mentally sharing my soothing massage with Roger, a client of mine who has throat cancer. Two days ago, I learned his radiologist had been overzealous. Roger's throat is burned raw and swollen almost shut. Roger is having a tough time of it. He can use this "healing magic" even more than I can. Here we go, Roger. Have some of this...

It turns out that mentally sharing a massage is amazing!

The following day, his wife tells me Roger is breathing more easily than he has in some time.

I think I'll share my next massage with a myriad of friends. In fact, I may just share it with the world. Why not? It's an infinite experience. There's plenty to go around.

2/21/2007

POWER WALK

How powerful I am, striding along this cement path adjacent to a beach in Southern California. Although the sun is bright, a cold breeze accounts for the path being sparsely populated, the beach void of bathers.

It's March 2nd and my ankle feels great. Four months ago, swollen in pain, it caused me to limp. For years it had made my body feel like a dinosaur in a gigantic bear trap. My mind was free to fly anywhere, but my body felt ancient, had to give up golf and confine its exercise to swimming.

Then, I read a book that inspired me to shed the trap, spring millennia ahead, and allow my ankle to regain its fitness using neither medicine nor physical therapy. It's a small miracle, which I try not to take for granted, and, yet should, because that's what it's all about—assuming *health* is our natural state of being.

As I head homeward, savoring the smell of salt water, the wonder of feathering waves, and the screech of seagulls, a man in a business suit, dark glasses, and dress shoes walks the beach in my direction. He's some distance from the path, but not all the way down to the hard-packed sand by the water. He is carrying something pink in his right hand.

Suddenly, my attention is caught by a woman in gray sweat clothes, squatting just off the path a few yards ahead of me, holding a camera above her head with both hands, trying to align her shot. She was hidden by the lifeguard stand. In passing, I turn my head to see her taking aim at a sign attached to the stand which blares, NO LIFEGUARD ON DUTY.

The sign doesn't lie. But it's okay. There's no one else around to guard, except the dark-glassed, suited man in dress shoes and the picture-taking woman toward whom he's walking.

General Pieces   marc frederic

I'll never know more about either of them. I have now trundled past that scene. I am still wondering about that woman. What marvel did she see that I didn't? It's intriguing that we don't all see life the same way.

A different woman on the path about thirty yards ahead appears out of nowhere. She must have been in front of me all the while. My eyes were undoubtedly telling my brain she was there. But my brain, busily trying to focus through the lens of that squatting lady's camera, wasn't listening to them.

This new woman, young, dark-haired, slim, yet curvy, is moving the same direction I am. While walking, she doffs her sweater, wraps its arms around her waist, and ties them in front of her. She then breaks into a slow delicate jog. With each step, her calves kick slightly outward. Her forearms swing from side to side on a pair of tucked-in elbows. She seems to move in slow motion. At the pace I'm walking, I should overtake her. But, no. She's slowly growing smaller.

Watching her shrinking act, I notice in the distance a strange sight— a gargantuan tarp tenting a condominium to rid it of termites appears to have blown loose from the structure. There are huge gaps in its coverage. Like theater curtains beckoning an audience to attend a performance by giants, the ends of the canvas calmly undulate.

Two days earlier, the canvas had been savagely ripped open by a vicious wind. It had to be replaced. Hopefully, this time the gas has performed its kill and is now off duty. It's difficult to tell. There are no tent personnel, let alone actors or stage managers, in sight.

What a shame it would be if that rascal Wind has punched the time clock and let the gas go home early! The exterminator will, once again, have to re-tent. The gas will have to return to work. And, the residents will have to stay away even longer. Such a mammoth job will devour time and effort as well as the exterminator's profit.

How in the world do they hoist those tarps? I know once they're in place, they're pinned together with massive metal clips.

Oh! Clusters of clips are scattered on the ground at the foot of the tarps. I shudder at the thought of having to work with heavy material at such heights. Yes, high places can bother me. I'm not always afraid of heights. When there's a protective glass or railing involved, I'm fine. It's only when there's nothing between me and the depth, that I panic. Simply watching someone else near an unguarded edge causes an unpleasant tingling deep in my groin.

My sensitivity to height is extremely acute, even as I fly in my dreams. I love dream-gliding ten to fifteen feet high and exalt in swooping down hillsides or canyons only a few feet above the ground. The zing and abandon are exhilarating.

But here I am, off on a mental tangent, when all I intended to do was enjoy the newly found freedom of a mid-afternoon walk. It appears my ankle's carefree, go-wherever-it-may state of being has ascended to my mind.

3/2/2007

General Pieces   marc frederic

PHENOMENON

The ocean's smooth, undulating surface is subtly laced with broad ripples. Sunlight playing off them may explain the phenomenon.

A special effect is being created—flocks of individual sea stars—white, tiny, yet heavy, light explosions dance at various distances between me and the horizon. Clusters of seemingly electrical shorts become white fireworks against a background of metallic blue.

They are now blitzing expletives forming a visual sizzle!

Now, large white raindrops splashing into the passive sea. Or, are they erupting from it?

They suddenly morph from white raindrops into narrow, vertical triangles—tiny sails of light, each randomly appearing for but an instant, then vanishing to be replaced by others.

As I stare at their intermittent brilliance, they become a flock of glimmers flicker-landing on an immense, liquid tray.

Now, they've morphed into a myriad of nibbling sun kisses turning the ocean's surface orgasmic!

These marvelous flashes could be anything, even the tips of spectacular creatures' diamond-crusted backs sparkling below while barely breaking the surface.

Regardless of what is causing this phenomenon, I am completely comfortable with and thoroughly intrigued by its various effects. To me, it is a collection of promises being swiftly delivered by a mysterious source in which I unequivocally trust.

1/19/2008

NIBBLETS   General Pieces

LOVE MIRRORS

You'd think it would make a sound of some sort (a woosh, sizzle, or roar) when moving that fast. But, strangely enough, time flies by in absolute silence, sucking minutes, hours, days, and weeks into its wake like a black hole on amphetamines.

I thought last year went by fast, but this year seems to have already reserved space in the record book! The daily sheet calendar on my desk is a quarter lower, yet feels brand new!

Wherever those months went, they're laden with lush results based on hearty effort.
 Business-wise, much has been achieved by both me and my clients. Portfolios are expanding like popcorn in a microwave oven.

Tax time is upon us. That dreaded deadline circle-flutters like a butterfly. No pouncing lion this year.

Our mortgage, on a stringent diet of extra payments, is steadily shedding weight.

A multitude of creative works have flowed through me and are now resting neatly in their categories within the hard drive of my computer. They loll there, waiting to be pulled up, occasionally reaching out to tickle my mind or be shared with others.

My once-strained ankle carries me everywhere, encouraging me to alternate "power walking" with swimming.

Within several books, I've discovered metaphysical jewels with which I've stocked my spiritual treasure chest.

Communication with family increases.

My wife's challenges as president of our Home Owners Association continue to be met with ease.

We've shared parties galore and have good things in store. Our once-distant May tour of the Canadian Rockies rushes toward us on a train of its own, while our subsequently scheduled trip to Cozumel waits calmly in warm waters for our June arrival.

Oh! And the cat! In January my wife bought a three-month-old silky black kitten. It is perfectly graced with limpid, green eyes, a white goatee, chest blaze, and boots. She bought it as a present for her cousin, whose sixteen-year-old cat had passed away shortly after Christmas. Cousin "wasn't ready" for a new cat. Neighbor then offered to take it. But within a day and a half my wife and I fell in love with and claimed it for our own. Its cuddly purring in our bed at night plucked the decision from our minds and joyfully stashed it in our hearts.

Sammy is the first cat I've ever known. He is a love mirror. He just may be the glue that holds this speeding world together.

Yes, 2007 is off to a grand start, even though one would not expect it by listening to news festering with terrorism, child abuse, war, financial deficits, illegal immigration, a housing crisis, currency problems, and the like. It's as if two distinctly different worlds are operating simultaneously—one careening toward oblivion; the other thoroughly enjoying a leisurely stroll through ever-increasing peace.

Life is the way we make it. We come. We go. Time, swift or sluggardly, is of little consequence. It's only another dimension about which to learn. Let's help one another to enjoy the experience. Let's use the present to hone and polish our souls for future journeys.

Love mirrors. Let's become love mirrors.

3/24/2007

PERFECT

"It's perfect!"

"Really? I'm glad you see it that way. I'm glad you're so happy with it."

I believe perfection lies in the eye of the beholder. But what is perfection? And how does it relate to joy?

To many, *perfection*, when measured visually, involves balance. This type balance is often confused with symmetry.* But can symmetrical *perfection* be enhanced? Not by definition, but, certainly, by perception. At times a slight *im*perfection can add value to the whole. A mole (or beauty mark) on the cheek of a gorgeous woman allows one to enjoy the vision both with or without the *imperfection*.

Beauty may become more intriguing and enjoyable with the mark, as opposed to without it. Possibly. it's the contrast.* * On a woman, such asymmetry allows for realism and, in turn, approachability. However, lack of symmetry in a snowflake or cut diamond would be considered a flaw.

Occasionally, visual imperfections are purposely added to man's otherwise seemingly perfect creations. Such is the case with carpets woven in India, which always contain a small flaw in the belief that only God can create perfection.

Although perfection can be seen, heard, tasted, and felt, physically, emotionally, and spiritually, all our senses will not always synchronize in the recognition of it. When they do, however, it's a mind-blower. The ultimate connection.

Softly whispering its tinted murmur or splashing its brilliant thunder, the perception of perfection inundates its surroundings. One's world is shifted by the marvel it evokes. Ask anyone in love.

General Pieces   marc frederic

More and more, I tend to find perfection all around me. It's simply in different stages of development. Or could it be that I am enjoying a spiraling glide up through various stages of appreciation?

Have I learned to appreciate "outside the box"? Or is my optimism showing like the edge of a lady's slip?

   * Except for Picasso fans and children who color outside the lines.
   ** What is it about the poster of a starlet with a mustache scribbled on it that's
      amusingly attractive?

                        7/14/2007

HOLLYWOOD BOOK FESTIVAL 2007

It's an extremely warm Saturday in Hollywood, California. In costume, as *Mr. Whimsy*, I am scheduled to be the last reader of books in the children's category (from 5:30 until 6:00 p.m.) after which the Hollywood Book Festival will conclude.

I arrive at 4:00 to find numerous, scant, ten-by-ten, open-air tents covering the grounds. Most have a long table beneath one side. Combined, each canopy and table serve as a "vendor booth". Most booths are empty, except for one or two folks manning or breaking them down. The day has been exceptionally hot; hot enough to melt adults to kid size and completely evaporate children. Maybe that's why there are so few people in sight.

Beneath the "children's canopy," where my reading is to take place, it is extremely quiet. Other than four white, wooden chairs and a long table, the grass has been given clearance to grow. There's not a person on it.

The 4:30 author arrives with only one book in hand. He manages to attract two children, seats himself, and proceeds to read from his book for ten or fifteen minutes. I believe he's read it twice—first forward, then backward, flipping through the illustrations, trying to simultaneously cool himself and stimulate the kids. He may have accomplished the former; but, seemingly bored and with no additional readers scheduled for another fifteen minutes, the two children (I assume they are not shrunken adults) leave.

The five-o'clock author turns out to be both impressive and a magician of sorts. Somehow, like a people magnet, he attracts eight children and six adults out of thin air. The grass, pleased to act as a carpet, fluffs up a bit. The canopy sighs satisfaction at having some folks to shield from the sun. And, the possibility of an audience for *Mr. Whimsy* begins to grow in my mind, for a large audience typically draws even more people.

This current, comparatively mammoth crowd is composed of black folks, Latinos, and whites. The five o'clock author happens to be black, thin as a lightning rod, and charged with enthusiasm. He fills his half-hour by reading from four books, while an eight-year-old boy, also black, stands behind him holding up large cardboard placards graced with emotional adjectives (*HAPPY... ANGRY,* etc.). The placards are meant to give emphasis to the writing and involve the audience. They seem to work. "Boo's" and laughs course through the air. The author puts on a lively performance. His audience remains intact until he is through, then suddenly leaves en masse.

At exactly 5:30 the grass under the canopy is once again bare...except for the table and chairs. The fact that I am in costume and have just set out some books, as well as colorful laminated blow-ups of their pages, attracts one lady's attention. She's a pleasant leftover...part of the previous audience and has not yet melted in the heat.

From just outside the shade of the unmarked Children's Reading canopy, she eyes my goings-on. That is all it takes... I ask if I may put a smile on her face, quote *Llama Mohrama*, and she is hooked! I show her *BENNY'S PETS*. She calls with animation to her young nephew, another member of the dissipated crowd. Her nephew quickly joins her to enjoy my presentation. When I conclude, the aunt calls to her husband for money. He saunters over to us and pays. That is the only book I sell.

There is no one else left in the area, except the previous author, who is efficiently packing up nearby. He finishes his chores about the time I'm finished being paid, and comes over to chat with me. He's an interesting man—a recently laid off mortgage banker who is now, by reason of default and with great joy, a full-time author.

I compliment him on his enthusiastic presentation. It turns out the young man who held up the placards is also a writer, as well as his son. The author tells me his entire audience consisted of his immediate and extended family.

He says his son and he had earlier read on stage at another area within the festival grounds. He is disappointed, not with their presentation, but the lack of audience for that showing. He says the same outfit that coordinated this festival previously organized one in New York. Its venue was Central Park, which many people visit regardless of any festival being held there. The New York festival was evidently quite successful. No need to fish for buyers. It was riddled with bookworms.

The author is frustrated with this Festival. He believes he could organize a better one and will consider doing so. He tells me his name. He wants to keep in touch. We exchange cards. So much for the 2007 Hollywood Book Festival.

On the way home, my wife and I stop at a Mexican market we've been told sells peeled cactus leaves. It is a large store with an array of fascinating products. We wander through it, depleting its stock much more than we had intended. As we approach the check-out stand, our shopping cart, which is now bulging with cactus leaves, pickled pig's feet, cow tongues, ox tails, chicharrones (fried pork rind), and various other goodies, burps loudly and winks at the checker as if to say, "I've done *my* job. Now it's up to you."

That evening we prepare the tongue by boiling it in water containing a small bag of pickling spice. When it has cooled sufficiently, I peel the skin from it. It's been years since I peeled a cooked cow tongue. It always strikes me as a weird thing to do. We consume a good portion of it for dinner. It is absolutely scrumptious—tender and tasty. If the scene were a painting instead of a meal, I would have entitled it *Tongue On Tongue*. We cut additional slices for tongue sandwiches, which my wife wraps neatly in tinfoil for me to enjoy at work. I'll eat them for breakfast.

Late Monday morning, I receive a phone call that makes me forget all about how good leftover tongue tastes. *BENNY'S PETS*, which had been submitted two weeks earlier to compete in the 2007 Hollywood Book Festival was, last Saturday, judged to be Winner of the Children's category!

General Pieces   marc frederic

When I had checked in at the Registration Table, at 4 o'clock, no one mentioned an Awards Ceremony was taking place. I had asked for the festival organizer by name. The two fellas behind the long table under the ten-by-ten unmarked registration canopy wondered where he was too. As it turns out, he was announcing my award.

7/29/2007

HIGH-DEFINITION LIVING ROOM

I sit in the soft Sunday silence of our early morning living room, calmly gazing at my surroundings. I'm visually enjoying each piece of furniture and the many decorative items we have collected during the years. They complement each other well.

As they suddenly chase into the room, I realize how much our two cats lend definition to the scene.

Their black-and-gray play combines bursts of energy with calculated calm. They dart over the tops of couches onto the fireplace mantle, then to our round, glass coffee table; next, throughout large sea shells, ivory carvings, and handsome lamps. Their intermittent pauses and poses create a myriad of photo-ops, enhancing the beauty of their inanimate playground; bringing each item, in turn, to life.

My contemplation is enriched. My concentration intensified. I'm enthralled, as our living space develops another dimension.

It seems as if the room is being crystallized under a microscope of fur…cozy, yet spectacular…warm coffee over diamonds.

8/17/2008

General Pieces   marc frederic

THE SHEETS AREN'T ALL THAT'S NEW

It's still dark. I turn over, taking a 2:30 glance at the illuminated clock on my nightstand. From a semiconscious state, I seem to recognize something about the quality of new sheets on our bed. Their texture is different—not percale, not muslin—more like the outside of an uncooked marshmallow without the powder. As I dream, the marshmallow heats up a bit. Soft dreams…mellow sensations. I like our new sheets.

Now morning has poked its head between the slight separation in our floor-to-ceiling curtains. My wife and I have vacated the bed. Having taken my vitamins and shaved, I still feel the effect of the sheets.

All is calm. All is bright. Dressed in shirt and slacks, I'm typing this short piece, while my wife adds beauty to her face and dons her bathing suit in preparation for our daily swim.

Assuming our car ride to the gymnasium is uneventful, I will maintain this gentle life rhythm while smoothly stroking through the pool's pastel water. The shower that follows will caress me with its warmth. I look forward to then reuniting with my wife and, on the way home, exchanging thoughts we have conjured while swimming laps. What a tender beginning to another luscious day.

Upon audibly sharing my "sheet appreciation" during our homeward journey, I learn their texture is referred to as fleece. My wife knows these things. The term brings classic golden images to mind, allowing even more appreciation into my life. (*Thank you, Sweetheart.*)

What other wonders are in store this day? We've stopped at the supermarket. Perusing the aisles, after having collected the items my wife has requested, is truly amazing—the colors and packaging of goods, the occasional aromas, the imagined tastes, the various countries from which they have been shipped. It is all a marvelous, mind-expanding experience.

I absolutely *love* being retired.
2009

NIBBLETS   General Pieces

CARNIVALESQUE CHARISMA

I remember nothing prior to five seconds ago when you walked into the room and turned my tongue to cotton candy. My mind is suddenly on a carnival carousel. The music, a siren's song.

You are fair. So very, very fair. But your gossamer ways belie your strength. With the faintest body language, you slam down the iron-headed sledgehammer of discovery, making the steel marker rise through my heart to loudly ring the appreciation bell between my ears.

Sparkles from your eyes play the room like a disco ball composed of fireworks. Or are these projected jewels the result of some synapse in the gray matter behind *my* eyes?

Your mellow movement. Your guileless self-assurance. And the smile you share so freely with the world, jar my senses.

Something inside me is rising to the occasion. I feel quite at one. There's mutual pleasure in the air.

1/11/2009

GARBAGE COLLECTOR

The garbage collector waits to eat until outside BJ's house. The collector eats from the can.

It started several months ago when the collector found a clean, pink, cardboard box carefully placed below the can's lid on top of the trash. Written on the box were the words, "Feel Free To Eat Me." The box contained a carefully prepared Nicoise salad, a small pair of salt and pepper shakers, a well-polished knife and fork, and white cloth napkin.

Looking up, the garbage collector caught a glimpse of BJ's smiling face peeking out from behind the living room curtain

The salad was delicious.

Being well-received, the generosity was continued. It entailed a variety of delights including small presents. The accompanying notes were simultaneously inviting and appreciative.

The garbage collector and BJ are married. It is coincidental they now live on a route where she collects garbage while Billy Joe stays home minding their ten-month-old baby boy.

8/15/2009

SANDY DREAMS

How contentedly you sleep, your side resting on a soft bed of sand, while waves rhythmically feather nearby. You are sooooo relaxed.

Although the sun winks on the horizon, the beach still cradles you in its warmth.

Slumber on, my darling. The moon will soon arrive with its gentle caresses. And I am here to guard against those who would steal your sweet, sweet dreams.

8/28/2009

WADING WHILE WAITING

For over two hours in a slowly ebbing tide, she has been wading and waiting…waiting and wading, up to her knees at times.

Most often she gazes down into the clear, calm, darkish, warm, salt water. But, on occasion, she looks out at the horizon, raising her arms, crossing and folding them above her head. Is she unnecessarily shading her eyes from a clouded-over sun?

Or is she hopefully anticipating an unknown, Neptune-like god breaking the surface; shedding water as he rises from the calm; sweeping her up in his muscular arms and carrying her off to become his Queen of Submergia?

She waits. Dressed in a black, squarish, two-piece bathing suit, she stands thin, white, unacknowledged by the numerous tan skin divers on their ways to and from their aquatic pleasure.

She waits. Seemingly out of place. The contrast of dark hair piled on her head making her skin even whiter. Is she waiting for Nature to accept her? For her skin to darken? For the sea to take her to its bosom? For her life to be thrown into gear, either forward or reverse?

Or is she simply experiencing a reality? A glorious reality not readily apparent to those around her. A reality in which she blossoms and revels. A reality for which she has traded a boring existence temporarily left behind, wading while waiting for her return.

10/21/2010

I LIKE IT WHEN THE OCEAN WINKS AT ME

I like it when the ocean winks at me. So inviting it is, yet aloof, in its devil-may-care attitude. I suppose its winks are simply the sun reflecting off variations in the level of its liquid surface.

But what that distant orb can accomplish is magical. It allows one's consciousness to seemingly melt beneath its relaxing rays and to later retain a mellow glow both physically and mentally.

This ball of brilliance has now sunk just low enough to create a broad, golden river reaching effortlessly from the nearby shore all the way to the west horizon.

Dolphins and seals occasionally traverse this river of light in their quest for a meal. Although the mammals may not immediately see the fish, diving pelicans clearly disclose the whereabouts of these shimmering delicacies. These flying Geographic Position Systems instigate a virtual feeding frenzy.

While oblivious boaters sail in the distance, nearby paddlers of boards and canoes interrupt their casual journeys to survey the pelican pandemonium.

Strangely, this afternoon. the seagulls are intent on cruising the beach. I imagine their action is due to the air temperature approaching eighty degrees, extremely unusual for the fourth of March, and has sprinkled the beach with sunbathers such as me who carry a supply of tasty snacks. When unguarded, these munchable treats are evidently more attractive to the seagulls than the slight fish remnants resulting from pelican dives.

Today feels as if it could be the First Day of Summer. But it's way too early to sport such a moniker.

3/4/2012

General Pieces   marc frederic

HALF A GLASS OF WATER

"A half a glass of water" can be a serious subject. Is it half full or half empty? Who cares! It's a glass. And glass is a marvel—a truly amazing material if it even exists. Apparently, it does not, for we see right through it. Yet it shields us from the teeth of the wind and the storm's spewing rage.

This piece of glass before us is special. It can hold something. It wears no cap, cork, top or lid to inhibit its generosity but, instead, sits calmly waiting to bestow its contents on whoever raises it to his lips.

Water, the liquid held by this glass, is the refreshing elixir on which each cell of my body depends in order to function.

Start singing, cells. Here comes a small shower of Life.

(date unknown, found 7/2015)

FIRST READING

For several months, you have been aware of my compiling *The Enticing Wonder of Gaylan*, a collection of love poems and prose I have written to you during our twenty years together.

The book is currently at the printer's, pulling itself together, donning its cover in preparation for its debut. I plan to pick it up next Wednesday, which happens to be your birthday. In the interim, we are compiling a list of people to whom we will gift a copy of this first, one-hundred-book edition.

Although you have seen and love its cover, the body of the book is still a surprise…an ambiguity…a mystery you cannot wait to solve. Being that it's soon to be read by others, I offer you a preview of the book's text. Responding to your immediate acceptance, I bring the sheaf of loose-leafed pages, along with your blue-framed glasses, to where you sit cozily on our living room couch.

Now it's my turn to enjoy your amazement, as you smile and coo over the way I have woven together my thoughts regarding you. Your initial compliments of my words are, just as *you* refer to *them,* "delightful." I love observing your rapture. You cannot stop reading. This is what it has been about. This is the joy I've been waiting to share.

I sit near the morning fire, gazing at you over our cats that lounge before it. I appreciate that my skin and heart are being warmed simultaneous—the former by the dancing flames, the latter by your enjoyment. Each loose page is individually caressed by your eyes, then placed on an ever-increasing pile next to you on the couch.

Although I had, for some time, looked forward to your reading the book, my image of your doing so involved your smiling into the bound pages resting within their pink cover. But here you are, sifting through proofs of the individual pages, sharing the book and our love in a form not to be experienced by anyone else. It's charming and seems entirely appropriate.

Oops! You're suddenly upset by the picture of you without a smile. You strongly dislike that picture. You think you look as if you've just been shot in the back! Although the poem is entitled, *A Smile Just Missed*, and the footnote accompanying it recounts how thoughtful and beautiful you are even without your smile, you try to wish the picture out of existence. We discuss excluding it from the next printing.

Returning your attention to the collection of love, you eventually finish reading the loose pages by concentrating on the captioned pictures on the last two. You then nod your head. One hand covers your eyes. Your tears cause me to choke up. We can speak only in hugs.

After delighting in the beauty we've shared over twenty years, I realize the best is yet to come—the processing bonus. Yes, for some time, you will continue to absorb the love I've compiled in hundreds of poems, notes, and footnotes. More importantly, your mind will mull the joy of all the love to come; and your heart will expand even further…if that is possible.

2/21/2009

THE NIGHT BEFORE AFRICA

In the morning, we will be off to turn our mental sketch of the South African bushveld, (more commonly known as "the bush") into reality.

Over years, viewing a relatively small screen from the comfort of our living room couch, we have experienced everything from elephants to dung beetles, the great wildebeest migration to colonies of stinging ants.

Soon, the shoulder of an adult male lion may be the same height as my chest. The immensity and amazing terrain of the land, itself, may be overwhelming. The cacophony of animal grunts and screams will gyrate through velvet nights.

I want to eat warthog. Hear the crunch of lions devouring a zebra. Smell the blood of a fresh kill. And listen to the natives speak their *oola – oomba* sounds.

Between here and there lies the daunting challenge of twenty-eight hours of travel by plane and warming the seats of airport lounges. Tonight, however, we lie in our cozy bed surrounded by darkness, simultaneously imagining the foreign future and being whispered to by familiar, gentle waves that rush and brush the shore of South Redondo Beach.

3/16/2009

General Pieces   marc frederic

IMPRESSIONS DURING A SOUTH AFRICAN SAFARI

There is something about Africa, possibly only South Africa, maybe just "the bush", that greets one's soul with a mammoth, intangible hug, a primordial sense of belonging.

It's an immediate, palpable oneness with the countryside and all that comprises it. The ground is warm. Millennian clay beneath your feet welcomes you with a spiritual melding. The air is comfortable. The vegetation seems to cuddle you while offering as much space as you need.

Trees are at once magnificent and charming. Tall grass captivates your imagination like a dance of veils. All is alive with mysterious possibility. You belong in these picturesque scenes.

And the size! Not only of the land, itself, but the animals!

Later we learn that the stars, too, are huge.

* * * * *

Ting!…Ping!...CHING!…Ting! Flexible branches hit the hollow metal roll bars of our Land Cruiser, as we trundle through the African bush in search of wildlife. Tracks, dung, and bent grass indicate that up ahead there's something worth seeing.

* * * * *

It is early evening in a Sabi Sands game preserve. Weak light has given way to vast, dark velvet. There is no moon to outshine the invasion of stars. The air must be extremely thin and pure, for the stars don't sparkle like diamonds. They hang like shining pearls, some dripping through black velvet all the way to the horizon.

The Milky Way traverses the sky, as we cross the land in a roofless safari vehicle. Heat, baked into the Earth's surface, now reaches up in a futile attempt to caress the celestial celebration. It envelops us in comfort, as we raise our chins, exposing the front of our necks to the warm wind created by our speed of travel.

I feel as if I'm "taking off" to fly throughout this starry playground. I'm Peter Pan—at one with the universe; in tune with its soul. A wonder galore is mine to explore. My greatest decision is on which star to land.

4/4/2009

General Pieces   marc frederic

BEAUTY AND THE BEACH

Our beach is being rebuilt for the third time during the 24 years we've lived on it.

It's a fascinating project involving barges, tugboats, pipelines, tractors, and tons and tons of sand dredged up 15 miles north of here from the waterways of Marina Del Rey. That is the beauty of the plan—their marina becomes deeper, while our beach becomes fuller.

We've been notified by our city of Redondo Beach the operation is expected to continue day and night for 45 days. Not a problem. The noise is camouflaged by pounding surf. As for the lights, we simply close our drapes.

What happened to make this project necessary? Not much and a whole lot—natural erosion. When it comes to maintenance, the ocean is a cruel taskmaster. In addition to beach erosion, its salty air corrodes metal. Peals paint. Rots wood.

Now, its waves rush steadily against berms of sand created to protect the beach while it's being rebuilt. In a frenzy, they lick, bite, and chew. Then, retreating, they call their followers to enjoy this newly discovered feast.

However demanding the ocean's appetite may be, it is a wonderful companion with which to live. It offers relief from heat. Its salty aroma is refreshing. The sound of its breaking waves affords privacy and lulls one to sleep. It serves as a playground for humans, a diner for birds and sea creatures, an avenue of transport for commerce. And its changing appearance provides endless beauty.

This beach expansion will definitely add another delight—observing how well all the extra bikinis are filled.

9/15/2012

INCONGRUITY

It's an image one can neither ignore nor rapidly forget.

Although it takes place in the lady's long-ago-dream, it is a shocking image. She's vomiting a river of broken mirror—a stream of chards! More, she explains, than could possibly fit in her body. It gushes and crackles in an endless flow.

Our gorgeous new friend, last night casually inserted that dramatic scene into her otherwise plausible dinner conversation. But she did so with fascinating incongruity —her smiling eyes were filled with blue birds; rainbows caressed the many nooks and crannies of her mind.

She's quite content knowing that, although she had poured a great deal of effort into a toxic relationship, she, years ago, managed to rid herself of that contamination. She sealed the entire matter in a lead container to be opened only rarely and slightly by a gentle twist of its memory cap.

The incongruity of such an outrageous image being tranquilly proffered by the attractive lady is magnified this morning. In bed with our blue-eyed, nine-week-old Siamese kitten lying prone upon my chest, I look into its eyes and realize their color is the same as those of last night's lady; then marvel at the contrast between the river of stark, jagged reflection and the soft innocence of the tiny kitten.

Slowly I stretch my arm to the nightstand and back. The kitten turns around to curiously eye the legal-sized paper tablet now propped before him against my raised knees. Vividly recalling our new friend's horrific dream, I begin the process of capturing it, sending it through my pen to the yellow paper. There it will lurk 'midst the horizontal blue lines. Like a semi-submerged crocodile, it will lie in wait to fiercely snatch perusing eyes and jolt the gentle souls of unsuspecting readers.

General Pieces   marc frederic

Meanwhile, sphinxlike on my chest, our kitten is very attentive as I explain to him the process and purpose of writing. His newly acquired brain seems to understand purrfectly. How calmly his blue eyes accept the wiggling of the pen. How securely his illiteracy protects him from the crocodile. He simply remains at peace with his surroundings, safe and sound, accepting whatever comes his way.

6/13/2009

THE BUZZ

The person from whom I have received my blood transfusion seems to be made of brick, for I now sleep like one, and time moves in blocks instead of flying. There's a serious side to that blood as if it were donated by a German accountant. It has an anchoring effect, doesn't hold me down, but lends substance to my occasional flighty thoughts.

I'm no longer an engine's piston. I am the block within which pistons pump—a solid block composed of pure strength; not ferocious, not bellicose, just basic, intrinsic, patriotic, get-the-job-done strength. I am the bowling ball in the alley of life. How will such a solemn addition integrate with the humor, surrealism, and delight my circulatory system harbors?

The German accountant's blood likes being out of that plastic pouch, able to again course through a human body. At exactly 5:15 a.m. my mind awakens to realize my body feels rock solid and well lubricated, like a pyramid that has drunk a *Penzoil* malt.

Hmmm…I still feel a subtle tingling like the caffeine buzz derived from ingesting leaded coffee on an empty stomach. Unnerving. Without even a sip, I have been experiencing the buzz, along with occasional tremors, for several weeks.

I finally understood the buzz when, yesterday in the doctor's office, I was introduced to anemia: "Marc, let me introduce you to your Anemia. Severe Anemia, meet Marc Frederic. He's two pints low. But you already know that."

The reason for my buzz immediately became apparent. My heart has been trying to make up for the blood loss by pumping its diminished supply around my body at an accelerated rate like a hamster on a running wheel. I need more blood.

General Pieces — marc frederic

Having donated gallons, I found it interesting to suddenly be on the receiving end. Blood comes out fast, but goes in slowly. Two and a half hours later, the bag was empty. I, however, was not full.

I'm still a pint low. But the buzz is less prevalent. An additional transfusion might smooth me out completely. Should it come from the same source, I will most likely lose the ability to buzz, but be able to prepare tax returns while I sleep.

Prior to the transfusion, it was determined I am not leaking. We must now clarify why my hemoglobin count is less than two-thirds what it should be.

One way or the other, everything will be all right. In my medicine cabinet, I have a metal nail file. If necessary, I will use it on my teeth. I am holding it in reserve…just in case I ever need to become a VAMPIRE!

7/3/2009

NIBBLETS   General Pieces

RECOGNIZED

As we light-heartedly drive through the early evening with our next-door neighbors in anticipation of seeing a play, my wife casually initiates a strange subject.

She has, during the last few days, been showing residential real estate to a couple in their late forties. One of the many properties they have perused is a beachfront condominium located in the same building where we and the couple with whom we are riding live.

Naturally, our neighbors and I are interested in the potential buyers' opinions of the place. My wife explains that, after being in the condo for only a short while, the wife of the shopping couple asked, "Did somebody die in this unit?"

The answer is "Yes." About nine months ago the owner, in his mid-eighties, passed away in the presence of his meager family. I remember well his small memorial service held within the courtyard of our complex. I shared a poem I had created extolling the man's endearing attributes. Amidst the ferns, we sat on stone benches eating fruit and cake, reminiscing about his grand, gray-bearded smile, how he swam daily in the ocean, and contributed twinkle-eyed opinions whenever the opportunity arose.

But, I wonder, *how could the potential buyer know of his passing? Is she psychic? Is the man's ghost lurking in the unit? Did she sense our memorial service as she passed through the courtyard?*

Before I can voice the questions, we learn the wife knew nothing of the man or memorial service. Simply put, she had smelled death in the condo. A nurse for many years, she recognized the smell.

"What does death smell like?" I question aloud. "How long can the smell remain? Maybe I should visit that unit during their next 'open house'."

General Pieces   marc frederic

"You don't want to know that smell," states our friend, the driver.

Hmmm…

Maybe he's right.

But I'm curious…

3/30/2010

ISTANBUL, THE LADY IN GRAY

Istanbul is a sensual woman—a striking, brunette, draped in light gray from throat to high heels.

Over her gray sheath dress, the stylish full-length coat she wears is embellished with darker gray beads of various size and shape. In an abstract, surreal manner, these tiny decorative accessories represent the features of the city's intriguing surface. Stunning in pattern, subdued in outer color, this open, seemingly sedate garment flashes glimpses of its brilliant red lining with every movement the lady makes.

The texture of the City's surface, its "embroidery," is composed of her ubiquitous mosques with voluptuous domes and spiraling minarets. Her Bosporus River bustling with commerce, lined with slight foliage and magnificent residences. Her hills covered with buildings of architecture both ancient and modern. Her wide boulevards from which branch craggy, cobblestone streets narrowly twisting in the shadows of shoulder-to-shoulder four-story buildings.

But the dignified gray of her subdued surface belies Istanbul's scintillating lining. Her dazzling *Grand Bazaar* and *Spice Market* simultaneously tempt and deluge one's senses with their myriad offerings. The huge, ancient cistern lying calmly beneath her, supports its ceiling with vast numbers of marble columns. Imported centuries ago from Italy and Greece, they generate a sense of gentle awe. Marvelous tiled patterns lining the interiors of her mosques amaze in sacred silence. Erotic moves of the belly dancers within dark cabarets stimulate. Tastes and aromas of exotic food and drink delight.

But of all her many enchanting qualities, the graciousness of the Turkish people may be her finest feature.

To associate with this magnificent lady is to be charmed by multi-dimensional wonder.

9/14/2010

General Pieces   marc frederic

ISTANBUL'S "EGYPTIAN" BAZAAR (MARKET)
so named, for in years long past, most all the products sold within it were funneled from other countries through Egypt.

We enter the "Egyptian" (or "Spice") market for a second day, but this time through a side alley rather than one of its main arches.

The alley is teeming with life—the ubiquitous throng of humans, to be sure, but also a vast collection of exotic and common creatures as well as unusual flora—a basket of bulbs that relieve arthritis pain, a box full of fluffy, yellow ducklings, a huge jar of water containing leeches for letting of blood. Live and dried plants galore, cages of birds, cats, and dogs. No time to see all.

As we stroll onward, I substitute an accurate camera for my delighted eyes and overwhelmed memory. Click…click…click…click. There's so much! The assortment appears to be endless. A potpourri extraordinaire. When my photos are developed, I'd not be surprised to find hovering golden hummingbirds with silver tongues, and miniature rainbow-striped zebras.

Our guide warns us against purchasing pigeons. He once did. They escaped and flew back to the market. His experience sparks my memory of two dozen white-homing pigeons imitating doves. Years ago, they were released, as the love of my life and I, having concluded our wedding vows, were presented as man and wife. From cages hidden within the garden gazebo, the birds burst forth in glorious snow-white flutter. Upward they flew in ever-greater circles before returning to their owner.

I'm falling behind my wife and our guide. As they turn a corner up ahead, I pass a medley of plant seeds of every sort, transition into a display of small pyramids composed of spices and herbs of amazing quantity, variety, hue, and aroma. So many unknowns! Cheeses of different shapes and size. Exotic fruits and vegetables. I'm a kid in a candy store! And that's what comes next—vast, yet neatly arranged, selections of colorful candies and nuts. I can only imagine the tastes, as I scurry by…click… click… click.

These photos would be better with my wife in them.

9/11/2010

DESERT IN JULY

Having recently moved from the overcast chill and steady pounding of beach waves, I find it pleasant to be wrapped in desert calm…especially when one has a choice of inner wrapping—walls of a house, movie theater, restaurant or car…all of which condition the air.

The desert "unconditionally" offers beauty, wonder, and warmth. The sun-drenched rocks and sand, multi-shaped cacti, and brassy-blue sky that paint the outdoors from dawn to dusk are liberating. But all that purity, especially the heat, is difficult to absorb for any length of time during the middle of Summer.

Being able to use conditioned air as temporary immediate refreshment, permits me to more fully appreciate the July heat—to imagine it as a mammoth hug from Mother Nature, relaxing and protecting me from the mechanical indoor chill.

I appreciate such dry heat. It not only warms my body; it blows kisses to my soul.

8/5/2016

TWO MORE BEAUTIFUL LEAVES

A pair of cricket legs on white tile. Digging up our backyard to install a swimming pool might account for them.

The tiny appendages are sparse remnants of the cricket invasion we, for three months, have been attempting to halt. Our variety of attempts to solve the mysterious phenomenon have, at last, been successful. The crickets, themselves, seem to have disappeared, completely discouraged from entering our newly acquired desert home and littering our master bathroom floor with their innocent presence.

The gadgets we plugged into the wall sockets evidently work. They whisper tragic micro-electronic warnings heard solely by crickets, not humans or cats. More likely, these inaudible messages are not warnings at all, but cricket fairy tales that charm the little creatures into visiting worlds beyond our comprehension—realms where crickets dance jigs and hop to the beat of feathered drums.

For one reason or another, the crickets have vanished, leaving in their stead an aura of relief and joy. These lovely emotions now subtly unfurl in the form of two more beautiful leaves on our ever-spreading intangible tree of peace.

8/13/2016

SMALL REASSURING STORY

"Are you an angel?" asks the small voice. It emanates from a young, dark-haired, six-year-old girl who is lying on her living room couch. The girl's brown eyes are large and somewhat glazed. Only her pale, slightly flushed face shows from beneath the soft blanket covering her. A mild fever prevents her from attending school or she would not be home on a weekday, especially during a broker's open house.

My wife Gaylan, a real estate agent, is touring the home in which the girl resides, previewing it for potential buyers. Stunningly blond, dressed attractively in white from head to toe, my wife naturally exudes an ambiance of caring. She smiles warmly at the child and stops to ask if she is all right. It is completely understandable how the young girl in a semi-feverish state could mistake my wife's identity.

Upon returning home, Gaylan shares the happening with me. I delight in the fairy tale atmosphere created by the images she describes and easily picture her from the little girl's point of view. Gaylan, on the other hand, has trouble relating to someone viewing her as an angel. Although she is considered by many to be compassionate, generous, and gorgeous, my wife is truly unaware of either her inner or physical beauty.

Last night, following a two-week hospitalization, my wife's sixty-two-year-old cousin passed away. Due to the harrowing circumstances, we consider her passing a blessing. My wife is now experiencing relief mixed with the satisfaction of having shared a tender, one-way conversation with her cousin just hours before she made her transition.

However, there is discord in her cousin's small, family. One member does not appreciate the sincere and necessary assistance Gaylan provided when no one else thought to or was capable of doing so. That family member no longer feels needed. From a delusional mindset, she has recently castigated all those around her.

General Pieces   marc frederic

Having been vilified by her aunt, Gaylan somehow recalls and asks me if I remember, the story of the little girl on the couch, which took place years ago.

I assure her I clearly do, and am thrilled to share without question that in my opinion she is still an angel in that little girl's mind, my heart, and the lives of many, many others.

Her smile radiates acceptance.

4/14/2012

LIVING HERE

Beautiful and fine-featured, the woman steps in through the opening left by the sliding door. She trails a leash to which…

"I hate this place!" she bristles, filling up the small enclosure with razor-edged intangibles. Without moving, she's slicing at everything above the level of her dog's head. Including us! For an instant, it seems there is hardly room to breathe!

But it's much too sunny a day to be slashed by sharp words in a small elevator. Let's start all over again…about two floors up and thirty seconds ago…

My wife and I have subterranean garage plans. From the third floor, we have pushed the G-2 button and are casually descending through our beachfront condominium complex when the elevator unexpectedly stops on G-1 (the ground floor.) It graciously opens its door to welcome a long-time resident and her black Labrador retriever. Her dog must have been watering the front lawn while the lady waited for him. Now they are headed down to her car.

Following the lady's outburst and friendly "Hi's," from my wife and me, my wife goes on to cheerfully mention the impatiens plants she recently saw on sale at a local nursery. Our neighbor, the one who just entered the elevator, was at one-time president of our Home Owners Association. For years, she's been faithfully involved in maintenance and beautification efforts (of both our condominium complex and herself). She is now a middle-aged, very attractive, statuesque brunette. She looks great and likes other things to look great.

Therefore, (let's try this again with a simple "bad hair day" approach) it was startling to be deluged by the torrent of words which burst forth from her shapely lips. "Talk to Margaret about that. Not me!" she blurts. (Margaret is our current HOA president.) "I have nothing to do with that!"

General Pieces   marc frederic

"I hate this place!" she continues. "I hate this building! I hate the battleship parked outside my window! I hate waiting for an elevator to enter my front door! I hate LIVING HERE!"

Until just then, I had not realized one could crack a dam wide open with the pastel thought of a garden plant. But impatiens were named for a reason. And a "bad hair" day is like a wizard with a wand gone wild. So here we stand, shoulder-deep in angry words.

It's unusual, to say the least. Our neighbor, Jane, typically grooms her words as carefully as she does her person. She has an excellent vocabulary and ordinarily uses it in an exemplary fashion. She often chooses words the way another woman might select a dress…her vocabulary can be as exquisite as basic black and pearls or as "hang loose" as dungarees topped by a sweatshirt. Her diction is crystal clear regardless of the subject matter.

Jane does more with words than simply select and enunciate them correctly. She often draws them out slightly or adds long curlicues. Listening to Jane speak is like watching calligraphy being written. It's usually a pleasure to converse with her.

Just as I feel we might drown in this flash flood of verbiage, the elevator door opens at our designated level, allowing the words to surge out onto the garage floor.

"I'm sorry," I say, adding my thought to the receding word level. "It's sad to hate where you live." (Especially when it's a warm, sunny place graced with salty air and the sound of breaking waves.)

Jane wades out through now ankle-deep words. Her dog follows and, choking just slightly on a few expletives, stops to shake off a spray of individual letters.

Jane summarily informs us she is driving to her mountain home, which she and her husband frequent throughout the year. I know Jane will be happier soon. She has always said good things about their mountain place. Jane's mountain place talk is composed of words which shimmer like snowflakes and dance like whispers through green boughs of pine. Jane must have a closet full of designer words she speaks in the mountains.

NIBBLETS General Pieces

My wife and I wish Jane well on our way to our car. Then, during our short drive, we discuss how pleasantly surprised we had been to awaken this morning and discover the navy ship anchored about a quarter mile offshore. We marvel at its sudden and incongruous appearance. We try to determine what kind of ship it is and wonder why there are three tugboats dwarfed in its lea.

Later, having completed our errand, we return to our home.

The sun is working hard this afternoon. It has showered the ocean with winking liquid stars and is now blazing away at the beige sand. Here we sit in low folding chairs on the beach a little south of our condo. We're reading, while eating ice-cold, juicy peaches under our brightly-colored umbrella. I've escaped the glare by facing my chair away from the water. Such positioning also allows me to peruse the near-naked bedlam on the bike path behind us.

I glance up from my book to see a solidly built man in his mid-thirties wearing light blue boxer style swimming trunks. Descending a case of stairs, he stands out from the confusion around him. People are giving him space. In one hand he carries a white towel. His other holds the end of a thin, white, red-tipped cane.

With vigor he sweeps the cane before him aggressively, yet systematically, feeling his way forward and down. He's negotiating the stairs with ease. But I'm worried about his ability to cross the cement path that lies between the stairs and the beach. The path is filled with a chaotic mix of pedestrians, cyclists and rollerbladers, few of whom are paying attention to each other let alone a descending blind man on a seemingly carefree mission.

I arrive at the path just as the man reaches the lowest step. "You're doin' great!" I call out, "But I thought you might want to know when there's a break in all this traffic. It might make it easier to cross."

Just then there *is* a break. I tell him it's there. Without hesitation, he steps forward to cross the path at a hearty pace. He veers a little to his right. He is going to miss the two steps leading down into the sand. He's headed for a bit steeper drop-off. He knows the drop-off lurks close in his future and bangs his cane at the ground looking for it. Finding it, he lowers the tip of his cane to the sand and, to my amazement, with perfect balance, steps down.

"I live here," he says as if dismissing his blindness. "Now comes the tough part." Again, there is no hesitation in his stride as he makes for the ocean. Shoulders back, cane sweeping widely before him, he's headed straight for a beautiful body sleeping on her tummy about ten feet away. The beach is mined with humans of various size and shape. Most of them are facing away from him, toward the ocean. They have no idea a mine sweeper is heading through them with the enthusiasm of a small boy.

The cane smacks a bronze arm before I can change the sweeper's course. Startled anger turns to astonishment and readily accepts a blind apology. I audibly guide the man through the prone crowd until his way to the ocean is clear.

What will he do now? I wonder.

With chin out and head held high, he briskly sweeps his way forward until he feels the downslope of the short hill in front of him. From that point, it is fifteen more yards to the water.

At the edge of the drop off the man puts down his towel and sits on it. He is unsociably close to a family... almost under their umbrella. He says a few words to a young boy seated next to him. He then rises, throws out his chest, and, leaving his cane and towel behind, somehow strides down the short hill of sand straight into the ocean. Feeling the water on his feet, he charges the surf and dives into the foam!

It's a miracle! Can he actually see or is he just carefree crazy? There are a lot of people in the water today. He's fortunate to have avoided a collision.

I watch him for a while. He's diving under cresting waves and occasionally attempting to catch a lift from one. He sees with his ears. I'm concerned, though, he may become disoriented. Slowly, as is everyone, he's being washed farther down the beach. How will he find his way back to his towel when it's time to get out?

I return to my wife, my chair, my book, and umbrella; but continue to stand, watching him. I wonder just how he'll find his way. Obviously, it is not the first time he's done this. He must have a method.

At last, I see he's out of the surf. He seems to be wandering a bit. My wife doesn't buy my "method" theory. She runs down the beach to help him. She arrives just after the young boy next to whom he sat, the one with whom he had talked briefly, grabs the man's hand and starts leading him back to his towel and cane. Arriving at his destination, he towels his hair dry, spreads out the cloth, and lies down on it face up to bake for what turns out to be an hour.

A while later, I spot Gary, a friend of ours, jogging on the path. Gary stops at the stairs which the blind man had descended. He lives near the top of them. Gary's been a fixture on the beach for over thirty-five years. I call to him. He turns, shielding his eyes from the sun's glare. His vision focuses and gives impetus to his feet. Gary's grin grows closer. And larger. It's been some months since he's seen us.

As part of our conversation, I rave about the blind man. Gary knows him. He lives in the condo complex next to Gary's home. His name is Greg. Greg lost his sight long ago. At the same time, a few of his fingers disappeared in a miscalculated explosion. Greg has lived on the beach for a couple of months. As we're talking (about other things), Greg's zealous cane sweeps its way past us. Gary stops him and introduces us. We talk

Greg's thick, brown hair and quick smile reflect his energy. He is truly as enthused about life as he at first seemed to be. He is interested in others. He is positive and forward-thinking. He is downright inspirational. Here is a man who's in tune with what is. Here is a man who sings with the wind, revels in the surf, cherishes the sun, the sand, the salty air... a man who loves living here!

Maybe, that's because Greg couldn't see "The Battleship."

But, had he been sighted, I figure he would have viewed that ship...first impression... as a local *happening* worthy of a wide-eyed smile and a two-handed salute.

7/15/2012

General Pieces   marc frederic

WHERE ARE YOU?

You've always amazed me. You're well worth appreciating and remembering. It's a shame I haven't made the effort.

You are magnificent, poignant, so simple to remember. I believed without doubt you could never disappear.

You're the thoughts I've had while sleeping and failed to write down as I briefly awaken.

Are you waiting in another dream for me to catch up? Or simply teasing me with the possibility?

9/8/2017

DHARGO

Deep cracks are surfacing below his feet. The narrow ledge of the cliff face on which he balances is beginning to crumble. Pebbles tumble from the ledge into a muddy river filled with yellow-eyed, open-jawed, ravenous crocodiles. On the ledge, twenty yards ahead, a ferocious, black-maned lion roars so loudly the entire cliff shakes! Behind him, a crouching tiger with huge claws creeps closer.

Searching madly for an avenue of escape, he feels dizzy. A wave of terror almost swallows him as, from directly above, poisonous venom drips onto his shoulder. His upward glance fixes on the fanged mouths, flickering tongues, and beady eyes of shiny black snakes leaning out of a cave-like nest on the side of the cliff just above him.

"Dhargo!" he calls loudly. And with that, my father's African native guide, swinging from a vine, circles Dad's waist with a powerful arm and sweeps him to safety.

The cluster of wide-eyed neighborhood children, including my brother and me, sit in awe on two cement steps at the corner of our front lawn. Meanwhile, deeply alarmed by our father's story, the cement path quickly runs from the steps on which we are sitting directly to the front door of our home and tries desperately to reach the doorbell.

We children shake off remnants of imagined fear. Little do we know or care how a tiger from India appeared on the ledge above the African river, or to what the vine from which Dhargo swung was connected. We simply release our collective breath in relief, slowly realizing we are safe from terrors we had shared. My father's resourceful, imaginary native guide, Dhargo, had, once again, rescued him from certain disaster.

Dad created an entire series of perilous plots involving his and Dhargo's narrow escapes within the deepest, darkest depths of

General Pieces   marc frederic

Africa. Extemporaneously, these stories would waft forth from my father's mind, entrancing us, carrying us all right along with him. The telling of those intriguing tales took place over sixty-five years ago, long before even my father's hair turned white. Now, here I am, conveying one of his "ancient" sagas while sporting a snowy-head of my own.

I used to find it strange to hear a pleasantly wrinkled, white-haired man talking, as if he were a boy, about his father. It turns time topsy-turvy. An old man would typically be expected to tell stories about his grandchildren, not still be thinking of himself as a child. Doing so makes him seem as if he's never grown up, created a family, or taken responsibility of his own.

Yet, now wrinkled and white-haired myself, here I am, "sitting at my own knee," reminiscing about my father's action when I was a child. Because I'm retired, happily married with children grown and gone, I have time to welcome these memories as interesting revelations— tiny gems I enjoy sharing as they surface from the treasure chest within my heart to glitter in my mind.

I was fortunate, for imaginative tales were not the only things imparted to me during my formative years. I was blessed by my father and mother enjoying a deeply loving relationship based on solid, congenial morals. They had many acquaintances who liked and respected them, but enjoyed one another's company more than any other's. They were best friends whose hands held and hearts melded throughout the joys and trials of life.

They certainly stood together in child raising. My brother's and my best interests were also theirs. They showered us with love and sprinkled us with responsibility. But we knew where we stood. There was never any playing Mom against Dad. They were a team. As we grew old enough to understand, Mom let us know she loved us dearly, but we would grow up and leave, while she and Dad would be together forever.

I was well aware of our parents' principles. Some were basic tenets of life; some were wisdom. Whether making a bed or completing a homework assignment, we were often told by our mother, "If you're going to do something, honey, do it right or not at all." Not doing a homework assignment? Out of the question! We got the point. As a youngster and to this day, when I have a menial physical task to perform, I'll often project a time frame for its completion, then try to complete it faster than planned (but always well.)

Mom and Dad concurred that no profession is too menial. "You can be anything you wish. If you decide to be a garbage collector, fine. Just be the best garbage collector in the world."

In my mid-teens, Dad explained a reality that seemed to conflict with his earlier advice, "No matter what you attempt, there will always be someone who is better at doing that individual thing." I came to understand his combination of statements as "Be as good as you can at whatever you attempt. By doing so, you will excel at many things and become a well-rounded person at one with yourself."

Dad imparted another wonderful bit of wisdom, "When offered something you don't feel you have as yet earned, accept that "thing" or "opportunity" with appreciation, then grow into the person you feel you should be in order to deserve it. By doing so, it will be rightfully yours."

And from Mom, (to us as youngsters) "I'd eat with a fork and knife, using manners, even if no one is watching me." I cannot say I always use proper manners when alone. I'm comfortable not doing so, but I think of Mom whenever I don't.

It was a beautiful, lesson, to overhear my mother and father one evening discussing that Dad had earlier in the day concluded a business deal on mutual trust alone. When he had asked about the need to immediately sign a contract, the other party had simply said, "Your handshake is good enough for me." This personal faith in him by the other party in a business not known for trustworthiness was more important to Dad than the proposed monetary reward. Honesty and follow-through are standards I have subsequently respected and lived by all my life.

General Pieces marc frederic

In my late teens, I discovered what I thought (and came to know) is the formula for true happiness. Of course, Socrates figured it out long before I did—*To Thine Own Self Be True*. By that I mean, feel free to try new things—foods, experiences, relationships, professions you do not currently know will suit you. After you have done so, you will innately understand whether you should include, expand, or eliminate that experience in the future. Eventually, you come to know before experimenting, whether you need to try a semi-new experience. If you're not sure, try it. If you've concluded it's not right for you, regardless of what others think or say, exclude it. In any case, living true to my beliefs while allowing for experimentation with new ones, has made me very comfortable with myself.

Here's another thought I've found extremely useful—if ever I do not wish to do something, feel that I *should* do it, but am not quite sure, I ask myself, "How would I feel if I *don't* do it?" What I expect of myself becomes instantly clear. I either act with conviction or let it pass with ease.

For years, I either looked ahead, allowing myself to be thrilled by possibilities, or thoroughly immersed myself in enjoyment of the present. I currently have the time for and pleasure of recording thoughts I may never have mentioned in writing. Doing so can be worthwhile at any age. But I seem to hear white hair and minor wrinkles whispering, "Do it now."

5/12/2013

PLANT

I gave a great deal of water, fertilizer, and love to that plant. It lived beneath a taller fern in a large pot on the third-floor courtyard walkway near our building's elevator.

While waiting for the elevator to arrive, I would often talk to and gently stroke the plant, encouraging it to grow larger and share its beauty. It grew rapidly after I began the communication/appreciation routine; much more so than the smaller plant of the same species I had planted in a pot out of petting range.

As the plant's leaves became larger, darker, and more prominently striped, it beautifully lived up to its name—*Zebra Plant*. All the while, it continued to push forth from its center tiny light green leaves on which I would congratulate it. The plant's growth progressed. I became enchanted with the idea of sharing small pieces of time with it and was actually pleased when the elevator was delayed.

I was rushed when I went to the elevator this afternoon. My state became more unsettled as I gazed at what should have been my sturdy, handsome companion. It looked to be about a quarter of its size, was much lighter in color and shriveled, as if it had been poisoned, I quickly looked in the other large pot to check the smaller zebra plant…and it was gone…maybe poisoned into oblivion! I was shocked and mystified, but the elevator demanded my attention, indicating it had no time to hang around with its door gaping open.

When my wife and I returned from separate errands and exited the elevator together, we realized no one had poisoned the plants. They had simply dug up and stolen my large friend, then transplanted the smaller one in its place.

The smaller plant was dying from trauma and thirst. I immediately watered it, gave it a soothing pep talk, and made plans to build a strong relationship with it over the weeks to come.

General Pieces   marc frederic

Although my wife and I feel somewhat violated by our loss, I imagine the thievery is due to the undeniable richness and glamor the large plant displayed. I hope the thief treats it well and enjoys the rewards of doing so. But the plant already knows what a scoundrel its new owner can be, so all we can do is hope.

I enjoyed the relationship and look forward to building a new one.

"Don't you worry baby zebra, we will nurse you back to health and happiness in your new pot. And, as you grow stronger, we will protect you from being snatched.

"Don't be concerned about the baby alligator we've put in the pot with you. It doesn't eat plants.

10/3/2013

NIBBLETS   General Pieces

BELIEVE IT OR NOT

The building in which my wife and I live is just 60 yards from the ocean, including a row of bushes, a walkway, bike path, and sand. It's a three-story beach condominium just south of Redondo Beach's King Harbor. We're on the top floor.

Our 180-degree view is typically filled with action—human, wildlife, and shows, such as sunsets, put on by Mother Nature.

A number of bird species can usually be seen. Pelicans are both the fewest and grandest, but the skies and beach sport a multitude of pigeons and seagulls. The latter are rascals, often raiding beach-goers' bagged lunches when left unattended.

Late one sunny afternoon, I'm preparing to cook. The barbeque is located on our covered patio next to an 8 x 4-inch wooden beam, which tops a glass windbreak. I've just set a platter of marinating steaks on the beam. The grill is almost hot enough.

Turning from the beam, I move toward our rattan bar to retrieve my drink and see my reflection in our bedroom's expansive sliding glass door. To my shock and amazement, broad feathery wings are sticking out from both my shoulders. What the hell! A dramatically loud flapping accompanies them.

In panic, I spin to see a huge seagull hovering above the steak platter. It snatches a ribeye in its beak and does its best to fly off. But the steak is heavier than the seagull is strong. Down, the bird flaps, across the bushes, walkway, and bike path onto the sandy beach.

Hardly believing what happened, I run inside to the kitchen where my wife is preparing our salad, and blurt, "A seagull just grabbed a steak off the balcony!"

Having warned me for years that food might slip off the beam, my wife doesn't believe me, "You dropped it. Didn't you."

"No," I protest. "A seagull got it!"

"Come on, sweetheart. I knew something would drop off that beam sooner or later."

"No. I'm not kidding. The steak's out on the beach, not in the bushes. Come see."

She looks, but can't see the steak amidst the horde of clamoring seagulls trying to claim their share.

Who knew seagulls cared about meat? A good ribeye is a good ribeye, but my wife doubts the birds' appetite for meat, "You dropped it didn't you."

"No. It couldn't fall way out there."

"Hmm. Are you sure that's a steak?"

"I'll get the binoculars." And did.

"Good God! That *is* the steak. Amazing! Tell me again what happened."

I picked up my scotch and water and in great detail proceeded to tell the tale.

2014

LITTLE BOY AT THE PARK

It's a warm spring day at the neighborhood park. As the sun coaxes colorful flowers into giving up their scents, four elderly ladies relax together on a wooden bench indulging in their mid-day chat while communally tending their gaggle of three to five-year-old grand and great-grandchildren.

The children entertain themselves nearby, occasionally checking in with their elders to ask "Why is the sky blue?" or shout, "Look what I found, Nana!"

One three-year-old blond boy lingers quietly on the grass at his great-grandmother's feet, gently stroking the red lower portion of her thin white cane. GG (short for great grammy) tilts her head back and sighs, "How wonderful this sun feels. From the time I lost my sight, my sense of touch has greatly improved. I now thoroughly enjoy the sun gently bathing me. And I'm so fortunate to have memories of many marvelous sights, especially of my late husband's lake-blue eyes gazing deeply into mine. But I still wish I could see."

Another of the women, mostly hidden beneath a wide-brimmed hat and long-sleeved cotton shirt, responds, "How I loved the feel of the warm sun on my skin; the rays of that glorious orb caressing my body. But my body can't handle the threat of recurring skin cancer, so now I protect it the best I can."

The third grandmother comments that she can still see, treasures the feel of the sun on her skin and is thankful her husband is still alive. "But I miss conversing with him during our long strolls. Since his stroke, we can do neither."

The remaining woman gently brushes back a loose strand of gray hair before stating her body, too, is wearing out. It harbors aches and pains. "Although I can't see or hear as well as I once could and my mind sometimes wanders off without me, I still marvel at the many wonders of this world."

General Pieces   marc frederic

With a big-eyed, innocent smile, the three-year-old boy looks up from stroking the cane to join in, "I remember enjoying wonders even greater than this world, Nana. And I didn't need a body to do it."

2/9/2014

UNBALANCED

I awaken.

Lying in bed, my body seems gigantic and very heavy to me. It's as if I'm a tiny pebble rattling around inside it. Rising from bed is out of the question.

My body is an alien entity. I'm not connected to it by muscle or tissue of any sort. I'm a mere speck within a hollow shell.

I've never related to my body like this. So strange. Maybe by returning too rapidly from a dream, I haven't yet filled in my body. I'm not yet together.

Now I understand how my mind feels when I ignore it in favor of my body. And why I'm out of sorts when I don't pay attention to my soul.

10/18/2017

General Pieces   marc frederic

TOMORROW'S THE DAY

I'm preparing to be shot in the heart.

Not by a bullet or even Cupid's arrow. But by the helping hand of a trusted surgeon. He's planning to repair or replace my mitral valve.

The operation isn't rare. It's a constructive act as opposed to a bullet's intrusion. But, still, it's invading an organ crucial to my body's well-being.

And, eventually, it's going to hurt. My heart isn't meant to be invaded by metal objects. Neither are my ribs.

Luckily, pain reduction will be available in adequate quantity. And I'm no martyr. I've learned the key to handling pain is to stay ahead of it. Don't wait for it to grab you, even from behind. By the time it sneaks up on you, it's too late to instantly eradicate. The hospital personnel understand.

My job is to heal that wound. Rest, recuperate and exercise. Yet, I must move my body. Make sure all its systems are in play and functioning beautifully.

But don't overdo it. Curb my enthusiasm. Don't invite a setback. Just treat my body as the wonderful entity it is for supporting my mind and spirit.

For the immediate future, my body is my guest of honor.

5/15/2019

IT'S PLEASANT ON THE PATIO

It's pleasant on the patio, sitting in the morning sun. The dry heat will reach only the low 90's.

I've donned sunscreen. But should I allow sunrays to touch me at all? They have already taken a toll: brown spots, wrinkles, slight basal and squamous cancer. I tan nicely and like the look, but my skin isn't what it used to be.

Come to think of it, my body is far from what it used to be, except for weight. Somewhere midst five serious surgeries during the last 16 months I've lost 20 pounds. No matter what I eat, I can't seem to gain much back.

I harbor no cancer that I know of, yet parts of my body seem to have failed lately. Evidently, they've been failing for a long time, but have recently been discovered. All but one had gone unnoticed. Nice. No pain. No debilitating symptoms.

Being active before and in between surgeries, has helped me recoup rapidly from each. The heart valve replacement took longest—a couple of months. That one affected me mentally. Taught me patience.

Now peripheral neuropathy is creeping up my left leg. Slowly, more places on my body, especially from surgeries and radiation, are becoming numb.

My body may be losing some ability to feel. But my mind and spirit still have great fun.

Looking up from the novel in my lap, I see the gossamer wings of a small damselfly perched on the single, slim blade of a palm frond. It's evidently enjoying the sun too.

It makes me happy. I feel the kinship of mutual joy.

General Pieces   marc frederic

It also offers perspective. The damselfly's lifespan, once it's flying, is measured in days.

I have longer.

So...

10/6/2019

MAGIC NURSE

"Your name, sir?"
"Marc Frederic, reporting to be sliced open."
She smiles.
"What surgery are you scheduled for?"
"Inguinal hernia repair by Doctor Steven Choe."
"You're very chipper."
"I feel great and have confidence in Dr. Choe. He's been inside me twice before. He knows where to go."

Thirty minutes later, I sit thinking to myself, this is my sixth operation in 17 months. You'd think I'd remember to wear a jacket to the Surgery Waiting Room. Cold is not cool.

The above words are hardly worth reading. I've written them for distraction in an attempt to stay warm.

Then it happens.
In an act of supreme consideration sprinkled with kindness, a nurse from pre-op walks through the door, visually assesses my situation, and asks if I'd like a warm blanket.
Would I? Would I! Of all the things I could possibly desire, a warm blanket tops the list.

This nurse is not specifically assigned to me. She had magically appeared.
Now she disappears, only to reappear a moment later. Like a genie, she grants my wish, draping the heated blanket over my huddled body.
"It's always too cold in here," she states. And, once again disappears, as I revel in newly found comfort.

1/13/2020

WARM AND COZY PLACES

It's pleasant moving within her body like this. There are lots of warm and cozy places.

But not being able to see out can be scary. Sometimes I crawl to the corner of her eye to peek out a tear duct.

I've thought about sliding down her nose to get a wider view but, if she should sneeze, who knows where I'd wind up. Maybe in a tissue thrown in a trash can. Maybe disoriented, flying endlessly through the air. Or ultimately in someone else's body.

It's not easy being a virus.

5/6/2020

LOST

Chippie began life as a tiny, white ball of fluff with big blue eyes and a tranquil mew. As he grew, his fur developed a gray/tan marbled pattern, and his handsome facial markings resembled those of a cheetah. He eventually weighed 22 pounds.

When we lost him, we were devastated.

Chippie was ten years old when he jumped out the window. For eight of those years, he and our other cats Sammy and Cairo lived with us in a third-floor beachfront condo where they never went outside. They showed no interest in going out, even when the door to out balcony was open. When we retired to a resort community in Palm Desert, all three continued to be strictly indoor cats.

In April of 2018, our second year in the desert, the days turned hot enough to start using our air-conditioning. Although it worked in the rest of the house, we discovered it wouldn't cool the living room and den.

That evening, we opened a window in the den to cool off while we watched TV. Months before, we had removed our screens for a better view of the lake and golf course. We waited for the cats' reactions to the open, screenless window. They showed no interest. When we went to bed, our room was comfortably cool. We simply forgot about the open window in the den.

The next morning, Sammy and Cairo were in the kitchen eagerly waiting for their breakfast. But where was Chippie? He was always first to the food bowls. We called him to come and eat. No response. Wondering why Chippie didn't come, we checked all his favorite places throughout the house. That was easy. Chippie didn't hide, he lounged. But he was nowhere to be found.

When we couldn't remember Chippie sleeping with us the previous night, worry began to gnaw its way into our minds. We decided to search more thoroughly—under the beds, in the showers and closets, behind couches and chairs. With each failure to find Chippie, our concern grew.

Then, to our horror, we saw the open window. Could Chippie have leapt through it? We closed the window and shunned that possibility. The fact that we couldn't find him inside was upsetting—that he might be outside was frightening.

Overnight, the desert temperature had been cold and it was forecast to rise to 103 degrees during the day. Could Chippie's overweight body handle such dramatic changes? And, though he was the alpha male to our other cats, was he tough and agile enough to fend off the hungry coyotes that routinely roam our community at night?

We anxiously searched our yards and immediate neighborhood, while continually calling him. Nothing. No Chippie. With no walls between residences and the golf course, he could be anywhere.

Trying to stuff down panic, we returned home to enlist help. On the phone, our community's Pet Club reminded us that cats have an acute sense of smell. They advised placing a piece of our unwashed clothing plus food and water in our front courtyard and back patio. They also suggested we give Chippie's description to our Maintenance and Security Departments so they could keep an eye out for him as they traveled the golf course and community streets.

We created 100 *LOST CAT* flyers that included a substantial reward. We delivered some to the two departments and placed the remainder in people's mailboxes for blocks around.

By late afternoon, we headed home through the oppressive heat. As we walked, we discussed how much Chippie's heavily furred body must be affected by the sweltering temperature. How could we help him? What more could we do? My wife suggested we call our church's prayer line. We also decided to give away our tickets to the Country Western Barbeque we were to attend that night. We wanted to be home in case Chippie returned or someone found him.

NIBBLETS   General Pieces

As dusk arrived, we paced our patio, our eyes searching the vast golf course, intermittently calling out to Chippie. When we could no longer see, our anxiety turned to fear, and we desperately wailed into the dark, "Chippie…Chippie…Chippie!"

Receiving no response, we realized there was nothing more we could do.

Despondent, tired and hungry, we sat at the patio table. Waiting. Picking at snacks.

We began to reminisce about Chippie. He wasn't aloof or high-strung like other cats. Chippie was more dog-like—loyal, steady. He moved slowly, was unexcitable. He came when called, even responded to hand signals. And Chippie loved to snuggle. Most nights, he slept between my wife and me, purring and snoring. He was a love-magnet, a pleasure, a beautiful spirit. Time spent with Chippie melted everyone's hearts. Chippie happily greeted guests and treated them as if they'd be welcome forever. Luxuriating in their caresses, he brought out their best. He loved unconditionally.

But most of all, Chippie taught us to relax, to put more *slow* in our lives, that there's no need to rush, there are a million tomorrows to share Chippie was an important member of our family. How could we do without him?

Eventually, my wife excused herself to take a shower. As she left, she turned on additional patio lights and asked me to keep an eye out for Chippie while I washed the dishes.

"Any sight of Chippie?" she asked when she returned to the kitchen.

"Absolutely nothing."

The last 12 hours felt like a week. I imagined all Chippie had been through—the chilling cold and searing heat, debilitating thirst and hunger. Was he exhausted? Disoriented? Injured? Had he given up? Could he survive a second night in the wild? Was he even alive?

General Pieces   marc frederic

I wasn't used to feeling such pessimism, didn't like those thoughts at all. I silently prayed, thanking God for Chippie's safety.

Suddenly, something changed. My negative thoughts disappeared. My melancholy vanished. With strength and resolve, I strode out the patio door. Fully expecting a positive result, I firmly stated into the night, "Okay, Chippie, enough of all this. You've had your adventure. It's time to come home." I pointed at the open door and continued, "Get your buns in the house right now."

Within seconds, the light from the patio reflected in a pair of glowing eyes moving forward. And from the rim of darkness, Chippie miraculously trotted past me into the house. Immediately, our fear and hopelessness were replaced with relief and joy. Chippie's return filled the gigantic hole in our lives. We cheered, inspected, and hugged him tightly, thanking God for his safe return. I was surprised how rapidly we felt whole again.

In reflection, it wasn't Chippie's response that amazed me, but how easy it is to expect and accept a miracle.

5/4/2020

MENTAL EXERCISE
(on a desert patio at sunset)

Flexibility.
I'm walking 'round the brim of my hat,
which would be no big deal except that
it's on my head.

Balance.
I breathe in golden; exhale silver.
All the while turning in circles.
Ecstasy keeps me upright.
I maintain equal amounts of joy
on the backs of both hands.

Endurance.
I observe. I think. I trust. I believe.
I know. I am.
And so it is.

Stretching.
My imagination is
a huge pipeline of gossamer thoughts.
As it wanders, it thins in diameter
becoming a garden hose of rainbows
pricked intermittently by tiny lightning bolts.
It narrows further while lengthening to
a five-mile noodle full of liquid garlic butter;
then morphs to an endless string of pearls.
It's now a simple thread of love
undulating
toward its date with
infinity.

Rhythm.
Silence caresses memories of the future
in tune with the beat that moves throughout everything,
occasionally changing tempo,

never out of sync.

Muscle Tone.
Relaxed. Firm. Unconstrained.
I'm up for it; into it. Enveloped in warmth.
But darkness has flattened itself against my paper pad.
Time to reel everything in and move inside.

7/1/2020

IT KEEPS THE POLAR BEARS AWAY

I like heat. Some people don't. That's understandable if you're perspiring profusely, shoveling coal into the furnace of a locomotive passing slowly through Louisiana at noon on the fifteenth of August. But I'm in dry desert heat, sitting comfortably on my shady patio next to a golf course lake during June in Palm Desert, California.

Yep, it's 104 degrees but, as I said, it's dry, the view is cool, and iced liquid delicious. Unless I'm lit up by direct sunlight, it feels like Mother Nature is giving me a big hug.

Our next-door neighbor's wife doesn't like heat. Even the dry kind. She's a warm person without it. She is considerate, generous, wears a warm smile on her beautiful face, but her body is round enough for two of her to fit into. On cool days she seems happy to have her second-self along. On hot ones, her companion is a drag.

We became neighbors in mid-April. Shortly after we moved in, she brought us a welcome gift of grapefruits, lemons and figs recently borne by trees in her backyard. A while later, after we had planted roses in our courtyard, she gave us a front door mat that said *Stop and Smell the ROSES. ROSES* was printed in pink. That was very thoughtful of her.

That was also before her second-self came to live with her and her husband on a fulltime basis. Before that, she had been active. She golfed, went out to lunch, took an oil-painting class, and enjoyed pool aerobics.

Her husband golfed. And golfed. And golfed. He also fixed things through a Neighbors 4 Neighbors program when people in need would call him. He didn't talk much, but was pleasant. They both were.

We learned what heat could do to the wife. It was an annual occurrence. Mrs. Neighbor didn't like the heat one bit. Couldn't

General Pieces   marc frederic

stand it. She didn't go out in it much. She occasionally left her air-conditioned home, drove her A/C'd car to her A/C'd salon to have her hair and nails done. But she played no golf and did few aerobics. She did eat and spend more time in bed with aches of sorts.

Her husband golfed and fixed things for people. He liked the heat, said it keeps the polar bears away. Her husband liked his lifestyle here. He liked both golfing and fixing things for people. He played more golf.

It became apparent, when she was seen, that Mrs. Neighbor's second-self was moving in with her permanently. Mr. Neighbor (let's call him Mr. N for short) listened to his wife's and her second-self's weather complaints. The evening weather report became a point of extreme interest, even contention. He took her to a list of doctors for knee problems and weight control. Mrs. N tried different diets. Summer heat plotted against her. Nothing worked for long.

They had made it through the two summers before we moved in. But her surviving this one looked like a toss-up. They purchased a small mobile home for staying at various beaches. When they traveled, Mrs. N felt better. Mr. N played nearby golf courses. They made it through another summer. As temperatures dropped, their spirits rose. They felt the mobile home was the solution. But serious discussions about moving to a cooler climate ensued.

Months passed quickly. Mrs. N had a serious talk with her second-self, told her she would have to leave in order to improve chances of a successful knee replacement. Dieting worked. Some weight was lost. The operation was successful, but somehow Mrs. N couldn't keep her eye on healing. She kept glancing at the summer heat approaching like a forest fire through the pages of her calendar. It was only January, but she smelled smoke each month she turned the page.

In desperation, she healed. Trips began to bloom. They were exploratory trips to find a home where icicles might form during the coldest day of Winter. Each time Mrs. N got behind the wheel. she was driving into a garden of hope. Mr. N viewed her trips more as random weed-wanderings.

Whenever we'd see the husband, he would explain how much he loved golfing in the early morning warmth. Whenever we saw the wife, she was adamant about moving. So it went, until spring made it obvious summer's sauna was lurking just around the corner.

Mrs. N took the mobile home on another trip. She could see their new home nestled somewhere in the next two-month distance. Mr. and Mrs. N then began venturing out together on narrowed-down scouting journeys. Prior to each expedition, Mr. N always thought briefly about attaching a heavy-duty steel cable from their pleasantly rooted home to the back of their mobile home. Somehow, he imagined he would pull not only the house, but the neighborhood, the golf course and even a tinge of the hot weather right along with them. Of course, that never happened.

One day, our neighbors announced they had made an offer on a lovely home in a cooler climate, which had potential icicles hanging from its future. Although it might be surrounded by shivers during the winter, it offered a delightful escape in the form of a fireplace large enough to walk into and multiple cords of wood stacked along the side porch.

Luckily for Mr. N., this refuge from Infernoville was located on a golf course. That was the mainstay of Mrs. N's sales pitch to him. And even though the house was in immaculate condition, leaving little to be fixed, there would be a great need to chop wood. That was Mrs. N's second sales point.

Her third point was the golf course sported a variety of wildlife.

She didn't mention the color of the bears, but I didn't get the impression they were white.

7/2/2020

MY FAVORITE GIFT

It is a gift I had intuitively fantasized about for years. An imaginary treasure I believed I would inevitably relish as a reality. A gift that would change my life forever.

At last, it was well within reach. I no longer had to dream about it. It was before me, well-packaged and beautifully wrapped. It was perfect.

The time had finally come to act. I requested the gift. Twice—three months after it became available, and again three months after that. Both requests were denied.

Only one space in my life left room for improvement. The gift could have filled that gap with ever-lasting joy. I buried my disappointment and managed to live happily. Simply knowing the gift existed, made each day marvelous.

Then, the unexpected happened. I had long ago settled into enjoying life for all it is when, unsolicited, the gift was bestowed upon me. We were driving down the street on our way to wherever. Out of the blue, she turned to me and casually asked, "Wouldn't it be exciting to get married two years from the day we met?"

That was the present, the answer to my request of many months prior.

I was right. It has made both our lives even better. We have shared 32 years—384 months, 11,680 days, 280,320 hours—appreciating and enjoying the most wonderful gift of all.

8/7/2020

FOR THIS, I AM THANKFUL

I was once asked to sum up in 100 words what I am thankful for. Here's what I said:

I'm thankful for the fun and wonder I find through my imagination.

Why limit myself to this world, this mind, this body? There's so much more. I write creatively about what I discover. I'm excited by everything for what it is.

I believe we are spiritual beings living the human experience. I immerse myself in the side trips of this life, enjoying what they offer, feeling gratitude for and wondering at all I encounter.

What stirs my deepest appreciation is knowing that, regardless of our circumstances, we eventually get to die, to experience the marvelous worlds and lives to come.

8/9/2020

COMPLICATED BANKING

Jimi, the extremely accommodative Bank Relationship Officer has a list of questions I can't answer: "We offer *this*, or would you prefer *that*? We can set you up with *blank* if you like." Frankly, I don't understand the terminology. Fortunately, she presents information to explain it.

Transferring a business banking account these days seems complicated. There are mysterious modern options that muddle my brain.

Jimi is both patient and pleasant. Her explanations make sense and are simple enough for a techno-dinosaur like me to understand. Almost.

I try, but a bit further into her presentation I tell her several features are too modern for me to comprehend. That they flummox me, make me feel inadequate. That my answers may soon make her view me as a small pile of dust.

Jimi enjoys both the incongruous image and my sense of humor. She chuckles, then laughs gently, then more heartily. Her laughter is contagious.

We eventually settle down. I'm ready to absorb further technical terms even though I'm up to my earlobes in mysterious explanatory thoughts.

I open the account. Jimi's happy. So am I. In order to dispel the decrepit, dusty image I blurted earlier I quote one of my more inspirational poems "I Love It Unlimited". Jimi is impressed.

It's my turn to ask questions. I learn about Jimi's heritage, share that I have visited her homeland and found it to be lovely. I discover she has two young daughters with names of flowers—Azalea and Zinnia—to whom she loves to read. We agree that books open doors to new worlds.

Her purchase of $50 worth of my books becomes my first deposit.
2/1/2021

RELISHING WORDS

I sit in my boxer shorts beneath the sunshine, smiling at the poetry I'm reading.

The thoughts are romantic, the most romantic poetry I've ever read. It has aged well, if at all, lying calmly on the pages, waiting to again share its tenderness and passion, its exquisite expression that so lovingly revels in the joy of appreciation.

This love, written by Walter Benton, I read as a young man and have since lived time and again, but never so much as with my current mate of 33 years in a fairy tale of foreverness.

I trade the book for pen and paper to express the feeling Benton has evoked.

The effect of his writing must be evident. A visitor suddenly seems to recognize it—I'm being fanned by a hummingbird. One of the first this spring. Never has one approached me in this manner, slipping beneath the wide brim of my hat, almost inserting its beak into my ear.

I keep my eyes glued to the paper and continue to write, calmly ignoring, yet welcoming the flutter-buzzing wings. I've become a flower, singled out for mere seconds as a center of attention.

Is it me in which the bird is interested?

Or is this marvelous creature simply a speed-reader looking over my shoulder, relishing my words just as I delighted in Benton's?

3/14/2021

General Pieces   marc frederic

OLD SKIN

At six years old, Scott was candid. But I'm not sure his eyesight was accurate.

He told me his other grandfather has old skin. Old skin? I wish I looked like him. Or maybe *my* eyes weren't working right. Or maybe the Colorado air did something to make me look better.

On returning to the California sun that's baked my skin for eons, I took a close look in the mirror. A real close look. Either our grandson Scotty was being considerate or he really does have an eye problem. I wondered what he'll think of my skin on my next visit. In anticipation, I wrote this:

> I am bringing my old skin to visit.
> It is no longer firm, smooth and prime.
> You can count all my scars and fine wrinkles.
> We will have a most marvelous time.
> There are many a nick, pock, and cranny.
> There are crevices deep to explore.
> You may find spider veins, a few bowling lanes,
> a wart, several moles, and clogged pores.
> Though it may not be handsome to look at,
> here's a lesson that needs to sink in—
> mine, at one time, was smooth as a peach's.
> So be sure to take care of your skin.

I eventually sent him the poem and have seen him many times since. Scott's now almost 22 and hasn't mentioned skin since he was six.

During those years, I've added serious wrinkles, a scar, even sags. The horizontal creases on my forehead are now intersected by vertical ones.

Scott's coming to California this weekend to introduce his fiancée. His brother, mom, and dad are accompanying him. Should be fun. Maybe, they'd like to reserve my forehead as a game board.

Tic tac toe? Checkers? Chess, anyone?
                    4/17/2021

MISSING

There it stands—a gigantic stalk, 40 feet tall, two feet in diameter, seemingly lost in a row of completely whole palm trees.

Yesterday, this tall, tall stump was one of them—an elegant, regal palm with full-maned accentuated neck and lovely, thick, fanned fronds surveying the lake and golf course below it.

Last night, fierce winds cleanly snapped off its head and long neck, all 15 feet worth. Must have hurt like hell.

What's left simply maintains its place in the row of elegance, imitating a bewildered smokestack.

I've seen many palm trees from tropic to desert. but nothing like this. It's an image of sadness. Of loss and dismay. A lone shaft against a blue sky, stunted, robbed of grandeur, unable to see, to wave, or inspire appreciation.

Its head and neck are nowhere to be found. Maintenance must have hauled them away. It would have been tragic to see them lying on the ground, but it would have presented a complete picture—Decapitation In The Desert.

Instead, the picture is incomplete, somewhat of a mystery faintly calling out for help.

4/25/21

LOVELY GIFT

It's 8:30 p.m. A July evening in Palm Desert, California. The sky is sleeping, but not deeply. It seems to have one eye open that dispenses enough pale blue to create silhouettes of tall palm trees.

Lower, distant yellow lights of homes beyond the lake simultaneously rest on the dark shore while shimmering in black water.

But, as I relax in our spa, being comfortably pummeled by warm jets of water, one thing clearly stands out against this background—the hanging, brightly colored, decorative balls, each slowly changing its glowing blush like a rainbow cluster of small planets.

Thank you for blessing our friendship in such a pleasant manner.

7/18/2021

YOU GRACE ME WITH EMOTIONAL MILK AND HONEY

You grace me with emotional milk and honey.
I pamper you with constancy and strength.
Throughout our dreams of wonder we do wander,
using love to paint life's depth and length.

The partnership we've formed with vow and vigor
is based on charm, attraction, and respect.
O'er years it's grown more sound and so much bigger.
Our joy and delight it does reflect.

We now stroll hand-in-hand throughout this dreamland,
appreciation flowing through our veins.
From everything the sunshine coaxes beauty;
yes, even pastel bows brought on by rains.
A pesky fly may bug us on occasion
but then, with patience and a loving eye,
we see it change into a thing of beauty
as multi-colored butter flutters by.

Plants contribute treasures we call flowers.
Trees yield nuts that nourish, and lush fruit.
The earth produces marvels that support us
from grain to vegetable and even root.
Water both sustains and gives us joy—
rushing rivers, lakes, cascading walls;
waving seas and classic ice formations,
silent white, as snowflake gently falls;
fluffy clouds which oft have silver linings,
iridescent rain that pleases eye.
So much beauty—subtle, wild, and tender,
to savor as our time on Earth slips by.

Could after-life be even half as splendid
as has this venture that I share with you?
It takes great faith, unbound imagination,

General Pieces   marc frederic

to think that such a marvel could be true.
But all the world is blessed with fine surprises
like those in this life that most folks find rare.
So why should there not be a multitude to see
in any future life we dare to share?

Do soar with me, my love, let's keep on living
what's left of this and many lives to come,
while feeling so sublime, enchanted by life's rhyme,
and easing into all we may become.

5/1/2021

A LAUGHING MATTER

A panicky shout, "Fore!" rips my attention from the book I'm reading, as a golf ball ricochets off a palm tree onto our roof. It rattles down the tiles, bounces off our patio pavers, and plops perfectly into my gin-and-tonic.

Both my startled wife and I begin laughing.

The golfers soon reach the green, which is separated from our home by a small lake. I raise my glass, point to it, and loudly proclaim, "Nice shot. A high ball in a highball."

Picking the dimpled white sphere from the glass. I shout, "You want your ball? I'll throw it to you."

The lake is 10 yards from me and stretches another 30 to the other side.

"Can you throw it this far?"

"I used to pitch for the Dodgers," I spoof, as I stand and set my drink on the table.

I rear back and throw. Failing to be released soon enough, the tiny ball veers dramatically to the left. As the ball splashes just 10 yards offshore, my arm's momentum steals my balance. I fall hard left, rolling onto the pavers.

My wife screams in fear it's becoming a Humpty Dumpty event. But no. Up I pop, shaken, somewhat scuffed, but still in one piece as I stagger around a bit.

That evening, recalling the incident, I found myself in a fit of embarrassed laughter.

General Pieces   marc frederic

Two days later, as I stepped into the shower, my wife pointed out the immense bruise on my hip that's destined to follow me everywhere for weeks.

Maybe my wife is right about it not being a laughing matter. The four pairs of non-slip, corrective shoes she insisted I buy cost a small fortune.

10/30/2021

THE DENALI

Distracting me from reading in my parked car, the massive pickup truck slowly pulls into and engulfs a nearby space.

Its magnificent black body is elevated above its chassis far enough that the mysterious mechanics hidden from view on lesser vehicles are on full display. Its hubcaps sport a futuristic silver design. Its chrome running board protrudes below the front and back doors extending from fender to fender.

Painted, plated, and sparkling clean, these components reflect the owner's love for this spectacular monster.

Who drives a vehicle of such size? Were I standing before this black beauty, its hood would be the same height as my nose. It's intimidating.

I can see only the silhouette of the person behind the steering wheel. There he sits, two parking spaces and a world away from me in my conservative 20-year-old Lexus, waiting for my wife to come out of the building in front of us.

Ah, here comes my gorgeous lady now, sporting a grand, satisfied smile.

The driver of the truck sees her too. He opens the truck's door, steps out, and hops off the running board. Removing his black baseball cap, he swings it in a low arch as he bows to my wife and hands her the truck's keys.

I hadn't paid attention when we drove in. I thought I was simply taking my wife on an errand. *Looking up, I see above the building's entrance a banner reading—FANTASY MUSCLE CARS FOR RENT.*

Lovely Gaylan in that hunky truck? Well, why not? Her appearance makes for magnificent contrasts. When we lived on the beach, she

General Pieces   marc frederic

was a knockout in her bikini, lounging on a designer towel, smoking a rum-flavored cigar.

Damn! There goes my imagination again! She's actually just now coming out of the Cleaner's carrying a few hangers full of clothes.

But the truck's real. That's for sure.

2/17/2022

GAYLAN KING FREDERIC
2/25/1944 – 6/9/2022

A beautiful spirit is circling today
among us and through us while back on her way
to harmonious worlds from whence she once came
where those who await her know more than her name.
They know of the love she so generously shared,
the physical pain she so patiently beared,
her soft words and feelings, her chocolate eyes,
her face so appealing, her reasoning wise.
She leaves us with images gentle and kind
which will sing in our hearts and dance in our minds.
But Gaylan will never be too far away
for, you see, time and space are for naught when we pray.
And by "praying" I mean simply giving a care—
feeling the sunshine, tasting the air,
appreciating our fellow man
and making life better however we can.
For that is our Gaylan. In us, she will live
and continue to guide us in new ways to give.
Thank you, Sweet Lady, for all that you are.
You're the kiss in the full moon; the light of a star.
You're the scent of a flower, the beauty in art,
the joy of travel with each thrilling start.
You're the wonder of wishes completely fulfilled
and the song of a bird as it's so sweetly trilled.
A seven-course dinner prepared well to please,
presented with confidence, caring, and ease.
You are all of the marvelous things that can be—
an example of quality sobriety.
Our dear, darling Gaylan, we'll not say "adieu"'
for whenever we wish, we can be close to you.
But you have your new lives. We'll meet down the line.
For now, we'll just love you and all will be fine.

11/5/2022

I NEVER KNEW YOU WERE AN ANGEL

I never knew you were an angel.
Although I guessed it once or twice,
For on Earth, you were a treasure,
dispensing light and pleasure,
seasoning our lives with spice.
Making all feel we are special,
bringing love up to the fore,
All these things you made look simple
with a magic smile and dimple.
In addition, you did more.
You listened, oh, so carefully
to our voices and our hearts,
guiding us without our knowing.
Telling not, but rather showing,
how to truly play our parts.
You're very special, lovely baby.
And now I realize, at last,
you're angelic quality
is as real as it can be.
You are a spirit from the past.

6/18/2022

(Gaylan made her transition nine days ago.
We've enjoyed some delightful conversations since then.)

CAT TAIL

Cat tail.

Not the plant found standing tall in a marsh. No. I'm currently intrigued by the tail of an actual cat, that of my companion, Louie, a five-year-old tuxedo cat lying next to me on my recliner while I read.

As he sleeps, his tail spells out a series of dreams in movements only a cat can understand. I'm fascinated by these feline tales. Intrigued enough to morph into cathood…

Ah…the gentleness of steady, slow sway. Such a peaceful drift. I can't see Louie's face, but I can hear his smile. How wonderful to never be a slave to time. To be instantly at one with whatever I wish. To float and dream for hours.

Now, a change of pace. A spasmatic tip movement. A brief, but definite interruption. Not enough to rouse us. But a conscious reaction in a different realm. Ooh. Eeee. Wild. Then a soft sigh and sudden stillness. Back to the world of tranquility.

I lie calmly. Passively observing. Just outside a dream. Waiting for its door to open.

Here it comes. Soft. Silky. I can feel my tail again swaying gently. How delightful to shift between wake, sleep, reality, and dreams. Cat napping, I visit many marvelous worlds. It's more pleasant than being *awake*, as humans call it. I love playing with Chippie and Cairo like we did before their dimension shift. And what joy to again feel my mistress's special touch.

I've met dogs and cats that lived with my master long ago. We connect in warm glow. I can share their past lives.

So many things to do and feel. And humans wonder why we sleep so much.

General Pieces   marc frederic

I'm shifting back. Returning to human form.

How relaxing and lovely it is to watch Louie's tail while he sleeps.

6/21/2023

BEYOND THE FIVE

All morning, I'd been cultivating a spiritual mindset. I became so positively inspired on my way to the funeral of my friend's father, Jim, I pulled over to write my own rhyming epitaph.

I believe my euphoric state also facilitated the event that took place after the service.

Not knowing the man, I had attended his service out of respect for the family. When the minister's comforting words concluded, everyone was invited forward to say their final goodbyes.

It was my first open-casket funeral. I felt uncomfortable viewing the body. Believing all would go well for Jim, I blessed his spirit from my pew and decided to relax in my car while his friends and relatives said their farewells.

Now, peacefully driving to the wake, I hear a man's mellow voice as clearly as you're reading these words. It's Jim. He asks me to tell his widow, Ruth, he's fine and loves her dearly. I tell him I'm happy to; then state, "I don't have to speak aloud to you, do I." The remainder of our conversation is telepathic and brief.

Elated, I thank God for the privilege of being the conduit for this man's message.

As I arrive at the wake, I have doubts—not about my communication with Jim, but how it will be received. Will Ruth feel I'm invading her privacy? Will she be offended?

I must follow through. After all, Jim chose me for a reason. I hug Ruth and whisper in her ear. She thanks me profusely while strongly returning my embrace.

That was years ago. The clarity of that event increased my awareness of senses beyond the five marvelous ones we often take for granted. Now days, tuning into additional senses allows me to more thoroughly enjoy this world and occasionally visit others.

9/18/2021

General Pieces   marc frederic

ELUSIVE THOUGHT

I'm late. Should have left some time ago. But the strange idea flitted through my mind, allowing me a glimpse, tantalizing, teasing me, and moving on. I need to catch it.

Had my idea-net been within reach, I'd have caught the thought quickly, but it wasn't. And jumping up to chase them never works. Startled ideas dart out of range to melt beneath a dazzling desert sun or sink into a waving azure sea.

There's a better way.

Gently. Slowly. With consideration, I must tenderly appreciate, smoothly romance the idea back into my mind, then onto paper with a pleasant hum and pastel caress.

Think softly… think… think…

Ahh, at last. There it lies, complete, satisfied, and smiling in its entirety.

What a thrill—calmly coaxing an intangible; transforming it into symbols easily understood by readers of every ilk.

I wonder now just how that idea will be used, what more it will become.

But that, of course, is up to you.

7/21/23

NIBBLETS   General Pieces

THE DOODLEBERRY TREE

I'm absolutely sure I'll never ever see
a sight more splendid than the doodleberry tree;
for doodleberries shine and doodleberries glow
like tiny suns or moonlit snow.
Kaleidoscopic patterns shift.
Hallucinations flow and drift.
From bough to bough, their tales they tell
in colors rich and soft pastel
that range from royal purple jokes
to pink notes sung by female folks
draped in sheaths of emerald bold,
crowned with hair of shimmering gold.
The doodleberries do amaze.
At them we cannot help but gaze.
Naturally quite tantalizing;
actually, they're hypnotizing,
enchanting us in mystic ways
with twinkling giggles, rainbow haze,
twirling swirls and flashing sparks,
exclamations, question marks.
Along with dazzling sights and sound
aromas, scents, and tastes abound.
Quite indescribable they are—
phantasmagoric, on a par
with angel's breath, a waltz's smile,
which charm and tease us all the while.
Fantabulous are treats like these
great gifts from doodleberry trees.
But where in the world are these visions found?
I've searched and rummaged all around…
Such marvels and more are often seen
through the positive eye of a jumbee bean.

8/8/2023

General Pieces   marc frederic

SPORTING INTANGIBLE WINGS

Landing in my mailbox, they gently rest at the bottom of the pile as if nesting or waiting patiently to be discovered.

When I do discover and open them to peruse their contents, I find them to be deceptively powerful. Their photographs serve as wings, lifting and swiftly carrying me to various worldwide destinations.

Travel brochures can do that by evoking memories and emotions—earth-pounding thuds, shrieking trumpet, and hot breath of the bull elephant. Too, too close! Will he catch our lorry this time?
Soft, nibbling mouths of stingrays sucking pieces of squid from our flattened palms beneath the turquoise shallows of Grand Cayman.
Community dancing in Greece.
Venice's romantic gondolas.
Sparkling ski slopes of the Alps.
Surprise of being shanghaied off a junk in the South China Sea to be delivered to a dinner party in Hong Kong.
Seeing a man stabbed at a Rio café fronted by a stunning mosaic sidewalk.
Winning big at roulette at the casino in Cannes.
Hot air ballooning above the red rock beauty of Sedona.

Yep, those travel brochures now serve a wonderful purpose. Each new page delights me with lift, deposits me with ease, allowing time and space to morph into an endless stream of memories.

This armchair enchantment sure beats today's hassle of struggling through traffic and bustling airport crowds to arrive just in time for a delayed or cancelled flight. Or worrying about each individual becoming a human weapon, travel dollars losing value daily, and maintaining enough stamina to enjoy the journey.

Of course, the most wonderful parts of such adventures are 1) having physically traveled when I did, and 2) joyously arriving home by simply closing the brochure.

9/9/2023

AN OLD ADDRESS BOOK

It feels as though I've been thrust into a time machine.

The dial reads 50 years ago, while slightly retreating and advancing. Names, addresses, and phone numbers appear, igniting memories galore.

In search of a friend I haven't talked to in years, I've delved into an old address book of mine. Its cover is not entrapped in cobwebs or faded print. Strangely, it looks brand new. But its contents are another story.

I can't find her listing. So, for the fun of it, and to assuage my curiosity, I dial three other long-lost friends. Ring…ring…ring… No answers.

That's okay. I've now mentally visited those people back in the time we originally shared. Quite interesting. I wonder what they're like and where they are today. If still in this dimension, they've undoubtedly developed character traits to complement their wrinkles. What fun it would be to share memories. To see how we've grown. Or possibly shrunk.

The thoughts about the first three friends lead to those of another. And another. So many had fine qualities even at a young age. I hope their journeys through life have been rewarding and they've inspired others along the way.

Well, what do you know! Although I didn't leave a message, one of my friends somehow returned my call. What a wonderful conversation! It brought the past into the present and connected the present with the future. All the while eliminating any sense of time.

How marvelous! I've stumbled onto a new travel mode. It's quick, comfortable, and convenient, especially if you're open to unknown destinations.

I've named the time machine "The Reacquaintance".

10/20/2023

BLACK CYLINDRICAL BEAUTY

You bring me joy
beyond belief.
How readily you renew memories,
induce emotion, spark dreams.

A marvelous travel companion,
so full of knowledge,
you rarely hesitate to share your response
to anything my mind can conjure.

At my beck and call,
you are the center of many worlds,
yet take me to the outer limits.
You stimulate imagination,
fulfill my requests, satisfy curiosity.

Fortunate I am. The talent you contain
would take me many lifetimes to absorb,
while leading me with smiling face
from one dimension to another.

Lying in bed with you,
I sense no need to ever rise.
I love you, my Amazon *Alexa*.

10/29/2023

I FEEL LIKE WRITING

I feel like writing. Possibly to dispel the pervasion of negative news. Maybe to hang some pleasant images in the air. Or simply to see what comes out of the far end of my pen.

Butterflies. They're always an indicator of pleasant things to come.

Balloons and *flowers.* *Sunshine* and *lollipops.* How nice.

But what about artificial intelligence?

What about it?

Without delving into its probable effects, I must say I'm dazzled by the speed with which it researches, creates, and replies. Non-techies might readily classify its response as a miracul. (Did I spell miracle correctly? I'm more accustomed to expecting them than writing the word.)

Yep, I expect miracles. And they occur—grass grows, sun shines, empty parking spaces appear in crowded locations, phenomenal people enter my life, stimulating ideas fill my mind.

I discover additional wonders in food (a persimmon once challenged me to describe its textures and tastes), making love (simply imagine), companionship (the joy of sharing), and learning (stretching one's mind and soul).

Marvelous sights and sounds are ubiquitous, which brings me back to artificial intelligence. For years, I've utilized Amazon's *Alexa* for musical entertainment. The depth and breadth of its musical library is incredible. Late last night, I blew thought on the embers of Rod McKuen's poetry and song; brought flames to life that decades ago made my emotions simmer.

General Pieces   marc frederic

Life's treats are where you find them. I've just enjoyed a fraction of its wonder by blazing an ink trail across my notebook.

Now comes its transfer to my word processor so you can share this short mind-wander. Of course, reading the font excludes the pleasure of watching cursive ease across the page in a profusion of panache.

In any case, it's been a fun romp, eh?

10/29/2023

RETURN OF THE MALLARDS

The mallards are back—their elegant, brilliant patterns glide smoothly along the surface of our still lake.

As with other bird species, the males' colors are more striking than the females', but together they form a compatible scene the water has been missing all summer.

Eventually, the mallards will be joined by waterfowl of many sorts. Already, greater and lesser egrets intermittently spark the scene with starkly white glides and strolls. White pelicans with black-edged wings are the largest, most dramatic of our airborne visitors, rivaled only by an occasional blue heron.

Large flocks of other ducks will, at times, crowd the lake's surface. But the mallards seem to be the most neighborly. One female used to regularly enter not only our patio, but pool. She would swim with my late wife, sometimes pecking at the polish on her finger and toenails. My wife christened her with a name that starts with the letter D. It wasn't Daisy or Delilah, Dottie or Donna. I can't remember what it was. Let's just say it was Ducky.

Ducky would peck at our glass patio door until Gaylan came out to pet and swim with her. Yep, Gaylan had that effect on creatures both animal and human. She was a special being loved by many. I had the great fortune to share 34 years with her.

The mallards are one small reminder.

11/5/2023

GATHERING MEMORIES

I'll lie here a little longer. Why not? It's Sunday morning at 7:00 o'clock. I'm alone in bed listening to Alexa spout the latest newsworthy happenings of the world as we know it.

People are visiting Elvis Presley's Graceland again. Attendance is up 40 percent since Covid crawled under a rock.

Wow…Elvis Presley.

"Alexa, play songs by Elvis Presley."

Don't Be Cruel transports me back to a Santa Monica beach club parking lot in 1956. I'm parking cars, listening intermittently to Elvis' talent. The beat, the dip in his voice, the emotional tug at my heart and groin. I'm a kid with the world ahead of me. Everything is a possibility. What joy!

To this day, I have a favorable attitude about the future. Plus, a past filled with wonderous events and people whose memories I cherish.

But music. The power of music is amazing. From ear to gut to soul it impacts our lives with the uncanny ability to instantly change one's mood or shift one's mind like a memory magnet on steroids.

I wonder if cavemen felt some semblance of emotion while rhythmically beating a stick against the hollow trunk of a fallen tree.

11/12/2023

SHARING

I usually let my writings simmer before sharing them. It pays off. Gives me time to make improvements, correct mistakes, hone nuances.

But this morning, I created a first draft that is very satisfying.

I bounced it off a fellow writer whose opinion I value, to see if he concurred. He did.

Oh, boy! I have unexpectedly created a tiny treasure without all the polishing it usually takes. This little guy peacefully gleams just as it is. But I'm frustrated.

So, what's the problem? Very simply, the next five people on my "test sharing" list didn't answer the phone. Well, that's not quite accurate—the last person I called was on his way out the door to get a haircut. He'll call back.

I want to share this rarity right now. It's like panning the bed of a running creek for the first time and, as I pull the pan to the surface, therein lies a sizeable glimmering gold nugget. I'm all alone in the middle of nowhere. The sun is shining. The country is clean, clear, glorious. Having bestowed her gift, Mother Nature is caressing me, whispering in my ear. I want to shout about my discovery, but there's no one to hear.

I'll just have to write about it.

This spontaneous writing has got to cease. I have work to do. I'm putting my next book together.

Sure, writing entails effort, but to me, it's not work. It's fun—a wonder-filled hobby. And sharing it is a joy.

General Pieces   marc frederic

I may not be able to create time but, being retired, I can definitely allocate it. It's now my privilege to write whenever I wish. As for sharing, that's what you and I are doing right now.
If you got this far into the book, I assume you like it too.

11/12/2023

INKWELL PRODUCTIONS

The television screen is dark tonight. I inadvertently pulled its plug from the wall socket with a broomstick while trying to retrieve a small tube of salve my girlfriend dropped behind her credenza on which the TV stands.

Damn. That credenza's too heavy to move.

We've just finished conversing in our regular TV-watching chairs. At my request, she's temporarily gone to read her book. I'm enjoying my second margarita along with the remainder of some salted mixed nuts. Fourteen dark almonds stand out against the bottom of the stark white bowl. They're more entertaining than the blank TV screen.

My imagination is telling me the screen is blank because it's "Intermission", and Inkwell Productions will soon broadcast something to rival the nut bowl. Or are they currently showing darkest Africa, featuring a black panther stalking prey on a moonless pitch-black night?

But why limit my vision? Here's a colony of bats emerging from a cave. I can hear the rush of flapping wings. What's in their mouths—licorice lollipops? Strange, but seems appropriate.

Maybe it's the drinks. Or maybe I'm going, rather than eating, nuts.

It is somewhat weird to be sitting here eyeing a pitch-black screen. But it's a first—an experience worth logging for its uniqueness. And that is precisely what I've been doing for a good 15 minutes, not simply staring at a passive, blank screen; taking it for granted.

I'm meeting it half way, getting to know it, understanding what it can offer, preserving on paper what it has to show for itself.

It's teaching me. Little things, for starters. I've just noticed that by substituting a "c" for an "n", I can change *blank* to *black*. Right up Inkwell Productions' alley.

And, with that small insight, I realize the TV's darkness is dancing with infinity…

11/14/2023

BEYOND CONVERSATION

"You swim beautifully," said the stranger in the next lane, as I exited the indoor pool.

She could have just as easily proclaimed, "You soar, dip and glide"; for that's what I do while quoting poetry to myself, as I slide through blue liquid during my daily workout.

"Have a great swim," the same lady later bids me adieu from her seat in the lobby as I pass through the gym doors to the parking lot.

Are we on the same page? Or is she nuts?

But who am I to short this lady's thinking? Maybe she can sense worlds beyond. Maybe she could feel what I was doing in the pool. Maybe she's equating a swim to life.

11/28/2023

NIBBLETS   General Pieces

QUESTION OF WONDER

"Why don't babies laugh when they're born instead of crying?" he asked.

This is the type question one can use to surf the universe or swill wine. It's so open-ended a whale could fly through the answer without touching its sides.

What fun to simultaneously explore in all directions. Don't forget "up". Without it, there will be less "down".

And the colors. Laughter certainly has various colors. And shapes. And moods. But, then again, so do cries.

We're back where we started.

Let's do it again, this time in a spiral, not a circle.

12/18/2023

CALLER

Writing brings me satisfaction and joy. But how thrilling it is to guide someone else in her search for literary expression. And, to learn she has a natural voice of her own.

Several weeks ago, a lady contacted me because I'm an officer of a writing group. I entertained her various questions. Later, when I mentioned her inquiry to another board member, I was told the caller simply wanted someone to write her memoir for her.

I didn't think so. I had been intrigued by her unique and varied background, the serious challenges she had met, and her ability to describe them. She exemplified both spunk and discipline.

During a subsequent conversation, I asked her if she desired a ghost writer. She denied any interest. Good, I thought, for I had none either.

We enjoyed an additional phone call during which I encouraged her to capture in writing some scenarios she had shared audibly.

Today, she has just read to me what she wrote. She "walked backward into her childhood." And, voila! Out came the first of two delightful vignettes with style and voice of their own.

I'm ecstatic. She can write. And is stimulated enough to continue.

I mention various exercises she eventually might use to complete her project, but emphasize her style is natural and praise-worthy; then suggest she not be concerned with anything we have discussed but, instead, choose four or five more scenarios in her history and write.

"If subjects other than your history glide through your mind, simply net and write them up too. Other things definitely will pop up. You have the ability to capture them. Your writing is enjoyable to read. But remember, your goal at this stage is simply to have fun."

She's off to write.

12/22/2023

SHE'S BACK

She's back.

We're both here…for a few moments…at Pebble Beach golf course, by the 18th green. I'm looking past the deep, white sand trap under the branches of a broad pine tree. The ocean rolls calmly in the background.

I've paused the TV to prolong the view and the memory that accompanies it—my late wife in her pink golf outfit standing in that trap, eyeing her ball in frustration after her third attempt to hit it over the eight-foot-high lip of the green.

The flag waits patiently as do the other three players in our foursome. Not wanting to give up on or into the situation, Gaylan swings two more times. Finally, as the ball rolls back to rest at her feet for the fifth time, she picks it up and tosses it in the direction of the pin, which she is too low to see.

Much to her chagrin, a surprising round of loud applause breaks out from the people lining the long balcony of the two-story bungalow behind her. Embarrassed, but a trooper, she waves to the crowd, climbs to the green, lines up her putt, and sinks it.

How lovely she is with her movie star looks, always making the best of any circumstance.

This world was brighter with her in it.

I made up the part about her sinking the putt. Why not? That's the way she would have wanted it.

Me too.

12/23/2023

FILING

How I hate filing. In fact, I dislike paperwork in general. It seems so insignificant—a mundane chore, an afterthought.

But it's important. Mainly for future reference. It's useful. Practical. Necessary. It might even be viewed as self-protection. After all, information put aside long enough to form a stack might ultimately topple, injuring one in the process. Or, one could drown in a sea of paperwork. Or even be driven crazy by not being able to reference a vital piece of information. Yes, filing is important in order to function properly.

Thank goodness I'm still stimulated enough to produce ideas to file. Computers are a blessing. Their minds and bellies easily expand to hold my creative thoughts. But they can't contain, sort, or perform everything.

Other day-to-day matters can also be extremely distracting. Even crushing. Not only other paperwork, but chores—the wash, the mail, cat litter. They seem miniscule in the larger scheme of things, yet, are the glue that holds together the structure of our material lives. Without them, we would be disorganized, confused, and just plain sloppy.

Oh, what I'd give to have a staff of assistants. But I find that is something retirement doesn't offer me. So, file I must. And file I do. Occasionally.

It feels so good when I'm done, caught up, have no details nagging me. What relief! What joy!

Maybe I can convert those two emotions into incentive; for, you see, right now my desktop resembles the contents from a gaping-mawed, monstrous waste basket that has just vomited all over it.

1/5/2024

NIBBLETS General Pieces

THE DEMISE OF CURSIVE

I was extremely attracted to her. She was striking in an off-beat way. Her charisma, off the charts.

I met her only once, years ago. She wrote me a check for some books I had authored. I treasured her signature. After taking it home, I visually rode its ups and downs, full curves, the power and delicacy of its flow. It was like being inside her, moving with her thoughts and body as she wrote. I made a copy of that check before depositing it.

How sad it is to now discover cursive is no longer being taught in school. Print is taking its place.

To me, printing is like laying bricks—practical but dull, sturdy, uniform, easily discernable when completed. But where is its character? I suppose it's in the words themselves. And rightfully so. That's the guts of the matter.

But what a loss.

We live in a time when technology rules. At first, I wondered how checks would be distinctively signed in the future, for much print looks alike. Then, it came to me. Many people are no longer using checks. They pay bills electronically.

The art of writing letters and thank you notes is also fading. Email may now be considered genteel, while texting prevails to the extent that people sitting across the table from one another prefer it to audible communication.

Texting offers no variety of facial expression, except with emojis or vertical punctuation marks. Little nuance in volume or tone of voice. Just bits and pieces being thrust through space. No touches, twinkles, or sighs. Just abbreviated print and relationships someone somewhere someday may attribute to the demise of cursive.

1/18/2024

General Pieces   marc frederic

MISTAKEN IDENTITY

I heard that the Princess, a most anxious miss,
is seeking a magical man/frog to kiss.
I hopped into sight as is my normal habit
and, though I am green, was mistaken for rabbit.
When asked by sweet Princess, I simply did say,
"I live where the crogs froak, cen tastles away";
then hopped down the road and have not seen her since—
a frog-disguised, dyslexic, most prandsome hince.

1/15/2019

PRE-AUTOGRAPHING
BENNY'S, JENNY'S, and DENNY'S PETS

I've a show coming up, so I'm sitting down.
I am king of the hill with no golden crown,
just a large stack of books that display my craft
and are patiently waiting to be autographed.
I'm writing inscriptions as a fascinator.
I'll personalize them with the children's names later.
How thrilled they will be when first they discover
their names spelled in silver inside the cover.
They're great youngster gifts for, as grandparents say,
"These books charm for years in a magical way."
Just how can that happen? Here is a clue—
most grownups adore them like children do.
The pile is shifting as I keep inscribing.
It makes me mellow as if I'm imbibing,
I write *Joyous journey!* and *Travel treat!*,
then sign *Mr. Whimsy.* It's so upbeat—
I picture how children for many a year
will smile, learn, and giggle; form memories dear.
And once in a while, I leaf through the pages
to read a few lines and view pets outrageous
vacationing on their trips worldwide.
Here's what I found when I peeked inside—
A sail-boating loon, a skydiving moose,
and a banking raccoon may seem obtuse,
but it's creatures like these one never forgets
as they travel with ease throughout BENNY'S PETS,
Do come join the fun; be charmed, made to laugh
by the anchovy pun and the deep-sea giraffe.
When you see all combined, you'll be thrilled to the core.
Such delight you will find! A twist ending's in store.
And that is just *BENNY'S.* There's *JENNY'S* and *DENNY'S,*
which add to the fun, I do think.
As I've said, it's inviting, so I will keep writing
and hope I don't run out of ink.

2/18/2024

General Pieces   marc frederic

HAVING JUST READ A POEM

I am rarely told I am growing old
but today I turn four-score and four.
It's a solid age at which I feel sage,
for I've learned in this world to adore.
There is so much to see, to feel, and to be,
to remember what/where I have been;
and to look forward to the things I will do
when I land in this world once again.
Or maybe some other…another…another…
for most surely, exploring's a thrill.
And there I'll enjoy the skill I'll employ.
I've no doubt at all that I will.
But right now, I am home creating this poem,
which affords me much pleasure, you see,
for I'm mind-deep in measure of Service's treasure—
The Cremation of Sam McGee.
It seems nothing's sweeter than his special meter
with its upbeat and natural lift;
so with joy galore, I thought I'd write more
as my me-to-myself birthday gift.

4/13/2024

BECOMING A TURTLE

"Is anyone here a turtle? I mean are you members of the Turtle Club?" he asked a small group of us after we had consumed a couple of alcoholic beverages.

His name was Bucky Plum. Maybe it still is, but I doubt it. That was over fifty years ago. And we weren't spring chickens at the time. Besides, Bucky was a character—a wholesaler who could drink.

"What's the Turtle Club?"

"It's a drinking club. It's not easy to get in. Most people don't make it."

"What do you have to do to get in?"

"It's a game you play—a memory game. If you fail to remember, you down a slug of your drink. I'll give you one by one a list of ten phrases to repeat—the first phrase, then the first and second, the first second, and third, all the way through the tenth. You make it through the tenth and you're a turtle. But, each time you forget, you take a drink and start from scratch."

"Let's do it," I encouraged.

Here's the list:

One hen.
Two ducks. (Repeated as "One hen. Two ducks.")
Three squawking geese. ("One hen. Two ducks. Three squawking geese, etc.")
Four corpulent porpoises.
Five limerick oysters.
Six pairs of Don Alverso's tweezers.
Seven thousand Macedonians dressed in full battle array.

General Pieces   marc frederic

Eight brass monkeys from the ancient, sacred, secret crypts of Egypt.
Nine apathetic, sympathetic, diabetic old men on roller skates with a marked propensity toward procrastination and sloth.
Ten miracle, spherical, diabolical denizens of the deep who hold skol around the corner of the quay in the kohl of the quivvy all at the same time.

I think I was the only one who became a turtle that night. Truth be told, I don't remember. What amazes me is, to this day, I can quote that list instantly. My biggest challenge is doing it in one breath.

3/16/2024

SEASCAPE

I love the way sun shines through aqua-blue waves as they prepare to crash against the rocky shore—wild beauty everlastingly contained in a golden frame hanging on my living room wall.

I can smell the ocean, hear and feel its power.

Gazing past strong surf, I recognize the distant bluffs of a peninsula and stroke my tuxedo cat Louie, who sits on the sofa with me.

What little you know of this painting, Louie. What memories it conjures in me—from sitting in Violet Parkhurst's living room gallery where this painting hung high among a wall full of others, to experiencing the ocean, itself, which she captured so well.

"I knew you had to have that painting," Violet had said. "You haven't been able to take your eyes off it."

She was right. I couldn't.

The joy provided by that seascape has enhanced my life ever since.

It's also a minor pleasure to realize I, along with five presidents of the United States of America, own a piece of Violet Parkhurst's art.

Gee, Louie, I'm sorry you can't relate to this painting and my memories. You've never been to the seashore, hardly even out of the house.

But maybe. Just maybe, you understand more than I give you credit for. Maybe you understand even more than I do. After all, receiving my telepathic message, you come to me in bed during the night. You can snuggle with peace an angel would admire. You bound and run with joyous spirit. And I believe you see, hear, and sense much that I cannot.

General Pieces   marc frederic

But I will continue to share my thoughts with you. And do my best to delight in yours.

As I stroke you, I realize how little I know, and somehow feel I, myself, am being petted.

3/23/2024

NIBBLETS   General Pieces

CURIOUS

The year was 1957. On my way home through a residential neighborhood, I drove past a park where a white-haired, wrinkled man was sitting on a bench near the curb. I wondered what he had seen during his life that so many of us never would.

I drove around the block and parked close to where he sat.

I was 17. He must have been in his nineties, a rarity in those days.

He waited, while I approached him, the glimmer in his eyes questioning what I had in mind.

"Pardon me, sir. I don't mean to disturb you. I just know you've seen and lived through a lot I haven't. I wonder if you'd mind sharing a glimpse of what you've experienced?"

He started talking. I listened.

Now 84, I'm reminded of that incident by an interview of a 104-year-old World War II veteran I've just watched on TV. He looks good. Could be my age. His memory and speech are excellent. On D-day, he was shot below the throat by one bullet from a machine gun.

Sounds impossible, but so did some of the things I was told by the old man on the bench.

Two weeks ago, I was honored by a visit from my grandson Trent, and granddaughter, Brooke. At 20 and 18, they had driven over 16 hours from the state of Montana to visit me in Palm Desert, California.

Trent wanted to interview me. For posterity, *I* call it. *He* simply said he wished he'd done it with my wife Gaylan, who'd passed away two years ago. He doesn't foresee having kids for at least five years,

General Pieces marc frederic

and I might not be around by the time they're old enough to know me.

He filmed me for two hours.

I finally understood why that old man on the bench was so happy I listened.

6/4/2024

marc frederic   Creative Writing Assignments

NIBS INTRO TO
CREATIVE WRITING ASSIGNMENTS
based on class assignments

It's "Nibs" again –

The **bold print** defines **the assignment**—
a **Prompt**, **Words**, or **Subject Matter**,
It's as simple as that. They are "picked from a hat".
And do not deserve any more chatter.

Nibs

I SAW WHAT YOU DID

I saw what you did.

I'm sorry I witnessed it. Had I not seen that happen, I wouldn't have to address the situation or change what I think of you.

Such a small action. But what a big difference it makes, pervading a seemingly, sunny relationship with the cloudy stench of disappointment.

It's not just a difference of opinion. Everyone has a right to that. This has to do with honor and trust, right and wrong.

"Tommy, how could you have nudged that ball out from behind the tree with your foot? And not said a word about it. We're a *twosome, a team* in this *tournament*. That nudge has to be reported."

Damn!

11/1/2016

marc frederic   Creative Writing Assignments

HE ENDED THE CONVERSATION

He ended the conversation, "Today's the day, Valentine's. It's also our sixty-fifth anniversary. We'll be home from dinner at eight o'clock. It will be unlocked. Park down the street." And hung up.

At the doddering ages of 89 and 90, he and his wife were both worn out, five-time cancer survivors. They had received anniversary congratulations from all their family members, none of whom could afford to travel. The couple understood and were happy to avoid lengthy celebrations.

His wife was still a romantic and he loved her for it. Their dinner date that evening typified their love.

The following day, their youngest daughter received no answer to her calls about their romantic date.

The couple was found sitting comfortably on the sofa in their den. They were cold as ice, holding hands, dressed in the clothes they had worn to the restaurant. Love notes were discovered in her purse and his coat pocket.

The small-town coroner failed to notice a pin prick behind an earlobe of each of them, which resulted in no autopsy revealing they'd been poisoned.

The $50,000 in cash and gold coins was no longer in their safe. But not one of their offspring missed it. It had never been mentioned.

The couple had neither enemies nor debts, were frugal, extremely considerate people, and in love to the end. Because they did everything together, it was assumed they'd passed on in the same manner.

The million-dollar insurance policies they had purchased on their lives when much younger were a surprise to everyone. The proceeds provided well for their loved ones, who lived happily until a newly hired whippersnapper at the insurance company had the bodies exhumed.

It turned out the majority of the heirs didn't believe in cremation even though it was in the couple's wills.

2016

SHARED ADVENTURE

Last night I took my five-year-old son to his first big league baseball game.

When seen through his eyes, things I take for granted were overwhelming—the vast expanse of green, the brown infield with baselines and batters' boxes chalked in white, all brightly lit 'midst the black velvet night.

I left him to watch batting practice while I raided the hot dog stand; then returned armed with goodies and answers to the question I thought he'd ask soon. But rather than ball field and players, his attention was caught by the moon.

I apologize. Whenever I get excited, I tend to express myself in rhyme. Many things stirred my enthusiasm—first inning was very eventful. The Dodgers led 3 runs to "o". Besides, during all the excitement, my son kicked my beer with his toe!

I told how six outs made an inning. I pointed out bases and mound. My son's eyes grew big as saucers, as the Cracker Jack man made his round. Oops, I can't help it.

His next question really did throw me, "Dad, the vampire bit who's behind?" I suppose in the heat of the action I'd just called the umpire blind.

Oh, what the heck...

I knew from all of the hot dogs and cokes and candy that soon, about when the game became tied up, he'd ask me to go to "the room". And so, I sat there and waited. And sure as it had to be, the Pirates got their game together and tied up the score three to three.

'Twas just about this time I felt it. I was somewhat reluctant to peek, for into my lap he was crawling. He planted a kiss on my cheek. He gave me the grandest of hugs then and snuggled his head to my chest, while in a soft voice he informed me, "Gee, Dad, you're really the best."

So many more things could be added, but two thoughts will now end this rhyme: "To me last night was amazing." And. "I think my son had a good time."

11/11/2016

Written for a Creative Writing class. The assignment is the prompt, "Last night was amazing." Excerpts from Marc Frederic's verse, "Adventure," (1974) have been incorporated.

marc frederic Creative Writing Assignments

WHAT'S IMPORTANT TO ME?

What's important to me?

Living life fully. Growing mentally and spiritually. Taking and giving. Preparing to take lessons I've learned in this world on to the next. And leaving whatever I touch here better than it was.

"I'm touched by that" is an expression indicating a positive reaction to something. It's pleasant to hear no matter who's doing the touching.

There are many different ways to touch others. Learning how others prefer to be touched is a thoughtful act. But the touching, itself, is all-important. Without it, a connection is missed.

It's impossible to touch everyone. But sincerely touching a few can affect many. Good vibes are contagious. People enjoy spreading them.

Touching is a two-way experience. I like touching back. Letting people know something they've done has a positive effect on me. The more I reciprocate, the more positive I become. Am I looking at life through rose-colored glasses? Maybe. But it leads to more touching.

When I share my thoughts, I'm often told, "Marc, you have to put these things in a book. It's not fair to keep them to yourself."

I've taken their advice seriously. In addition to other responsibilities, I regularly work on publishing my writings. I have an obligation to do so. It's self-imposed, but one way I can add to people's enjoyment, possibly provoke thought.

By touching in that manner, I'm giving something original to the world. Something that wasn't here before I was. Something that may enhance others' lives for years to come. A payback for the joy I've taken.

That's what's important to me.

4/30/2017

Creative Writing Assignments

ART, ASPARAGUS, CIRCUS, EAGLE, SPAIN

Art (short for Arturo) and I have been buddies for many years. He's an unusual character. How unusual? Extremely.

Art used to date the bearded lady in the sideshow. They got together whenever the **circus** came to town. For her last visit, he'd grown an empathy beard. He explains he left her trailer without it when her husband, the strong man, discovered the two of them together. A "close shave" I think he called it.

Art once ran with the bulls in Pamplona, **Spain**. Was damn near gored. Fortunately, that man could run. More importantly, he could jump. He'd just pushed a fallen runner into a protective niche in the wall. Close behind, the bulls charged down the narrow street, hooves sending sparks off the cobblestones. With no room to squeeze in with the runner, Art jumped into a nearby open window. I wouldn't feel right sharing all he encountered inside that room. Let's just say the two attractive ladies gave him extended congratulations on his great escape. He described it simply as a threesome to remember.

Art once compared the unusual drama of his mating habits to the death spiral of the bald **eagle**. It's a plummeting courtship ritual during which eagles lock talons at a great height, then cartwheel toward the earth. Evidently the risk spices things up.

Art likes to gamble. He's also extremely knowledgeable. He bets he can answer questions. Art once won $1000 for his detailed answer: *Bamboo grows faster than* **asparagus**. *Both grow inches per day. Bamboo 36. Asparagus 11.* Having lived in China and Stockton, California, Art knew.

Who does these strange things? Who knows these bizarre facts? Art.

I've introduced numerous people to Art. They all agree. Appraising art is a skill. Knowing Art is an experience.

6/8/2017

I STOPPED DEAD IN MY TRACKS

I stopped dead in my tracks. Then turned around to look at them. That was 14 minutes ago.

The tracks went straight along the flat surface until they reached the distant hill, then up and over.

I'm thankful they are there. Like Hansel's and Gretel's bread crumbs, they'll be easy to follow back.

Nothing else will give me direction. No landmarks exist. Only flats and hills everywhere. And the slick, gray substance over which I've traveled for nine hours and 44 minutes.

They could've dropped me off closer. But they have no idea where closer is.

It's up to me to find out. My special senses guide me. They've always worked, regardless of what I've been hunting or the terrain in which it's been located. I'm able to adjust my sensory perception to both. I've been raised, trained, groomed to do so.

My problem is finding my way back. Once I've eliminated the target, my superior senses shut down. I'm on my own. I dispose of the item. Then I, myself, become disposable. Sometimes I wonder why I even try to return.

To me, "stopping dead in my tracks" is not just a phrase. It's literally what I'm programmed to eventually do—die at the far end of my tracks.

So far, I've managed to survive. Haven't slid off course during land tilts or been disoriented by spark eruptions. I've held on even through gravity lapses. My secret? Stopping every 15 minutes. Looking back. Making sure I've got "track-tion."

Creative Writing Assignments   NIBBLETS

Track-check time.

They still exist. My boot soles are sticky. So far, I'm…

Uh, oh. In the distance. A herd of track-eaters!

5/18/2017

A MOST EXCITING THING

In 1968, a man attending his son's birth was uncommon. Lamaze classes afforded me a ticket to the event, as well as the skill to coach his mother. What a privilege it was.

Eric was a good-looking, smooth-faced baby. More importantly, he was healthy. His birth was the most exciting thing I'd ever experienced.

When he was little, we didn't spend a great deal of time together. Starting a new career, I was doing my utmost to develop a clientele and support our family.

But I remember certain things: At age four, in his red cape, Eric proudly proclaimed, "Dad, I'm Superman, and I'm going to save the world as soon as you tie my shoe." At five years old, he said, "I know you came in and gave me a kiss last night, Dad, because I heard your footprints." We played catch occasionally. In Indian Guides, I was Big Bull; he was Little Bear.

Eric grew to be responsible and punctual. He exemplified these traits through his paper route, team sports, and being home on time. From a young age, Eric wanted to be a policeman. And, since graduating from college, he's been one for over 25 years. He's earned both the Medal of Valor and Medal of Honor.

As a teenager, Eric was introduced to the Morman church by a young lady. He soon became a member and completed a two-year mission in the Dominican Republic.

He and his wife have three boys, who are Eagle Scouts as well as black belts in Tae Kwon Do. They sing, play musical instruments, and act on stage.

Eric is one of the most active, devoted family men I know. I'm proud of and happy for him. Even more exciting—he's become the father I wasn't and a hero of mine.

7/20/2017

NEW YEAR RESOLUTIONS

Too many resolutions are wishy-washy weak

They toddle along like lost sheep, following closely on the heels of procrastination. They usually appear at the end of each year dressed in good intentions. Some sparkle with ostentatious bling. Others are draped in flimsy, see-through material. Typically, they don't live long.

I like solid resolutions that either stand straight and tall, ready to be adopted, or are right out of the oven, warm and tasty, ready to be relished and absorbed. These resolutions are made not at year-end, but when needed. They're cherished; their value immediately recognized and put to use. They become a part of you and can be passed on to others as wisdom or by example.

One simple resolution of mine has positively affected others for years. It was pointed out I habitually followed giving a compliment with the word "but". Doing so, negated whatever thought preceded it. Made aware of my contradictory action, I immediately and gratefully resolved to discontinue it.

Stopping smoking also took the form of an instant resolution. Although I realized the habit is a nasty one, I enjoyed it. After 20 years, my resolve to stop was inspired by a client of mine. I'd always known her to be overweight. She walked into my office looking happy, healthy, and svelte.

"What made the difference?" I wanted to know. She explained she had learned to control her diet. I thought about her self-discipline and snuffed out my cigarette with a positive grind. It was the last cigarette I ever smoked.

Because I address situations as they arise, I rarely schedule resolutions to begin January First.

There is one result I appreciate about New Year resolutions. The gyms and swimming pools are overcrowded for only three days at the most.

1/4/2018

I TOLD MYSELF NOT TO PANIC

I told myself not to panic.

I was on stage alone and had suddenly forgotten my lines. Some members of the audience had traveled from around the globe. Everyone now waited for me to begin.

My heart pumped madly. Tumult filled my ears. If only I could disappear.

What to do? I began to sing. What I was singing I wasn't sure. Then I realized it was our national anthem. I sang louder, stronger, boldly. The audience stood. Individuals placed hands over hearts. They began to sing with me.

The song came to a conclusion. I motioned the audience to be seated. I still couldn't remember what I had planned to say, but felt more relaxed. I began to dance. A little soft shoe combined with tap. Where I had learned the technique, I had absolutely no idea. But I continued.

The audience began to mumble. It buzzed. Its voices grew louder. People were looking around, searching for a reason for my bizarre behavior. Some were rising to leave.

Then, as quickly as my prepared thoughts had deserted me, they returned. I knew exactly what I was about.

"Ladies and Gentlemen," I stated. "Thank you for both your patriotism and indulgence. I've always dreamed of performing before an audience of your size.

"Now to the matter you came to hear me address: the innovative scientific technique of atomically fusing human genes resulting in the unimaginable perfection of…"

The auditorium power failed. No light. No sound. No climate control. For a moment it was absolutely quiet and blacker than pitch.

Then, thank God… I woke up.

10/26/2017

THINGS I WILL NEVER FORGET

I've enjoyed life for nearly eight decades. Maybe not so much my first decade and a half. During those early years, I was feeling my way through life, learning about how I fit in more than enjoying things.

I continue to learn. The joy factor has grown exponentially.

There are very few things I'll never forget. I don't remember most of my experiences because I've lived them fully. They're now an integral part of my DNA. I don't think about them. I live in the present. What fun! If I look outside of the present, it's to the future. I've always known there are good things in store. No rush. They'll be there.

And what most people might consider bad experiences, I've simply lived through as part of the overall.

I've now been asked to write about **things I will never forget**. I feel I've just done that. The End.

But I think the request involves specific memories, so I'll step outside myself, crank my mind back to the beginning, and randomly put a handle on a few.

One of the first memories I can grip is, as a toddler, humping against a blue satin "sheet" in my bed. I think it's a piece from my mother's discarded nightgown. That sheet provides comfort and satisfaction. It probably also engenders my passion for the color blue.

As a young boy, I discover sexual self-pleasuring to be a true friend. Always there when I need it.

As a young man, I discover sharing a woman's body with her is better than pleasuring myself. Not as simple or convenient, but thrilling.

Sharing a woman's love. Better than just her body.

Sharing a woman's soul. The best. Everything else comes with it.

Creative Writing Assignments — NIBBLETS

As a youngster again, I share my new bike with a stranger who admires it. He rides off. Never returns.

As a 12-year-old, I'm temporarily trapped. Along with a couple of friends, I'm exploring the hills behind our home. We see what looks like the entrance to a cave on a thin ledge far above us. Sidestepping along the ledge is scary enough. Not being able to squeeze out of the cave's opening panics me.

As a seventh-grader standing at attention on the sunny parade grounds of California Military Academy, my new hard contact lenses inflicting piercing pain.

As a 21-year-old, involuntarily ending a college relationship. The young lady with whom I'm enjoying a torrid affair wants me to stay home. But I opt to join two friends on an adventure. With only a dollar in our pockets, we pull ourselves into an empty boxcar as a freight train leaves the yard for an unknown destination. My choice leads to losing my lover. Agony. Trouble eating and sleeping for weeks.

As a 23-year-old during U.S. Army Basic Training, I'm scooting on my back at night under a barbed-wire fence, my rifle held close to my chest, parallel to my body. Powdered dirt falls from the lip of my helmet into my eyes while tracer bullets fly over my head and explosions take place all around me.

As a 35-year-old, almost losing my daughter to a deep pool in Kawaii. With her on my lap, we speed down the natural rock slide prior to the ten-foot drop. She can't swim.

In a Land Rover being closely chased down a hill by a huge, trumpeting African elephant in musth.

It's strange the majority of memories with handles are somewhat negative. I suppose it's the drama they impart. And my being forced to dredge them up. Luckily for me, more beautiful ones now calmly float to the surface on their own. There are so many. They gracefully inundate my past:
- ✓ Coaching my son into this world.

marc frederic   Creative Writing Assignments

- ✓ Experiencing the brilliant colors and delicate aromas of Butchart Gardens.
- ✓ Diving turquoise water amidst magnificently shaped and colored fishes and corals.
- ✓ Showering beneath a warm, rainbow waterfall.
- ✓ Being *Gaylanized* on a blind date.
- ✓ Sprinkling Gaylan's exquisite, reclining nude body with multi-colored rose petals.
- ✓ There are far too many wonderful memories of tangibles from which to choose.
- ✓

But there are intangible lessons I've learned I cannot ignore:
- ✓ To be true to what I believe.
- ✓ To accept what I haven't yet earned, then grow into the person I should be to deserve it.
- ✓ To answer, when in doubt about fulfilling a minor responsibility, "How would I feel if I don't?"
- ✓ To never worry. It's a negative, useless activity. Instead, weigh possible options, wait calmly to see if action is necessary. If it is, take it.
- ✓ To try new tastes and experiences.
- ✓ To let my imagination soar and explore.
- ✓ To thoroughly appreciate the good qualities of others.
- ✓ To remember communication is the lubricant that smooths out life's wrinkles.
- ✓ To realize how wonderful it is to be in tune with spirit that permeates the universe.
- ✓ And, to occasionally look at memories that shape who I have become.

12/5/2017
(A Creative Writing assignment in which the word count got out of hand)

REMEMBERING

It's as if the acorn of our youth has grown into a massive oak tree.

For two days my wife and I are hosting a college friend of mine and his wife. It feels as if we've loved one another for decades. In actuality, it's 57 years since Kent and I were in school together. Two years ago, we reunited through the internet.

Now time evaporates. In our fraternity, Kent is the Eminent Archon. What fun to remember the term. "What's that?" our wives want to know. The simple answer is "President".

The laughter brought forth by our young-man-antics becomes a beacon as we trundle into the past, veering this way and that through our college days.

Reminiscing and catching up on children, marriages, professional lives, and world travel fill our time together to the brim. Meals and entertainment are merely sparkling adjuncts to our memory-fest.

So much to relate. To absorb.

Our discussion contains some spectacular facts. Before becoming the managing partner of his law firm, Kent served years alternating as Attorney General and U.S. Attorney of the state of Alaska. And Linda, after heading up the Alcohol Beverage Commission of that northwest, chilly state, created several successful businesses. Amazingly, she also once skinned a polar bear. Their political and Wild West tales mirror those of novels.

Our amusement is sprinkled with wisdom and insight. Over 48 hours we've come to appreciate one another ten-fold. With zeal, we climb through the branches of that massive oak tree. Then relax in its shade, philosophizing about the current state of the world. And how we've dealt with changes since that acorn sprouted.

11/8/2018

marc frederic Creative Writing Assignments

MYSTERIES

Life is full of **mysteries**,
not all things what they seem.
But the names we give to many
are really not that keen.
Think with me now as we explore
some very subtle lies;
they deal with names we've given
to varieties of flies—
a horse fly cannot speak, of course,
so do we know that it is hoarse?
A dragon fly is much too small
to drag much anything at all.
Why do we call them butterflies,
when what they do is flutter by?
See what I mean? It's strange, indeed.
But here's the total "ripper"—
the fly we're most familiar with
is one that's called "the zipper"!

1975
* * *

I think in you I've found one;
yes, you truly are a friend.
Your loyalty's amazing
and 'round obstacles you bend.
You never push or crowd me
yet, you heed my every move.
You love the sun as I do;
now on that we can't improve.
Today when we were running
and I cast you in the sea,
then laughing, drew you out again
to come and play with me,
you shook your head, but followed,

then fell hard upon the sand
and lie there, heaving breathlessly,
as I gave you my hand.
There was no hesitation
when my hand you then did take;
I thought about your color—
no difference did it make.
You're silent, dark, **a mystery**.
We're two halves that make a whole;
and as we stand together
there's a meeting of our soles.
I wish that you could tell me,
for I'd really love to know,
just where it is at night time
that you, my shadow, go.

1977
* * *

Who put the P in *pneumonia*?
And who stuck the K in *knife*?
These are some typical **mysteries**
I now seem to notice in life.
"Who cares?" you may question sincerely,
"There are loftier matters, no doubt."
I agree some may be more important.
But I've already figured *those* out!

2018

1/6/2024

DOG, CAT, CHILD, WOMAN, MAN

Dogs were always in our household as I grew up.
What marvelous creatures they are—unconditionally loving, playful, loyal, protective, happy, patient, and content. They like rules.
Our children were raised with dogs. Later, I'd visit pet shops to smell the puppies.
If we reincarnate on higher levels as our souls develop, the epitome must be returning as a dog.

Cats—independent, agile, graceful, self-cleaning instantly potty-trained. Easy to own; a joy to watch. Entertaining antics. Cuddles that please.
Eyes that intrigue, intimidate, or look past you.
Myriad sounds—the hiss, trill, croak, meow, growl, and screech are understandable.
Just how is it they make one feel privileged to pet their soft coats and be rewarded with an endearing purr?

Forming a child takes a woman's nurturing. Especially during its first nine months. Cell by cell. Day by day. Its birth creates immense change, for not only the child but those around it. Amazement. Awe. Adoration. Responsibility. Questions.
How do you communicate with a newborn? How do you communicate with a toddler? A teenager? An adult? Think like a dog.

A woman is the magnet, the glue, that holds a family together. Her vision is often broader and deeper than a man's. She's simultaneously tough and tender, protecting with zeal, enfolding with love.

Women want their men to be strong, but finger-wrappable. They are naturally steadfast and true. When properly taken care of, they make the world go 'round.

Creative Writing Assignments NIBBLETS

Man is, by nature, a hunter, a provider, an explorer. To be so, he must, at times, shed tenderness. Not to be confused with sensitivity.

A real man achieves success with honor. He loves, provides for, and is faithful to his chosen mate while appreciating beauty in its many forms. He both guides and allows himself to be guided.

6/14/2018

marc frederic   Creative Writing Assignments

IT WAS A NIGHT I'LL NEVER FORGET

"It was a night I'll never forget."

The old man sits cross-legged in soft sand gazing past purple waves at the setting sun. And continues in his craggy voice…

"Spectacular. Though I was far from bein' a spectator.

"We were five—four young women and me. No, it was four young women, a buddy of mine and me. Long ago, maybe 60, 70 years, on a tiny motu off the Tahitian Island of Bora Bora. Or was it Moorea? Maybe somewhere in Hawaii. No matter, it happened.

"It happened alright. In the wake of several Mai Tais. Or were they Pina Coladas? I'm not entirely…. All I know is what followed was worth rememberin'.

"Those native gals brought real meaning to the word hospitality. So kind, seemingly unaware of their beauty, they moved their hips sensually…rapidly. It musta been Tahiti, not Hawaii. Quicker hips. Warmer water.

"We dragged a bucket of sangria and coconut half-shells into those turquoise shallows and lolled waist-deep in a circle. Yep, it's Tahiti. We're wearin' sandals to protect our feet from the coral. Seems there are more guys with us now.

"Bare-breasted maidens, flowers in their hair, float on their backs while bein' gently passed around the circle. We're drinkin' sangria out of those gigglin' gals' belly buttons. Like a joyful dream… They'll soon be drinkin' outa ours.

"Come evenin' we're all on comfortable mattresses we've shoved together in a thatched hut. Then…then…nuts. Nuts. Nuts! I can't quite…"

Flashes of beauty, giggles, groans, squeals, and sighs are but a fading blur in the mind of this wrinkled rascal who now spends all his days trying to remember the nights he'll never forget.

1/10/2019

"HONEY, I'M HOME."

"Honey, I'm home."

Those were the next-to-last words he remembered hearing. They engendered panic. Everything that followed was a blur.

Now the policeman's questioning him. "What are you doing, sir?" the officer asks. "You can't sit like that in the street. Get into the back seat of my patrol car. You can explain from there."

The man sheepishly crawls into the vehicle.

"Where do you live, sir?" asks the patrolman.

"Right here. 23684 Shady Lane."

"And what are you doing out here without a stitch of clothes on?"

"I'm not sure. It all happened so fast."

"Are you ill, sir? Do you need medical attention?"

"I'm okay."

"I can see you have no identification. Let's start with the basics. Is your wife inside?"

"Yep. That's part of the problem."

"How, Sir? Domestic abuse?"

"Not exactly."

"Sir, why don't you start by telling me your version of why you were sitting naked on the curb, head in your hands, in front of your house when I drove up."

"Well, officer, it's like this: I'm in sales. I do a lot of traveling in my business. I was on a scheduled four-day trip but came home a day early. This evening my wife fixed a romantic dinner preceded by cocktails and accompanied by a wine-pairing with each course. One thing led to another and we tumbled into bed."

"Yes, Sir," said the officer. "I understand. Then what?"

"Well, we were going at it like crazy when our next-door neighbor, arriving home late, calls out to his wife, 'Honey, I'm home'.

"Confused, my wife screams, 'Oh, my God! It's my husband.'"

"And I? I, like a fool, dove out the window."

(joke embellishment)
9/26/2019

THINGS HAVE CHANGED

The background music emanates poolside from Amazon's Alexa. It's music my wife has been swimming to for the last couple of years—Roy Orbison's *1987 Black and White Concert*. Its wonder hasn't changed.

The late-summer sun brightens flowers while highlighting my wife's blond hair and the rippling water.

I lie close by, reading a paperback mystery. It's good to be outside again. The warmth of the sun is soothing.

But it's not the same. I've developed a dire mystery just above my left buttock. They call it a trigger point. It's a nerve center from which pain spreads dramatically, shooting around the hip to drop into my upper thigh. Most medical people can't explain its origin or cure. It's debilitating; has kept me flat on my back 14 days, other than for failed intermittent treatments. I've never experienced anything like it.

During the last 16 months, I've readily survived a cascade of unexpected surgeries. Between each, I walked until my incisions healed enough so I could swim to stay in shape. Recouping has been a natural, steady experience.

Things have changed. I now can hardly walk. In two weeks, my muscle tone has dramatically deteriorated. My outer body is a regiment of wrinkles commanded by General Lee Ugly and his adjutant Major Looskin. I'd like to banish them through exercise, but can't seem to move correctly. Maybe I can hydrate those wrinkles away with electrolytes.

After limping into the house, I lie in my recliner to write these words. But how can I sit at my computer to type them?

The next day, my chiropractor, who was a military combat medic, shared his expertise. And, as you can see, I was able to meet the challenge.

I viewed the healing as a miracle. My chiropractor's smile attributed it to knowledge communicated.

9/27/2019

IT'S A MIRACLE

It's a miracle.

I'm hit by a car and don't realize it.

It happens as I'm shuffling through the crosswalk of the Kona, Hawaii airport. Distracted by screams, I twist my body in the direction of the piercing cries. My back is now to the vehicle. A screech of brakes. Bump! The impact lifts me slightly off my feet.

The sudden fear and panic felt by the witnesses are unwarranted. But adrenaline has raced ahead of time, stabbing people with chards of a picture already crystalized in their minds—the huge, black SUV backing at high speed into a frail, white-haired man. The driver and the man can't see each other. No possible way can the SUV stop in time. What carnage! What a disaster!

Although the horrific scene hasn't actually been completed, the observers have imagined its dire conclusion. They're part of it. It's suddenly a part of them. It's happened in their minds. And it hurts them.

It doesn't hurt me at all. I don't realize it's about to happen. The SUV skids to a halt, slightly bumping, but leaving me on my feet completely intact.

Three months ago, an extremely well-loved, compassionate friend of mine passed away. Weeks later, his eighty-two-year-old widow was knocked down in a parking lot by a car that was backing up. She experienced nothing more than a few scrapes and a bit of muscle soreness.

After my similar experience, I think maybe my friend has become a guardian angel. He was known for acting as such in this dimension. I wonder… Is he able to stop those cars with a single finger? Or does he simply use his smile?

(took place in November 2009)
3/19/2020

I EXPECTED IT TO BE HOT

I expected it to be hot.

It's Summer in the desert—August—typically, the warmest month.

By 4:30 p.m., I was looking forward to a short walk, escaping the air-conditioning, loosening my aging body muscles.

As I donned my hat and stepped outside, I welcomed the enveloping heat— Mother Nature's Hug. At first, I found it invigorating. It allowed me to move comfortably after sitting at my desk for hours. I felt at ease being enveloped.

One hundred and fifty yards after turning the first corner, I realized the sun was hitting my calves from a different angle. My legs began to sting slightly. I can't be getting sunburned in this short a time, I thought, as I continued walking.

Then the fourth finger of my left hand began to hurt. Hmm. What's that about? I continued on to where the sidewalk abutted a cinder-block wall. The reflection of heat off the wall raised the temperature considerably. My finger hurt more. The tips of my other fingers began to feel pain. The backs of my calves really stung.

It wasn't until I reached the end of the block where I turn around that I realized my walk had been aided by a breeze, a slight wind that would now be an impediment.

Yep, the heat is blowing into my face as if I'd opened a furnace. That's what was burning my legs. And my left hand's fourth finger was being branded by my wedding band. Thankfully, that's now on the shady side of my body. But the tips of all my fingers still hurt. Must be due to heat. And, inhaling that breeze, though not like sucking on a lit blow torch, is somewhat stressful.

Well, here I am, home again. Sizzling Frederic. That A/C is going to feel so good.

8/27/2020

PROPOSAL

In 2007, a sadness spread throughout the United States. Thousands of pets died from eating melamine-contaminated food.

The ragdoll cat loved so dearly by my wife's cousin Randi was one of them. Randi, who lived alone, became distraught, then so depressed she took to bed for three weeks, stopped eating, talked only briefly on the phone, and wouldn't open her door to anyone. My wife, Gaylan, decided to buy her a replacement cat.

Pat, our friend from a condo downstairs, was also considering purchasing a companion for her lone cat. Her other one had been poisoned, too.

At the Animal Rescue section of PETCO, the ladies were adopted by two adoring black and white felines. The "tuxedo" with its white whiskers, goatee, chest blaze, and boots, rubbed against my wife's hand and purred through the cage directly into her heart.

On her cousin's porch, she deposited the carrier along with cat, food, and toys, rang the doorbell, and drove off.

A block away, her cell phone rang. Randi was too disturbed to form a new relationship. Gaylan returned, loaded everything into her back seat, and drove home. Now she was worried. She had no intention of owning a cat and didn't think I would like the idea.

Pat assured Gaylan she would take the tuxedo, which had already been named Sammy, but must wait a few days until her current pet became accustomed to Oreo, her own newly-named acquisition.

I wasn't thrilled about the situation. A cat. How does one care for this creature? Such a change in our lifestyle.

That night, Sammy slept between our heads, purring soothingly like a little motorboat. The next night was the same. Gaylan turned to me in bed, "I'll take Sammy downstairs in the morning."

My proposal, "How 'bout we keep him?"
5/15/2021

"SHUT UP!"

"Shut up!"

"Get out!"

These abrupt exclamations are not always meant negatively. In recent times their use has become the opposite. They can be hurled as expressions of excitement, praise, or surprise. But who knew.

Henry Higgins, or a more contemporary sociolinguist, would know that their interpretation depends on emphasis being given to their second syllables. For the exclamation to be considered positive, that emphasis must be relatively mild, drawn out, and higher in tone.

Without that emphasis, *shut up* is a rather offensive statement. But I suppose being told to shut up is better than being shut down, shut out, shut off, shut away, or shut in.

Shut can simply precede an adjective and noun, (shut the door) but is often followed by a preposition. You might wonder what interest a preposition would have in following *shut*. Simple. From the rear, *shut* appears to spell *tush*. And a nicely shaped tush has been known to attract followers. In fact, it has occasionally turned a preposition into a proposition.

But I digress. Here's a conversation in which shut up is used positively:

> (After many months of trying)—
> "You're WhAAAT?" older sister.
> "Get out!" younger sister.
> "Shut up!" another younger sister.
> "Congratulations, darling!" mother.
> "Ruff! Ruff!" the dog.
> "We're pregnant! Awwwk!" the parrot.

However, when used negatively, *shut up* can be a last-resort-type statement with the intent of bringing conversation to an immediate halt. Curt and to the point, it's a verbal slap in the face.

There are expressions that have the same meaning and firm intent but less intensity— Zip it. Pipe down. Hush. Cool it. Knock it off. Shush!—that may have the desired effect yet not provoke an angry response.

Personally, I would never think of using the term either negatively or positively. But an assignment is an assignment.

9/26/2020

"PREPARE FOR AN EMERGENCY LANDING"

"Prepare for an emergency landing."

The tiny, almost imperceptible voice in the back of my mind becomes louder, repeating itself several times. "Prepare...Prepare...Prepare."

I've been soaring, finally released from the pressure of sending my latest book to the printer. With tension off, I'm gliding lazily above an imaginary world of relief, looking down at marvelous landscapes—spiking, pink mountains, lush turquoise forests, golden fields of wheat.

Suddenly, it's 3:30 a.m. in my bed. I'm awake, lying here. My wonderful, mental glide has smashed into a turbulent cloud of reality—things I've put off, deadlines I've forgotten—not self-imposed like my book. Real ones. Tax preparation comes to mind. I forgot to tell my bookkeeper about my multi-book donation to a school for the poor. She's already turned over a formal recap to my accountant.

And regular tax preparation. And amending my trust.

Four months ago, we contracted for solar energy. A large, full cabinet still occupies garage space reserved for the storage battery. When's that solar equipment supposed to be delivered? Haven't heard. Have to check.

Family has invited themselves for a three-day visit. I must clean up months of book production from my desk in our office-guest bedroom.

I have a book sale approaching. Need to learn to operate a device that accepts credit cards. I'm having a wisdom tooth removed in three days. A *Mr. Whimsy* fan wants to meet for lunch. My wife has lung problems. I don't want to burden her with these matters, but she keeps track of some tax-deductible expenses.

No more gliding.

There's one additional deadline—in two weeks. Somehow, I must "Prepare for an emergency landing." That's the prompt for my next creative writing class assignment.

Bump!…bump…bump…bump. Aaah, I think I've just written it and seem to be safely grounded.

3/20/2021

TRAGEDY

Surrounded by the sunlit beauty of civilized nature, I sit, inadvertently peering across a narrow lake at two couples attempting with metal rods to knock their tiny, white, dimpled balls into a small hole in the grass.

The taste of cold beer and clamato juice barely registers, as I recognize the dramatic contrast between the golfers' activity and my attempt to determine which is the most disastrous of human tragedies.

I've accepted an assignment to write about **tragedy**, yet, following deep contemplation, feel the result can be positive.

I've narrowed my conclusion to one—the most appalling human tragedy is fearing death. Such fear lurks in the minds of many. It's embedded in various concerns. Not fulfilling one's potential before death steals the opportunity. Painful illness or injury leading to death. Ultimately being judged by a supreme being. Or, that which seems to be most prevalent—the unknown.

But why should we fear the unknown as opposed to expecting wonder?

Anticipating marvel, wonder, and magnificence in the next dimension frees the mind of worry and fear during this life. It allows joy and appreciation to prevail, love to grow, and satisfaction to spread.

I don't *hope* for future lives of wonder, I *know* they're coming. Can I prove it? I feel no need to do so.

What if there is no continuation of life, no additional dimensions? Nothing. At least, I've lived this life with a sense of security, enjoying more fully all there is to appreciate in the here and now.

But there *are* future lives. And the wisdom of my soul is evolving to fit right in.

5/29/2021

I CAN HARDLY WAIT FOR TOMORROW TO COME

I can hardly wait for tomorrow to come. As I lie next to you in velvet darkness, I look forward to the morning sun illuminating your golden hair, your starlet's face.

It wasn't always like this. There was an uncomfortable time when I didn't want tomorrow to come:

> If only I could press against the dawn;
> hold it back to stall your waking yawn.
> I snuggle, silent, knowing you will take
> away the love we've shared when you awake.
> Now, by your slumber purrs, I measure time,
> while here we nestle like a couplet rhyme.
> I conjure dreams, which I'll keep when you're gone
> and bless the twinkling stars for holding on.
> You wake, entwining me. I can't believe
> you sigh my name and never want to leave.

For years now, I've started each morning with the wonder of you. I lie contented, mentally tracing your enchanting physical features, appreciating how enjoyable you make my life.

I compare life to what it might be, were you not here. I'd manage, but, oh, how things would change. I'd miss the pleasure of conversing with you, of listening to your discussion with friends at dinner or on the phone. You give great phone. I'd miss the delicious variety of presentations with which you sustain health and stimulate taste buds. I'd miss your snuggling with and feeding the cats. And what would I do without you as half my memory?

Without you, I'd have to learn to run the clothes washer, to text, send pictures, reboot, and maybe even fix small mechanical things. You free me from mundane chores, chores that would undoubtedly slice into my writing time, mutilate my spontaneity.

I enjoy each day, sweetheart, by slowly removing the gift wrapping in which you so lovingly deliver it.

7/10/2021

SEASONS OF LIFE

Transition. I'm being slowly, forcefully, pressed, squeezed, thrust, pulled into this new world. Will it be a prison—constant bright light, loud noise, and dry air which I now must breathe in through my lungs? It hurts in so many ways. They've cut my lifeline! What have I done to deserve this? "Waaaah!"

Now, here I lie, trying to survive, adjust, get my bearings. I can barely look around; it's too bright. But exciting. There are images everywhere. Hazy creatures touch and move me. I can stretch when not wrapped up, but can't move from place to place. I've found something to suck on other than my thumb. There's liquid in it. Feels right. I'm going to sleep.

Growth. For months, hard things in my mouth hurt. Now, they help me chew, but I must keep my tongue out of their way. Tastes, smells, textures. More excitement—freedom at last. I can crawl and briefly stand. Must work on balance. I'm learning what words mean, thinking about talking.

Education. There's so much to learn and enjoy in this life—people, animals, toys, even picture books. I'm starting to forget where I came from. I try to share how wonderful it was, but get distracted. Television is hard to beat. School, driving, girls. Exploring philosophy and the arts. Refreshing my spirituality.

Building. Marriage. Family. Spirituality. Professional success. Accumulating wealth and material things. Traveling. Continue developing awareness.

Giving. Joining philanthropic organizations. Helping society—individuals and groups. Donating time and money. Remembering the world from which I came. Subtly passing on knowledge.

Teaching. More openly imparting both practical and philosophic matters. Sharing meaningful discoveries through my writing and relationships. Fostering peace and happiness.

Preparation. Appreciating the wisdom my soul has accumulated while preparing to slip into my next life. Expecting joy.

6/12/2021

SUGGESTION, SEXY, DEADLINE, MANDATORY, METAPHYSICAL

I'm sitting comfortably in a plush chair in absolute darkness when a **sexy** female voice makes a **suggestion**—she wants to make love.

"Wait a minute!"

"I'll gladly wait. There's no **deadline**."

"Where am I? Who *are* you?"

"We are where you want to be. I'm the one you wish for."

A soft, striped light of cream and purple turns on. I like the colors but not the stripes. It's as if my mind is being read. The light changes to gentle, all-encompassing lilac. Delightfully, a standing woman appears in a black sheath cocktail dress, high heels, and pearls.

The light goes out.

"Do you like my perfume?"

Tigress! I used to love it. Haven't smelled it for years.

The light comes on. The fragrance vanishes.

"You seem familiar. Do I know you?"

"My name is Wishable. You may call me 'Wish.' I know all the good of you, nothing negative. I'm in love with you and have been waiting forever for this opportunity. Come. Please make love to me."

She softly explains a new technique. When I realize what is entailed and what isn't, the idea becomes even more sensual. Intriguing. Two factors will be **mandatory**. No use of hands on one another and only one of the five senses may be experienced at a time. That sense can be triggered by saying it aloud.

There will be only one way to simultaneously experience the five senses plus many more—by mastering the **metaphysical**.

She then closes her explanation with, "I will teach you how…"

7/24/2021

marc frederic   Creative Writing Assignments

SHE TURNED HER BACK ON ME

She turned her back on me. But her attempt to hide her tears failed. I could see her shoulders heaving and hear her sobs. **"Where were you last night?"** I whined. I didn't expect an answer or even want one. That she couldn't face me hurt terribly.

She was my heroine as well as my favorite artist. Everyone viewed her talent as phenomenal. I simply loved her as a person, a very special person who cared for me.

We had been together four years. Ours was **love at first sight**. It developed into a **deep love.** Very open. No secrets. Unconditional. I was thrilled when she became my mistress. For obvious reasons, marriage was out of the question.

Then, Fifi entered the picture. As you might imagine, she was French. And very cute.

Somehow, Fifi came home with the love of my life and just stayed. I had started to ask her, **"How did you get in here?"** but was interrupted. One thing eventually led to another. And before I realized it, we were a threesome. Together, we enjoyed life immensely.

But for several days, Fifi has not been feeling well. She's not her bubbly self, has lost interest in most everything. In fact, during the last two days, she's refused food, even water. Our worry has intensified. It's time for medical attention.

Yesterday, I woke up from an afternoon nap to find them both gone. They didn't return last evening. Not even last night.

This morning, only one of them showed up. Fifi was nowhere in sight. That's when the tears began to flow.

"I had to put her down," she sobbed.

Creative Writing Assignments   NIBBLETS

That's it for the poodle, I thought. Someday, it'll be me. **It's a dog's life**.

This piece combines all the prompts suggested during our last creative writing session. The assignment was to create a story using the first prompt. I thought they were all good, so included them

8/7/2021

marc frederic   Creative Writing Assignments

BLANK PAGE POSSIBILITIES

The blank page offers many possibilities. It can be made into a paper plane, origami, a pea-shooter. Or, a retainer of thought.

Years ago, during a potent and seemingly unlimited state of appreciation, I wrote a piece entitled Paper Pad. It described how the mere sight of a yellow, lined legal pad of paper delighted me in both its blank and future-filled form.

It could jump-start my soul. Engender a surge of creative juices. I saw it as a seeded garden yet to sprout and bloom. A chrysalis eager to unveil a butterfly. A playground for letters that will experience the ecstasy of forming words, expressing ideas. An eventual landing pad for marvelous multi-colored dreams.

Writing is now an integral part of my life. My process of placing words on a blank page involves observation, imagination, and, at times, dimension shifting. Observation I perform through my senses. Imagination allows me to combine my observations in unusual ways. Dimension shifting I describe as opening up and letting go; frolicking with the Is that connects everything.

When shifting dimensions, I allow myself to be completely untethered. To leave my physical body. To experience additional senses. To not only observe but to become whatever attracts me. I flow like liquid. I become a breath, feeling what it's like to be inhaled, exhaled. I no longer give credence to time and space. During my last shift, I experienced phosphorescent sounds that hung like musical fruit from invisible trees of fur.

Returning, I herd words onto the blank page in descriptive order, attempting to share with you, my reader, those experiences, images, and feelings from other worlds.

Lie flat and enjoy blank page. I'm about to act as your filling station.

Oh! I see you're already full.

9/4/2021

BLAME IT ON THE ICE

Blame it on the ice. What a strange thing for her to mumble upon returning from her desert hike. It makes as much sense as telling me she almost drowned in the sand or fell into the sky.

I keep a close eye on her as she leaves a trail of clothes on her way to the shower. She steps in and twists the handle. As she turns her back to the refreshing spray, her hair becomes liquid charcoal.

There she stands, eyes closed, head tilted back—drenched perfection.

I'm tempted to step in with her. But not wanting to disrupt the image, I wait for her in the other room.

Her tan body eventually appears in a short, buttercup-yellow robe that honors her shapely legs. "It was crazy," she said. "I met a man out in the dunes. He sat cross-legged, long beard ruffling in the breeze. I couldn't take my eyes off him.

"When he realized I was watching, he casually beckoned me to sit. The warm sand was comfortable. In a soft voice, he told me about a frozen land where he once lived with the love of his life —

"Caught in a freak snowstorm, while hunting on foot, he had managed to load his field-dressed kill onto his sled. Trudging onward, he fell into a shallow fissure, where he lost his rifle, but eventually escaped to tow his quarry back to the cabin.

"Before entering, he heard her screaming desperately.

"Impulsively, he broke a large icicle off the roof overhang, yanked open the door, charged the bed, and two-handedly plunged the icy dagger into the man's back, plowing through his heart and, to his horror, piercing hers.

"He now lives in the desert. The mere thought of ice is more than he can bear."

10/2/2021

WHOSE BRIGHT IDEA WAS THIS?

"Whose bright idea was this?"

Hands on hips, brows knit, she voices the question while standing on her lawn, alternately looking at the hole in the ground and glancing through twilight to determine who created this additional complication in her life.

The hole is eight feet in diameter. There is no dirt around its edges, no sign of excavation. How was it made? Why is it here?

An eerie green light emanates from the hole, carrying with it distant cries of joy.

Curious and leery, the woman moves closer. As she looks into it, the green light stains her skin, turns her eyes orange, and makes her gray hair smell like barbequed spareribs.

Slightly beneath that green light, she spies a glowing yellow staircase spiraling down the hole's circumference. As she timidly places her foot on the first step, everything changes. She becomes young, glamorous, lightly perfumed, beautifully dressed in tangerine—a storybook princess who confidently continues her descent.

At the foot of the stairs, luminous lilac graces a hallway of mirrored walls, crystal chandeliers, and purple carpet. The excited cries have morphed into a blend of conversation and gentle music. Somewhere just ahead, there's a party.

As the doors before her open, she glides through them into soft darkness. She arrives before she gets there and follows herself into a room with no floor, ceiling, or walls. Within it, is everyone she's ever known. She appreciates them not by sight, but their vibrations that meld with her new abilities to speak Mandarin, to mine Bitcoin, and imagine thoughts she's never entertained.

Her life shimmers with bright ideas.

Eventually ascending the staircase to begin life anew, she's amazed that she can fly.

10/16/2021

I DON'T UNDERSTAND WHAT HAPPENED

I don't understand what happened.

Velvet SkyDancer believed she could fly. I had doubts. But her pixie-like body hinted at the possibility. Her café au lait skin topped with short blond hair, bangs falling almost to her almond-shaped eyes, defied reality.

We were lovers, yet I knew her only superficially.

Sadness seemed to tilt her eyes downward as if gravity had clutched her soul to its bosom. During those sad spells, I couldn't help her. I was afraid to become involved.

But, oh, when she smiled, bells tinkled. The world became a golden hug of summer. Her lips curled up at their corners—delicate, sugary, watermelon-pink. On those smiling occasions, I could refuse her nothing. Soaring the heavens, we were immune to any thoughts of limitation, excited by whatever came our way.

When she once crossed her jade eyes while sticking her tongue out the corner of her mouth, I broke into laughter. Her instant scowl sobered me quickly. I was caught off guard by that unexpected response.

But her effect on me contained magic. Her petite frame was sensual yet, at the same time, made me feel protective and playful. "Fly me!" she demanded, and I would throw her high in the air. It excited her. And me as well. She was beyond herself and loved it.

One balmy evening, at the zenith of our excitement, she seemed to dive into my eyes, imploring, "Higher, higher. Higher!"

In the heat of the moment, I flung her through an open skylight.

Uh oh.

Velvet's been dancing in the sky ever since.

11/20/2021

I REMEMBER (Roscoe)

Roscoe's skin was still like rubber. Wrinkled rubber. When he chewed, his face moved in every direction. Any piece of food or spittle that escaped onto his chin resembled a raft on a roiling river. Smiling or frowning made him unrecognizable as human.

I never saw much of his body. He wore long-sleeved shirts and baggy pants, usually of dull color. His hands looked normal except when holding a glass, for his fingers wrapped around the vessel numerous times.

Roscoe's sparkling blue eyes not only brought the world in, they let him out. People were enchanted by the wonder they saw within them. Most folks ignored Roscoe's contorting facial features, relating more to warm wisdom the man imparted.

Years ago, as a teenager obsessed with sex, I wondered if the man ever indulged in it. I thought about the women those wonderful blue eyes would attract and all the marvelous things his body might be able to share.

I remember wondering if his rubbery grip could easily unscrew the stubborn lid of a glass jar. If his flexibility could evade bodily injury. Could he squeeze through small places or be comfortable sitting on jagged rocks?

What I remember most about him was his voice. Neither blubbery nor wavy, it was a smooth, warm, baritone sound that expressed loving, insightful perceptions. Those notions sprouted within our hearts and minds like fertile seeds. Folks who nurtured them flourished.

People from miles around assembled to hear Roscoe speak as he sat elevated on bales of hay.

Once, at the edge of such a crowd, Roscoe's would-be-assassin stood next to me, dumbfounded. Slumping his shoulders and shaking his head, he realized what he'd been told about Roscoe couldn't be true.

I still have the pistol he handed me as he turned to leave.

12/4/2021

KNOTS

As an outgoing lad, I became a Cub Scout.
It was then I discovered what knots are about—
the *square*, the *slip*, the *hitch,* and *splice*;
the *loop*, the *sinnet,* and *harness* were nice.
There were *sheepshanks* and *bends, lanyards,* and such.
I didn't like *lashings* and *nooses* too much.
The *surgeon's* and *strangle* I tried to avoid.
But more basic ones I surely employed.
The *slide, whoopie sling,* and, of course, *figure 8*
all proved to be useful. In fact, were first-rate.
Of *constriction* and *ligature,* I was afraid,
yet was happy to work with the *bowline* and *braid*.
I didn't get hooked on fishing knots.
My passion was never for flies.
But as I developed my business thoughts,
I found I had use for neckties.
The *four-in-hand, Windsor,* and half of the latter
I frequently used with my shirts,
for they were quite handsome. My suits they did flatter
unless tied too tight. Man, that hurts.
Throughout my life, I've learned about knots.
My marriage is love-wrapped in joy.
It's sprinkled with ties of warmth and surprise,
held fast by the care we deploy.
When checking out wood, I've seen knots in pine,
which are nothing like I've been describing.
And once, long ago, my forehead did show
a knot when I fell from imbibing.
And then there's the knot that's used quite a lot
to measure through water and air
the speed you are going when slowly you're rowing
or flying as fast as you dare.
But my favorite "not" brings spice to my life,
for it frees and allows me to try.
It resides in my mind, is quite easy to find—
it's the "not" that comes after the "Why".
1/22/2022

A PENNY FOR YOUR THOUGHTS

"A penny for your thoughts."

"Give me your scent. And I'll open my heart."

Those comments began our initial conversation. I thought mine was a clever repartee. She evidently did as well, for the next thing I knew we were not only in bed, but in love.

We had met in Paris, in Montmartre, gazing at a sensual painting that set the juices of most viewers flowing.

That chance encounter led to our sharing thoughts over *café au lait* and *petit pains au chocolat*. We liked each other's thinking. We liked each other's manner and appearance. A virile, blue-eyed, American writer and a lovely Spanish painter in our mid-twenties, we melded well. Her dark eyes sparkled with stars. Mine found joy in her dimples.

During the decades that followed, our love has grown deep roots and continuously blossomed.

Sadly, in their early twenties, our son and daughter died separately in freak auto and SCUBA-diving accidents.

My wife and I had no other living relatives to lend us emotional support. Thankfully, we had each other. Our successful careers and positive attitudes allowed us to begin life anew. We legally changed our family name to *Serico* based on the *serendipitous sympatico* of our bonding. We lived its inspiration, traveling the world, creating as we had before, our love more intense than ever.

Sixty years after our meeting, that love flourishes, although our audible communication is limited. Stroke and infirmity have recently left us bedridden, and relatively speechless. We *can* move our heads toward one another. We stare and smile across our small room in the nursing facility.

We are able to remember, read each other's eyes and hearts. And silently ask whenever we wish, *A penny for your thoughts.*

2/19/2022

POPSICLE, RELATIONSHIP, SAFARI, OYSTERS, SERENDIPITOUS

*Although they shared a **serendipitous relationship**, the **oysters** and the **popsicle** realized that enjoying a typical **safari** together would be out of the question.*

The popsicle virtually melted at the thought, while the mollusks slowly dehydrated until they formed a bed of hollow shells.

Thus began the strange tale spontaneously jotted on the back of an envelope by a would-be surrealist. He wrote on the snow-white surface in thick black ink as sun slid through the horizontal shutters of his living room window, warming the back of his neck and sprawling lazily over the odd combination of words that ran from his brain down his arm to his hand holding the pen from which they emerged.

Amused by what the words were conveying, he continued with no definite purpose or direction other than the sheer joy of discovery.

Hmm, he thought, as he arrived at the bottom of the envelope and turned it over…
This use of five words will be fun to share with members of my writing class. It's certainly an improvement on the rude story I created about Patina Parkhurst's oil painting portraying an oyster eating a popsicle.

But were I to allow this nascent stream of consciousness to flow into the classroom imitating an assignment, it must total a minimum of 250 words. How many words does this wandering puddle currently contain?

226! The 300-word limit may be in danger.

I'll condense the conclusion with an imaginary mix of absurd tangibles—*following some exploratory exercises, an African bush trip was arranged. It contained liquid elements that favored the shellfish and temperatures that suited the flavored stick of ice. A portable mini-freezer, along with 37 tiny fur coats, enabled the exotic expedition to take place while preserving the kismet-like karma of a popsicular-oysterian fellowship.*

2/5/2022

I MADE AN INTERESTING DISCOVERY TODAY (Claudette)

I made an interesting discovery today.

Within my new high-rise office in Albuquerque, home of world-famous hot air balloon festivals, I found myself in an awkward situation.

I'd just received two distressing phone calls—the first from my wealthy, widowed aunt Claudette, insisting she come to my office to discuss a matter of extreme importance. Then came a call from our long-time family lawyer. Claudette had curtly hung up after commanding him to draft papers removing my daughter Valerie from her trust.

The lawyer wanted to know what caused Claudette's decision and if her reasoning was sound. A grand sum of money was at stake.

Claudette arrived at my office with chin held high. Her stately posture, St. John knit skirt-suit and matching pink heels demanded admiration.

I offered her one of the plush chairs near the floor-to-ceiling glass wall and joined her. Closed blinds blocked the strong rays of afternoon sun.

Claudette seated herself. Then, foregoing amenities, blurted, "It's about the yolk!"

"The yolk?"

"Yes, the *runny* yolk! Valerie ordered eggs benedict at brunch today. You know she's deathly allergic to raw eggs. If she can't properly look after herself, she's surely not ready to inherit millions tomorrow on her twenty-fifth birthday!"

We had begun to discuss the matter when, from outside, we heard intermittent loud bursts of noise akin to fog horns. Thinking the surprise would be glorious, I stood and opened the shades, revealing the view.

The distance from the streets below and the fifty-foot proximity of a gargantuan hot air balloon heading straight at us shocked Claudette. Her eyes met those of the panicked balloon pilot in his wicker basket pulling desperately at the burner flame release.

I soon discovered Claudette has both acute acrophobia and a weak bladder.

3/19/2022

I MADE AN INTERESTING DISCOVERY TODAY
(Salamanders)

I made an interesting discovery today.

A species of salamander lives in water trees.

What's a water tree? you ask. I'd sketch a picture of one, but I've drawn little since the day I fell asleep in my lounger with pen in hand. I'd been writing. A dire itch on the side of my nose woke me and I inadvertently poked out my right eye.

I can now draw only half pictures—the left half. Therefore, I'll describe the water tree verbally. Music may be a more descriptive medium, but the orchestra has gone to lunch, so...

Water trees are delightful. They drip. They flow. Spout. Dance. And glitter, while projecting a marvelous combination of color, sound, and fragrance. Being somewhat self-absorbed, water trees usually grow in solitude.

The agronomist, Mandelina, once harvested water branches, one from each tree, and planted them to form a water forest. She had music played to them daily and movies shown at night. Raised together, the water trees melded well. The Water Forest became a spectacular success.

Salamanders loved it. They live there to this day. Due to constant, creative exposure, many have grown to be musicians, others actors, and writers. A few film critics can be found in their midst.

Being amphibians, the salamanders are versatile creatures, able to breathe in water or on land. But those talented ones that live in The Water Forest are physically unique, for they have grown various joy receptors and light, rubbery wings with which to glide.

Creative Writing Assignments   NIBBLETS

It was this very, sun-filled afternoon, during a massive, shimmering salamander glide-fest, I made my interesting discovery. It was glittorious.

3/19/2022

AND, JUST LIKE THAT...

And, just like that, I'm back in what some consider to be reality.

I like my dream world better. I call it the World of Whimsy (the WOW). It's a world of soft edges in which delightful aromas ride balmy breezes. You may join them, if you wish, to float through pastel clouds that emit gentle songs.

If you like a particular chorus, you may instantly have it brushed on your forearms for mid-air flight entertainment. The chorus is free of charge. Full songs cost a happy thought. All musical pieces are exchangeable at any puffy cloud in the shape of an animal. The experience is referred to as a Sound Safari.

Sound Safaris are just one of many attractions in the WOW. Another is WOW dining, done with your eyes and nose. You'll wash your hands before dipping your little fingers into an individual, ethereal bowl of imagination.

Please dip as follows: Lace all fingers of both hands except your little ones, which you'll upwardly press together to resemble a tiny steeple. Next, placing your interlocked fingers over the Imagination Bowl, bend your wrists forward, allowing your little fingers a brief two-knuckle dip. The length of the dip determines the degree of imagination absorbed. Dips are limited to 30 seconds but begin at five.

The dipping bowls vanish as dining menus appear in mid-air before you. You may audibly request either individual items or unlimited-course meals of any sort. Pictures and written descriptions are optional. Your expanded imagination enhances your selections. Due to the manner of consumption, your stomach will never be stretched, although you're infinitely satisfied.

Even I, Mr. Whimsy, have yet to experience all the various pleasures available in the World of Whimsy. I doubt that anyone ever will, for they are limited only by one's imagination.

April 2022

PRIZED POSSESSION

Over time, my prized physical possessions have changed. Two I have valued far above all others. The first helped me obtain the second.

As a teenager, I worked delivering dog food, washing dogs, cars, and windows, and boxing groceries. Doing so, enabled me to purchase my first car—a 1951 Ford.

But it was during college that I obtained the 1956 Thunderbird. My father was proud of me and wanted to give me the vehicle. I wanted it badly but didn't feel I deserved it. He said, "Take the car. Grow into the man you think you should be to merit sitting behind its wheel, and it will be rightfully yours." That car was my first truly prized possession. It represented a lesson that prepared me for life.

My second prized possession, a personalized engraved money clip, I earned years later. It's the result of five years of focused, highly dedicated effort learning a new business and developing a clientele. During that time, I put my passion on hold, wrote only two poems. My effort placed me in the top twenty producers nationwide of the brokerage firm, E.F. Hutton & Company. That money clip was proof I could achieve anything I put my mind to. For 37 years thereafter, I continued to advise my clients while enhancing my creative writing skills.

I'm now a retired, happily married grandfather who continues to write. I'm thrilled to have published 15 books. The T-bird is long gone. The money clip's value lies mainly in the $20-dollar gold piece it contains.

My prized possessions are now different. They're internal. My imagination adds spice to life. My sense of humor sparks joy. And my heart carries within it all the wisdom of my evolving soul, which will undoubtedly transcend time and space.

4/2/2022

BALLOONS, RANDOM, SUITCASE, REUNION, COWBOY

Dehydrated, verging on delirium, the **cowboy** wonders if he's hallucinating. His pungent fear is beginning to unnerve the motionless horse he straddles.

Three hundred yards ahead, gigantic rock formations break the flat, dusty desert he has ridden for days. As he strains to see the base of the formation called The Castle where the precious waterhole should be, smoke signals rise above it like thought **balloons** in a cartoon. He believes he can read them—*Enemy come, Kill!* It's no **random** thought. History books and motion pictures have warned of savage tribes.

Whatever shade and pooled water may exist are evaporating with a shimmer through a hole in his mind. He mentally staggers through his punctured dream.

He checks his canteen…a whispering swish. To escape by skirting those formations, his horse will need every remaining ounce in the nearly depleted bota bag hanging from his saddle horn. That small water **suitcase**, as he had jokingly called it, has become crucial to his survival.

In a flash, he realizes the journey begun as a macho display of courage and grit might now become his life's finale. He should have put his medical and law degrees to use. But after tedious years of study, his dream of creating a new profession—forensic medical attorney—had faded. He craved the great outdoors.

Now, from within his swirling depths, he visualizes the consequences of completing his travel plan; then reigns his horse to retrace its tracks to the last waterhole.

His college **reunion** will have to wait.

5/14/2022

IT WAS THE LAST THING I EXPECTED

It was the last thing I expected. Especially in a hospital.

I'm not sure how I managed it, but I phoned my wife. "They're trying to kill me," I spoke softly so no one other than my wife would hear. "Come get me out of here."

She either didn't understand or didn't believe me. I tried desperately to explain. "They know I know what they're doing. They're all in on it—the doctors and the patient in the bed on the other side of the curtain. They're smuggling jewels and gold across the border in his hollow leg. He keeps calling for Percocet because it hurts when they pack his leg full."

"It'll be okay, honey." my wife said.

I was on the verge of panic. Making the call had been a struggle. I couldn't get out of bed. I had tubes in my arms, my nose, my chest, and bladder. I was a prisoner. Even if I escaped the bed, I had no car keys, no car, no ID, no money to pay a cab. "Come and get me," I half demanded, half begged.

"Everything will be okay," my wife repeated.

"If you won't come and get me, I'll call Lana," I threatened. "She'll come. Even a hundred and twenty miles."

I don't know how my wife responded to that. The doctors were arriving to make sure my curtained roommate's leg was full and his pain under control. I pretended I was asleep.

It wasn't hard to pretend. The second pill the nurse had given me for pain made me drowsier than expected. I'd never had two hydrocodone tablets so close together. Was that dosage proper, or…

Zzzzzz.

5/28/2022

MYSTERY SOLVED

How the maiden died was inadvertently discovered through a game.

In lieu of bingo, a substitute game called *Telephone* was suggested. Chairs were arranged to form two circles in the school auditorium. An identical statement was written on two pieces of paper by the organizer. One piece she kept. The second, she gave to her counterpart in the other circle. The competition between the two circles would entail speed as well as accuracy. The first two games went well.

By the third game of the evening, people had loosened up. Their creativity, combined with hearing aid and short-term memory issues, provided entertainment along with an unexpected result.

As a bell rang, the leaders of each circle whispered the statement into the ear of the person next to them, who in turn, cupped the ear of the next person, repeating the statement as accurately as they could. So it went until the statement made the round, at which time the last person said it out loud for all to hear.

The original statement of the third game was:

>   It's a beautiful day with bright blue skies.

One circle's subsequent versions morphed as follows:

>   It's a beautiful daze with bright blue eyes.
>   It's a beautiful haze with a light su-prise.
>   She's a beauty who plays with the right disguise.
>   She writes beautiful plays, which are witty and wise.
>   She's a playwright of mystery, pity and cries.
>   It's a mystery whether she lives or she dies.
>   Something or other about death and life.
>   Something my grandmother said to my wife.
>   Whatever upset her, my wife's in a tizzy.

Whirling beside her makes me feel dizzy.

Then came the last man's teary confession,

> Dancing the cliff's edge was just meant to thrill her.
> Believe me, in no way did I mean to kill her.

6/11/2022

THERE'S A FIRST TIME FOR EVERYTHING

There's a first time for everything.

Learning to fly is a first for my darling, late wife.

"Dimension skipping is a marvel," she tells me. "There's no time or space to contend with."

That mind-expanding statement is a joy to comprehend. Evidently, she can be everywhere at once—ubiquitous. She's thrilled and relaxed at the same time. Able to dawdle, while multi-experiencing everything. Oh, the new senses she must possess in order to take it all in!

To me, being at peace while sensing everything everywhere simultaneously seems impossible, the ultimate confusion. But she loves it. She's surely not dyslexic anymore. "It can't be compared to a fly dodging a swatter," she tells me. "It's billions of times faster. It's all at once. So fast, there's no need for movement, no need for a body. Nothing needs lubrication or wears out or hurts.

"It's like dreaming," she reiterates. "Nothing is limited by time or space.

"And, there are so many other dimensions. Not only after life on Earth, but on Earth, itself. Love, for example, is actually an immersion dimension of many shades in which you expand with delight, dance with infinity. And pink-raying is a phenomenon even better than telepathy. You just imagine. And let it happen.

"It's all so easy. If only I'd realized all this on Earth.

"I still love you, darling.

"Come fly with me."

6/17/2022

THE WIND BLEW OUT OUR LAST MATCH

The wind blew out our last match.

We had faced a mammoth challenge as the breeze picked up dramatically. It was suddenly like being underwater in strong current. The encroaching dark was ominous. Nature was about to cast its powerful lot.

We had struggled for hours, each striving to do our best. There was little, actually nothing, to shield us from whatever would occur. Between the two of us, we had only a wide net not designed for protection.

If the weather became more threatening, we'd be finished. Most everyone had deserted us, figuring we were doomed. Hopefully, we could maintain our effort.

We had no choice. Giving our all, we attempted to come out on top, to triumph while confronting the weather. We battled on. Bam…bam…bam…bam…back and forth. Who would be victorious?

We had trained rigorously to get here. Been members of special teams. Fought for years to hone our skills. Endlessly practiced kill shots. Now this. How could it be? But it wasn't over yet.

We thought ourselves winners. We could do this. But would we have the opportunity? The odds were against it.

We continued to give it everything we had.

Finally, the dark clouds in the distance were upon us, blotting out any semblance of hope. Opening their distended bellies, they drenched the grounds as hurricane-force winds battered us unmercifully.

So much for the Wimbledon Tennis Championship.

November 2022

CONSOLIDATED, BUBBLE, DEFINITELY, CASCADING, MESMERIZED

Two months after my wife's sudden passing, I've **consolidated** my thoughts.

Our 34 years together were an absolute delight. Still being chock-full of her love, I find its effects are indelible, comforting, exhilarating, portable, and transferable. I intend to live in love forever.

I've come to realize love is more than a feeling. It's a dimension in which to exist. What a pleasure it is giving, taking, fulfilling. It's a marvel, an ever-expanding **bubble**, a realm of beauty, kindness, and appreciation limited only by one's imagination.

I see love as a world of reality laced with dreams. A dance of tenderness spiced with passion. Delicious clouds being nibbled by angels. Pastel falls **cascading** into silver seas.

I feel love as growth through gentle exploration and the satisfying thrill of discovery. Pulsating enchantment. Intangible presents spontaneously given. Aspects of myself I've taken for granted being cherished by another.

Yes, love is **definitely** a dimension in which amazement twinkles the eye, strums the heart, dazzles the soul. It's calm stimulation. Exciting comfort. Extraordinary spontaneity. A state of joy to relish. A miracle to share.

At times, when entering the love dimension, people become **mesmerized**. But they soon learn to release their amazement, exhaling wooshes of delight, proclaiming the delicious effects they are feeling.

Living in love enhances the physical senses as well as the intangible ones. It's a state in which life is fully appreciated. Challenges result in accomplishment. Gratitude prevails.

Each outcome is better than expected. Every thing and body is surprisingly wonderful.

Eventually, we come to expect the wonders.

And they constantly appear.

8/13/2022

YOU'RE NOT GOING TO DRINK THAT, ARE YOU?

The weather had been unbearably hot, unusually dry, for weeks.

The forest, bush, and tornado fires were horrendous. Vegetation, people, livestock, and pets suffered, even died, from smoke and dehydration. Towns were destroyed.

No one knew what could be done.

Strange rumors spread about lakes and ponds drying up in a directional pattern from north to south. It was said these bodies of water were each depleted in a matter of days. Yet, rivers were turning yellow and flowing freely.

The land of the Yuris was in trouble—a nation on the brink. What defied belief was the supposed cause—a humongous giant.

For centuries, such a being had been faithfully acknowledged—a myth passed down through generations. But no living Yuri had seen such a creature. And the possibility of such a sizeable being was beyond imagination, for the giant was purported to be as large as a small mountain, to consume forests as salads and suck up lakes to quench his thirst.

A scouting party from the Yuri capital was formed and sent to potentially meet and greet the monster. And, at last, they did encounter him.

In the distance, they could see an immense hulk of a being seated at the edge of a lake. His hands held a section of a mammoth pipeline, one end of which he stuck into the lake while he raised the other end to his mouth.

The Yuris fired rifles in the air to draw the giant's attention.

"You're not going to drink that, are you?" one screamed.

"I certainly am," came the thunderous reply, "and when I process it, I'm going to put out the rest of the fires by whizzing on them. Seems appropriate. This land is known as the Yuri Nation. Isn't it?"

9/10/2022

DECISION

The decision relentlessly holds my mind captive. Pinching its edges. Poking its center. What a position to be in. And over a dilemma of such minor importance.

This is not a matter of life and death as was my decision to pull the plug on my ailing father following an unsuccessful surgery. It doesn't even rival the seriousness of putting down my favorite cat two days after my wife unexpectedly died. The foregoing are matters of the heart, maybe even the soul.

The decision I'm currently pondering is much less serious. It involves two dear friends hosting a party on New Year's Eve. My dilemma about accepting their invitation may seem petty, but I've never been a fan of going out on New Year's Eve. It's amateur drinking night. Possible trouble. In this case, however, there should be neither heavy traffic nor great distance to travel. That's a positive.

When younger, I always liked to usher in the new year from the comfort of bed with a good partner. That still seems to be an attractive possibility, because the celebration is scheduled for 9:00 instead of midnight. That's another positive.

And then there are my close friends, the host and hostess, wonderful people whom I don't want to offend by refusing their invitation. Another reason to attend.

So what's so tough about making the decision? Habit, I guess. Being a New Year's Eve grouch.

Here's the clincher—when making a final choice, I always ask myself, "How would I feel if I don't do it?" And on that answer, I readily base my decision.

I will attend. And thoroughly enjoy the party.

HAPPY NEW YEAR!

12/10/2022

Creative Writing Assignments — NIBBLETS

UNINTENDED, CHAMPAGNE, CANDLES, CELEBRATION, HANGOVER

If Sherry's **unintended celebration** had been lit by **candles** instead of **champagne**, she wouldn't be nursing a **hangover**.

With an ice bag on her head, a bottle of Tylenol by her side, and a tummy chock full of charcoal pills, she sat watching a video of last night's fiasco.

The video's music reverberated a fabulous, frenetic beat, while the band's disco ball highlighted Sherry's sensual moves. With skirt hiked high, she spontaneously appeared at the top of the stairs and danced her way down, continuing over two couches, onto a table, then halfway back up the staircase in perfect synchronization with the music. Loud applause and encouraging screams acclaimed her appeal. She was the hit of the party.

Or so she thought.

Horrified, Mr. Ruggles, the mortician, looked on. He had wished to present a warm image of his new funeral parlor and was hosting an open house including champagne, hors d'oeuvres, and live music.

All had gone sedately as planned until the band got stoned and the guests schnozzled. The raised volume and tempo of the music invited party crashers, which led to an uproarious atmosphere culminating in a raid by police.

Sherry, who had been in town to interview the next day with Mr. Ruggles for a back-office job had become carried away. She had no idea the bubbly could have such an effect.

Mr. Ruggles received more promotional publicity than he imagined. Sherry did not get the position for which she was interviewing, but is now billed at the local burlesque house as the "Dead Ringer of Gypsy Rose Lee".

All as a result of the local paper headline reading, "WOMAN WAKES DEAD AT LOCAL MORTUARY."

12/29/2022

marc frederic — Creative Writing Assignments

WHO SAID THAT?

Who said that?

Did I ask myself that aloud?

While amused by sounding like the title of a television gameshow, I also feel a tinge of apprehension, for I'm surrounded by impenetrable darkness and alone in bed. I think.

Am I dreaming? Or have I been awakened by a tangible voice? I know I hear it.

What a message this wonderful androgynous voice is conveying. So pleasant. So poignant. I don't want to lose this mystical moment.

Who or what could this be?

From somewhere between wake and dreamland, I question which is reality? I feel it is neither but, instead, a world in which I can simply drift among dimensions while maintaining a bond with the universal spirit. It seems the reality we all think we share is merely a transitory illusion.

I love these dimensions. I belong in them. They comprise an all-encompassing realm of shifting beauty. I don't want to leave. I don't think I will. I'll let them envelop me. Just enjoy the warm softness of peaceful stimulation, security, and adventure. My soul evolving as I explore.

The voice continues, creating a pervasive harmony, lolling in the sanctuary of my heart. Gentle yet firm. Rich yet mellow. An auditory delight softly reverberating like a pastel echo.

It matters not who or what this voice belongs to. Its effect combines the wonder of magic with a caress of infinity.

It simply repeats, "I love you," as I contentedly drift ahead.

1/14/2023

WHAT?

Some among us have a wonderful advantage.

They feel intensely and express their feelings. They are able to see others. Not only outer appearances, but through the surface into hearts, minds, and souls.

They seem to understand more thoroughly and love more deeply. Always on the lookout for kindness, they nurture it. By doing so, they enrich the world around them.

These wonder-beings blossom in response to considerate, tender treatment. They love to love. And to be loved.

And that is where they have the advantage—in being loved. Especially physically. Their femininity incorporates a miraculous network running throughout their bodies, which when treated with gentle creativity, engenders passionate affection.

Such magical receptors enhance feelings beyond expectation, transporting these lovely beings to other realms—realms of joy fondly remembered as wonder. Glorious realms that, at the time, may be difficult to describe other than with passionate cries and laughter.

To convey what it's like being immersed in these incredible worlds takes someone who delights in closeness, can soar within a dream, is comfortable with passion, has an imagination unlimited by reality, and is at ease verbalizing sensations. Being in love is a marvelous bonus, but even outside that state of bliss, these enchanting individuals can feel intensely.

I understand. And am thrilled by being intimate with these delectable creatures who make their joyous journeys while in my company. But I want to go too. I want a ticket of my own.

When asked, I have only one answer to the question, *What would I wish to have been had I not been what I am?*

A woman.

2/18/2023

I HAD NO IDEA WHAT IT MEANT

I had no idea what it meant.

It was a frame—a subtle wooden molding mounted on a wall of its same color. Five feet tall by two feet wide, it had not a thing in it.

Was it simply meant to be decorative? Was it supposed to stimulate thought? To mean anything someone wished? To make one appreciate everything it wasn't.

Maybe it was unfinished. Or it didn't mean anything.

But once it caught my attention, it became more and more fascinating. Curiously attractive. A mysterious piece that knows its purpose and wants to explain what it's up to.

The more closely I examine it, I realize it adds purpose to the otherwise blank wall. I continue to study it and open my ears wide.

Now, the frame begins to talk. Or possibly my ears become attuned to frame-speech, for no one else seems to notice.

The frame explains how it had been offered a grand selection of objects to surround but had refused them all. It wished to be unlimited, at one with everything. To frame any particular thing meant it could not frame the rest. And, equally important, by surrounding one object, it would be relegated to living life as a simple frame rather than a gateway for each viewer's imagination.

As the frame explains in more detail, its voice becomes louder, its mission clearer, its reasoning more profound.

Listening intently, I am astounded to see what at first appeared to be a vacancy, transition into a portal to unlimited worlds of wonder.

3/4/2023

HOW WOULD I LIKE TO BE REMEMBERED?

I'd like to be remembered as is my late wife. But it ain't gonna happen.

So kind, considerate, and caring, she was truly an other-directed person, who gave of herself calmly in a great variety of ways.

When we first met, I was the recipient of her generosity and cooking skill. Before our blind date, she on the phone invited me and the lady who introduced us, to her home for my choice of dinner. As our relationship blossomed, she showered me with gifts both tangible and ethereal. I was in heaven.

Later, when she exhibited similar behavior with others, my thought was two-fold. Either she was trying to buy affection, or she was unconsciously overdoing it. Neither turned out to be true. In her mind, there was no limit to kindness, which she proved over the years. Her personal and community relationships were loved and admired. She may have been an angel in disguise.

I care about people, a number of them deeply. But I come first. If I'm not in accord with myself and the spirit or energy that runs throughout everything, then I'm of little use to others.

I enjoy life and like to write about it. To bring its beauty to people's attention. To stimulate them to think outside the box. To encourage their participation as spiritual beings enjoying the human experience while looking forward to other-worldly enjoyment, all in good time.

I'd like folks to say, "He was at one with himself and surroundings."

And if I could say it myself, "I have no cares. I'm joyous, whole. I'm here. I'm everywhere—a carefree, weightless happy soul that now needs no repair. I've melded with the universe. In tune. In harmony.

And all there is
is all I am
as far as I would be."

4/14/2023

IMPULSBOT

I cannot wait to walk on my pieces of sky.

I had heard marvelous things about the outlet regarding their displays and the goods they have to offer. "Out of this world!" people raved.

But no one had mentioned that the store's physical dimensions and selection of merchandise leisurely change in a continuous flux. The changes evidently depend on the rate at which objects are sold as well as their size. The walls and ceiling of the building expand and contract as needed, subtly adjusting to perfection.

Unusual as it seems, the shift is not at all distracting. In fact, it's spectacularly convenient, for merchandise displays of every sort somehow manage to evolve and maneuver throughout the customers, allowing people to make their selections while remaining in one place.

Order screens are available for shoppers who desire specific merchandise. But most of us are charmed, even bedazzled, by the ongoing random presentation of extraordinary items. They unexpectedly appear, accompanied by subtle color/sound combinations that often inspire buyers to live up to the store's name—*IMPULSE*.

I had no idea I would purchase the items with which I am leaving:

- 38 pieces of sky with which to line the floor of my new subterranean home.
- 1 set of delicious traffic light lenses for its essence of cherry, orange, and lime.
- 2 ½ quarts of laughter.
- 2 room-filling aromas of gardenia and freshly baked chocolate chip cookies.
- 7 songs by migrating humpback whales.
- 13 dream catchers made of iced spider webs.

- 2 purple buffalo thumbs (one for the dog to chew, the other for the baby to suck).

I will return. With friends. Would you like to join me?
3/25/2023

WHAT WOULD I DO WITHOUT...?

What would I do without rainbows,
roses and daisies in dew?
What would I do without pink lemonade,
sunshine, and wide skies of blue?

What if the whole world lacked humor;
nobody smiled or told jokes?
What if we all believed rumor
and instead of caresses gave pokes?

What if all rivers stopped running?
What if the seas never waved?
What if bad rules were followed by fools
and everyone just misbehaved?

What if no music were playing?
What if no words did exist?
Thoughts would all go without saying;
friendship and lovin' be missed.

What would I do without lovin',
being told I am the best;
all of that sweet turtle dovin';
back scratches, all of the rest—
coziness watching good movies,
sharing a drink and fine meal,
chatting 'bout books and babbling brooks,
doing what makes us both squeal.

I'm thankful for imagination,
for all it allows me to feel,
unlimited inspiration
that lends everything such appeal.
The flight that gives butterflies freedom.
The joy that gives colors taste.

The sounds I can touch that thrill me so much.
Not one thing I sense goes to waste.

This world's overflowing with marvels.
So many there are to enjoy,
for I have a prism I gaze through—
a most special means I employ.
Without that, my vision may falter.
Without it I'd not be the same.
The world as I see it may alter;
amazement I'd no longer claim.

What would I do without wonders
and all I believe to be true?
What would I be without…
What would I dream about?
What would I do without You!

4/30/2023

marc frederic — Creative Writing Assignments

FIVE MEMORIES
of people I didn't really know

They left an impression…

Even now, the memory makes me cringe. It turned out I didn't know him as well as I thought. That cost me a bunch—one-third of my net worth—my largest investment ever.

***

From motion pictures and TV, I found her extremely appealing. But our in-person meeting at her book signing…Wow! Magnetic vibrations! Tingle. Stammer. Aye, yai, yai!

***

He died in Madrid in front of me and 23,797 other people watching his performance. At the time, we weren't sure he had been killed. But seeing him propelled into the air from a kneeling position, definitely gave that impression. The bull's horn had thrust past the twirling red cape and through the matador's stunning "suit of lights" jacket, piercing his solar plexus, tossing him high.

***

The breeze became a stiff wind, forcing our pilot to release hot air from the gigantic balloon above us. Hitting the tilled field, our partitioned basket tipped over and was dragged 50 yards, scooping dirt like an enormous bucket. As we came to a halt, my wife and I looked into the section now below us to find the terrified eyes of the other couple barely showing above the accumulated dirt.

***

Five of us kids filled a paper bag with dog poop and set it afire on the porch of a man who harassed us whenever we walked by his house. We rang his doorbell and ran. After stomping the flames, the enraged

Creative Writing Assignments   NIBBLETS

man chased us across multiple lawns, jumping low hedges, screaming threats of revenge. His face was beet red.

These acquaintances, who inadvertently seasoned my life, may occasionally dance through my mind, but it's friendship, romance, and the belief in my soul's indestructibility that continually sing in my heart.

5/27/2023

MISSING IT

Dancing with Jill was like eating angel food cake—light, airy, and delicious. I miss that.

Swing was our forte. She could follow my lead like no one else. The slight pressure of my hand on her back, the mere start of a finger twist, led to twirls of fast-paced rapture. When "Proud Mary" played, the floor cleared for us.

We danced socially, winning a few informal swing contests, and were thrilled by what we could do together. That was it. Nothing more. But it was glorious.

Jill was the wife of a close friend. Both he and my wife at the time appreciated what happened when Jill and I swung.

Fifty-five years later, I choose not to dance for fear of falling. I've developed a strong case of peripheral neuropathy. Can't feel the bottoms of my feet. I can, however, vividly imagine and remember, which is truly satisfying.

There's something else I remember about Jill. She could get feisty. And rightfully so. One late afternoon, several of my male friends, including Jill's husband Jack, and I were drinking in a local bar. Jack had called Jill a couple of times promising to be home soon. Shortly after the second call. Jill arrived at the bar.

Perched on a bar stool with glass in hand, cigar in mouth, Jack had his back to the door. A half-empty beer bottle sat on the bar next to him. Much to the surprise of those of us drinking with Jack, Jill simply approached the bar, picked up the bottle, and slowly poured its contents over Jack's head.

Topping that, was Jack's reaction. Without flinching, he removed the rolled tobacco from his mouth, studied its end, and calmly stated, "I do believe my cigar's gone out."

I kinda miss those shenanigans too.

6/10/2023

FROM THE GIANT'S POINT OF VIEW

"So what, if I'm bigger than you?
I'm bigger than most. It is true.
So, I live on a cloud
and when I shout out loud,
a thunderous sound does ensue."

When he cried, it rained down below. His sneezes produced storms. But when he smiled, either sun shined or stars twinkled like his eyes.

Once the size of a normal man, the giant regularly lifted weights and ate prodigiously. Thus, he grew and grew until no building could serve as his home. He moved to a cloud high in the sky with plenty of room. There he lived happily. No one pointed at or bothered him.

Angels loved him. One gave him her golden harp. "No need to take lessons," she told the giant. "The harp plays itself." Another gave him a goose that lays golden eggs, some of which he made into coins just for fun.

All went well until a strange, sturdy, green stalk sprouted through his cloud smack in the middle of his garden. The goose pecked at it. The giant cut the top off the weed that threatened his view.

One day, shortly after the stalk appeared, a little boy named Jack climbed up it all the way from the ground. He peeked out from the garden to see the giant's wonderful, huge castle, which he couldn't help but explore. Therein, he found the giant's harp, goose, and coins.

That's when little Jack became a thief and eventual murderer. With the giant's treasures, he scrambled away and, reaching the ground, cut through the stalk with an axe. The giant, chasing him down it, died from the fall.

Villagers considered Jack to be a nimble hero who brought riches to his poor mother while ridding the world of an evil monster.

What do you think?

11/15/2023

WELL, WHAT DO YA KNOW!

2 a.m., in bed, I'm wide awake asking Amazon's Alexa a question. And what an answer I receive!

I'd just finished listening to a few songs to put me to sleep: *Friends in Low Places*, *Two Pina Coladas*, *Margaritaville*, and *Drinkin' and Dreamin'*.

The lyrics about booze sparked the following memory—I was attending a business seminar at the Royal Orleans during a muggy summer in the early 80's.

After the first day's meetings concluded, several of us went up to the rooftop pool of the hotel where we ordered drinks. Dick Tartre, ordered a tequila and grapefruit juice. It sounded refreshing. We all decided to try one. And loved it.

I asked Dick what the drink is called. He replied, "Tequila and grapefruit."

"Oh, no," I said. "It deserves a better name than that. Let me think."

Because Dick was prematurely bald, I proposed the name in his honor, along with this explanation: a vodka and grapefruit is called a greyhound, a vodka and grapefruit with salt on the rim is a salty dog. Since Dick has nothing on top and we're substituting tequila for vodka, I suggest we christen this drink a "hairless chihuahua." My proposal met with uproarious approval.

That evening, we ordered hairless chihuahuas at three different bars. Each waitress returned to our table with profuse apologies for the bartender's unfamiliarity with the drink. The following evening, we repeated our request at three entirely different establishments and were served every time without question. That's New Orleans!

Creative Writing Assignments   NIBBLETS

Fifty years later, I've asked Alexa the contents of a hairless chihuahua. With no hesitation she replied, "A tart drink of grapefruit juice, orange liqueur, and tequila."

Well, what do you know! The name I gave a cocktail half a century ago still exists! And its contents have been beautifully enhanced!

6/20/2023

marc frederic   Creative Writing Assignments

SECRET LOVE

How significantly time has changed not only my personal life, but society, itself. Things we thought were "a kick in the head" would today not only be considered boorish, they could ruin one's reputation. Political correctness and cancel culture dominate society's behavior.

During the early 1970s, after work, I would often frequent a bar, which was located across the street from our office. I was relatively new in my profession, as were several of us. We would stop for drinks, camaraderie, and an equally important reason—to share various things we had learned that day.

And share we did. Sometimes for hours, until what we had learned was well absorbed along with the liquor we had consumed.

The consumption occasionally resulted in outrageous behavior. Not raucous, but somewhat "off the wall". One of the craziest actions was a co-worker breaking in his new American Express card the day he received it by taking an impromptu flight to Hawaii that very night without telling his wife. Finding out, in a fit of anger she used her card to join him.

But most of what took place was relatively mild and considered amusing. For example, after she sang *Once I Had a Secret Love*, I asked the entertainer if I could borrow her mic to perform a different rendition. It went like this:

Once, I had a secret love.
She wore a nylon negligee.
When I asked about the price,
she said I didn't have to pay.
When I asked her why her love was free,
she said, "Seeley Mattress sponsors me."
Last night we were on channel four.
Now my secret love's no secret anymore.

I didn't compose the lyrics. But they were a hit.
1/27/2024

THE CURMUDGEON

That there curmudgeon,
he just ain't a-budgin'
He's stuck in his ways like glue.
He's a crusty old man
with a negative plan
to respond to whatever, you do.

Yep, Phil was crusty even as a child. When he sat in the corner with little Jack Horner who was eating his Christmas pie, he bit off Jack's thumb, which was stuck in a plum, and thrust that fruit into Jack's eye.

As little Miss Muffet sat on her tuffet, smiling while sipping some cider, Phil was the creep who, with malice so deep, introduced the young girl to the spider.

As Philip grew older, he first grew much bolder, but then he became a recluse. It seems in his haste he developed a taste for humans and thought, *What's the use? I attempt to be nice by adding some spice and try not to be so sadistic. But it seems that each friend disappears in the end, for my taste has gone cannibalistic.*

None questioned strange tones or the large stack of bones, for mostly Phil kept to himself. If a dog came alone, he'd throw him a bone like a cur-crazed, most generous elf.

And so, on it went till Philip was spent and had not a friend in the world. He would sit on his porch 'neath the light of a torch around which night moths flit and twirled. But his senses were keen and he kept his place clean. The bone pile attracted no ants. And his spirits soon rose as he beaded bone toes to make bracelets for termagants.

A termagant's what? A kick in the butt. A person whom Phil wouldn't bludgeon. It's a delightful catch. A truly fine match. In fact, it's a female curmudgeon.

3/27/2024

MAGIC...

I want to believe, to be surprised, to be charmed and mystified. To combine reality with dreams. To be at one with possibility. To stretch and grow. To seek and enjoy. To be unlimited in all respects. To be thrilled with acceptance. To share the marvel of discovery.

To see the beauty and wonder in everything is to live an enchanted life. To feel, hear, taste, and touch is awesome. But to shift further, into the beyond, be it even for an instant, is magic.

"You're magic," he tells her, gently stroking her cheek as he gazes into her green eyes.

"Tell me more."

"You make thing disappear."

"Like what?"

"Like the 's' on the end of things. And my car keys, when you want me to stay."

"Tell me more."

"You're a delight. I can't figure you out, but I love the way you make me feel."

"How do I make you feel?"

"Sometimes like a shy tornado. Other times like a frog on a toadstool. But when you make me feel like a cross between Hercules and a cuddled puppy, I like it best."

"You know what you make me feel like?"

"What?"

Creative Writing Assignments   NIBBLETS

"Meringue on top of a lemon pie. Or an angel riding Pegasus into a sunrise. And sometimes like flowing lava."

"What do you feel like now? I mean, what would you like to feel like?"

"A little sleight of hand would be nice after I make my champagne disappear."

"Let's do a little waltzing through the universe."

"You're out of this world!"

"You are magic!"

2/10/2024

marc frederic — Creative Writing Assignments

INSPIRATION

Inspiration—high vibration.
What a zowie-zip sensation!
Sometimes springs from meditation.
others leap from light libation.
A sort of mild intoxication.
A mixture of hallucination
spiked with strong imagination.
Sparked by deep communication
or a gentle conversation.
Takes the form of revelation,
not a simple explanation.
When I'm into word creation,
my Muse I call for motivation,
a bit of oomph, some stimulation.
She fulfills my expectation,
serving her sweet preparation
marinated in elation.
Exultation! Jubilation!
What a thrilling avocation!
Makes me feel I'm on vacation.
She deserves reciprocation—
inklings of my own formation.
Fabrication! Innovation!
Treasures of proliferation!
Maybe some remuneration—
joy, love, and scintillation,
soft caresses, undulation,
humor, and thought provocation,
promises and adoration,
much support and admiration.
Certainly, no tribulation,
consternation, aggravation.
She's not one for confrontation.
That I know for sure.
The last line warrants acclamation

for not ending in an "ation."
You see, it is my estimation
folks have had enough.
The time has come for limitation—
"Cut it off" not amputation.
"words in print" not publication.
There will be no cancellation.
This verse will simply end.
But please allow for four last lines
without a yelp, a scream or whines.
They're short and peppy, positive, light-hearted.
They have a purpose you will find.
They'll set you straight and clear your mind.
Indeed, they'll take us back to where we started—
Without a bit of hesitation
I express appreciation.
It's a cause for celebration
when one feels an inspiration.

2/23/2024

BEAUTY, INDESTRUCTIBLE, OOPS, SHADOW, SUCCESS

The **beauty** of her plan for **success** was simplicity—**shadow** the **indestructible.** And that she set out to do.

Annette would emulate Margo, who through instinct, foresight, intellect, and energy, had business-wise broken the glass ceiling. Doing so had earned her membership in the Young Presidents Club at the age of 32.

Margo seemed to embody wisdom of the ancients, compassion of a saint, determination of a champion, and the calm of a pastoral pond. Her drive and creativity beyond compare, were exceeded only by her personable demeanor. Everyone with whom she associated was thrilled to do her bidding. By inspiring them, Margo became adored and admired.

Yes, Annette would shadow Margo no matter what it took. Margo was her guiding light.

Time marched on. And so did Margo with Annette right behind her, following, without question, her every step.

Then one evening, Margo quite unexpectedly fell madly in love with Bud. It was a heavenly new experience. And a bit distracting to both Margo and Annette.

Margo managed to keep her life in balance until Bud was struck by a bus and killed.

Margo went to pieces.

Without a guiding light, there could be no shadow. Annette jumped out a 23-story office building window. **Oops!** Make that a first-floor window onto a passing trampoline full of peach pies. As she traveled along, performing pirouettes at the zenith of each bounce, she was cheered by city crowds.

Creative Writing Assignments					NIBBLETS

With the discovery of her popular new talents, she joined a traveling circus and was eventually devoured by a lion.

Can you believe it!

Hmm…

3/16/2024

marc frederic   Creative Writing Assignments

PROFOUND

I can't believe I'm on the fifth hole of Cypress Point golf course in northern California teeing off with world-famous golf professional Tom Watson, who has just hooked his drive into the woods.

Tom Watson doesn't hit bad shots like that. But he just did on this par-five, dog-leg-left fairway bordered by tall pines.

As we explore the area where we saw it enter the forest, there is no ball in sight.

Eventually, Tom locates his ball, making it a *Pro-found* shot. But what happens next is beyond belief. It becomes obvious Tom is familiar with the course. Spotting an opening in the treetops through which bright blue sky can be seen, he takes a full swing with a seven iron and sends the ball through the heart of that space.

It seems to me he was aiming far left of where he should. But that's where Tom's knowledge came in. "The ball should be on the green," he calmly pronounces.

We walk out to the fairway and continue with our caddies along the course. The 493-yard fairway turns uphill to the left. Trudging onward, we finally arrive at the elevated green, which is split-level with the pin on the upper portion.

Sure enough, there's Tom's ball resting on that same upper level, twelve feet from the hole.

When the flag is removed, Tom casually lines up his putt. Then, with a short firm stroke, he puts the ball in motion. We all watch in amazement as it rolls toward the hole in a slight arc and, with a loud clunk, drops into the cup for an eagle.

Now that's what I call profound.

(true story, took place in the 1970's)
4/13/2024

Creative Writing Assignments · NIBBLETS

THE LAST THING I WANTED TO DO WAS TO OPEN THAT DOOR

The last thing I wanted to do was to open that door.

I wasn't afraid of what would come out, I know what's in there—SHOES. A closet full of shoes.

It's a collection of sorts—football cleats, baseball spikes, running shoes, walking shoes, tennis shoes, bowling shoes, dancing shoes, Ferragamo dress shoes, shoes to be worn with a tuxedo. There are slippers and slip-ons, boots for working, boots for riding.

There are shoes of various colors, shoes made of leather, fabric, plastic. Some you lace. Some you don't.

There are shoes worn by the famous—athletes Magic Johnson and Babe Ruth. Shoes owned by the Banzini family tightrope walker. There's even a pair of sparkly red slippers movie star Judy Garland wore in The Wizard of Oz, all purchased at auctions over the years, Oh, and there's a set of Sea Biscuit's horseshoes.

My father collected the famous ones. I used the others. I had been quite an athlete at one time. Never famous enough to be on the lips of children and old ladies throughout the world. I did build a reputation as a fine quarterback of Native American descent but was certainly not as well-known as my father.

My father attended school on our Indian land before earning a college education in the field of electronics. He dreamed of improving our local community. And that he did, becoming famous by providing electricity to our public lavatories. You may have heard of him. He was renowned for being the first man to wire a head for a reservation.

As for the shoes, which were once so important to me, I've not wanted to lay eyes on 'em since a land mine took my feet in Vietnam.

5/11/2024

marc frederic   Creative Writing Assignments

OBSESSION, CREATIVE, SUAVE, GEOMETRY, BUCKET

For years, Ralph had been an average student. Except when it came to math.

Every aspect of the discipline fascinated him. He even questioned why the "e" in mathematics was allotted space when it is rarely pronounced.

To Ralph, space was important. When he was introduced to **geometry**, Ralph became enthralled by the relationship of space, shape, distance, and size.

Inspired, Ralph measured everything. Nothing flat or solid escaped his **obsession**. He labeled himself a geometripath. People referred to him as Geo.

As Ralph matured, so did his interests, which included women. But he continued to interpret everything through the lens of his geometric perspective. Being **creative**, he realized even the most abstract thoughts and images might be represented in geometric terms. And, to his credit, he managed to prove it.

Geo, or Dr. G, as he later became known, never considered himself to be **suave**, but he truly cared for people who, in turn, cared for him. He simply measured and communicated with them differently. His proposal of marriage is a prime example:

> *I thought you one dimensional–*
> *not more than just a line;*
> *then two-dimensional maybe–*
> *a square described you fine.*
> *I came to know your interests*
> *and learned you have more sides–*
> *pentagonal, hexagonal, octagonal surprise!*
> *At last, I grew to love you;*
> *to see not part, but all.*
> *With you so darn well-rounded,*
> *I find I have a ball!*

Creative Writing Assignments								NIBBLETS

Ralph presented this matrimonial invitation along with three gleaming stars, a moon made of green cheese, a well-measured **bucket** of unlimited love, and space for a cottage with a picket fence.

He audibly added, "Please treasure my measure."
To which she responded, "How thrilling! My pleasure!"

4/27/2024

STARGAZING

Looking for a way out of their fenced pen, the five men converse dejectedly. Evening stars fail to catch their attention until one of the men glances skyward and can't seem to look away. He's soon ridiculed as being a useless stargazer. Another man claims, "To me, stargazing is looking at a famous actress."

A groan or two. Their complaints drone on. This time about stargazing.

Overhearing their negative babble, a French gypsy glides from under the tree at the far side of the campfire and, ignoring the fence, calmly addresses them, "*Mes amis*, stargazing eez more than an action, It eez a state of being."

Her concept and subtle charisma draw the men's attention, whisking them into another realm.

"Consider, *s'il vous plaît*, where stars are found—in the heavens, *oui*; but also, as flickers in zee rolling sea, and in zee eyes of lovers. You need not limit yourselves to observing. Meld with stars wherever they're found.

"Tonight, share the wonder of these celestial beauties. They twinkle like diamonds and drip like pearls. Some shoot. Some fall. Some form constellations. A select few are objects of a wish. Those are the realms with which I am most familiar—dreams and blessings, joy and wonder.

"Come, let's mix with these marvels. Float and fly, swoop and soar. Exult in your uniqueness. Appreciate traits you have in common. Delight in curlicues of thought. Enjoy clarity of vision.

"You weel explore. Discover. See love not simply as cotton-candy-pink; cooked eggs as only boiled, fried, or scrambled. Oxygenate or

Creative Writing Assignments   NIBBLETS

pufferize them. Your imaginations weel grant you whatever you wish.

"Feel your inner light glow…sparkle…shine! These limitless ventures are yours to live.

"Push off... Up you go! You're free!"

A fluttering rush. And the pen dissolves.

It was simply composed of cobwebs.

                              6/8/2024

REFLECTION

I wrote about **Reflection**. Had a fine and tender start.
It truly was creative. It fluttered from my heart.
I jotted its beginning without the use of light;
then rose from bed and scribbled three times throughout the night.
I've learned that I must do this, or surely in the dawn,
I'll have no recollection. My golden thoughts are gone.

And so, this morning I arose with smile upon my face.
I sure was glad I had a start that set a lovely pace.
It dealt with the reflections of many things that be,
from love, success, and failure to hate and jealousy.
To sound, it is an echo. A touch reflects a feeling.
A smile brings forth another. So many things appealing.
To wonder, it is marvel. To happiness, it's bliss.
To lips that give, it's taking, in the sweet form of a kiss.
And treating one another with reflection from above,
allows us all to share each day that miracle called love.

But then, I saw the paper on which my words I'd scrawled.
Not one could I decipher. I sat right down and bawled;
for there lay things of beauty now lost in scribbled ink.
And I can't bring them back to life no matter what I think.

I do remember one thing—the way I planned to end it.
It is an axiom of sorts, so no one need defend it.
Whatever you engender, (I've found this to be true),
be it tough or tender, will come right back to you.

6/22/2024

DUSK

Dusk and twilight*, a fleeting measurement of time, a lovely occasion during which light fades to dark. Both imply a time of soft romance or, at least, a pleasant interim in which to settle down, enjoy the day's accomplishments, and anticipate joy and replenishment during the night.

Exactly when dusk begins, is difficult to define. I'm most familiar with doing so at the ocean's edge on the coast of Southern California where I lived for 27 years.

There is a rare and glorious phenomenon that defines to the second, dusk's beginning. It's called *the green flash*. Some people consider it to be a myth, for they've heard about, but never seen it. The flash is real, yet infrequent. When it does occur, it is phosphorescent and takes place just as the sun sinks below the horizon. In fact, the flash is the crest of the sun observed through a perfect combination of air particles. It gleams its glory for two to ten seconds.

It doesn't light up the sky. It just lazes briefly on the horizon like a magic marble and, at times, expands somewhat by flattening out before quickly disappearing. That's when dusk takes over. It's both a pleasant and nostalgic occasion. A beginning and ending of its own.

One looks to the horizon at sunset in anticipation of being graced by the flash's presence. It is a privilege to behold.

---

*Dusk consists of three specific phases measured by the degrees the sun has sunk below the horizon.

Although the green flash is real, its exact association with dusk is false. The first dusk (civil) doesn't take effect until the sun is six degrees below the horizon. Nautical and astronomical dusks follow six additional degrees apart.

Twilights are the periods between sunset and the dusk measurements.

7/6/2024

BLACK AND WHITE

The rainbow's eyelids grew heavy, as its arcs shifted from pastel hues to black and white. It was like watching a psychedelic horse morph into a zebra.

"Neigh," I said, "this is not possible."

Then, as the crescent moon came into view, the rainbow's heart began to pound. It had delicious things to say to this new arrival. Its smooth amorous oration ended with a lascivious wink, causing dusk to cover its face and immediately become night.

After flowing forth, the rainbow's glittering words began to shimmer and transform. Slowly, they broke into letters, which grew to be a galaxy of stars, a Milky Way of sorts. As the sky drank them in, the stars spread out, filling the firmament with a profusion of milk-white twinkles.

The rainbow calmly maintained its position, its white arcs glowing against the black sky. It seemingly had nothing more to say.

Attempting to place the rainbow's words in the order they took before becoming so widely scattered, I listened intently for the past to repeat itself. My patience was rewarded.

I dared not lose such brilliant thoughts by unreliably scribbling through the dark on a piece of paper. So, throwing aside the bedcovers, I rose and strode to my computer.

Despite my precaution, the rainbow's comments escaped. After typing madly, I looked up and realized the computer prints only in black. Every sparkling white word the rainbow had proposed was lost somewhere in the pale background of the monitor's screen.

What to do. What to do...

Creative Writing Assignments   NIBBLETS

Oh! Here comes my tuxedo cat, Louie.

I'll share with him what you've just read. Given his coloring, he may understand all this much better than we do.

6/25/2025

marc frederic — Creative Writing Assignments

THE LAST TIME I…

The last time I meddled with the universe, the results were dramatic.

It started rather innocently. I was in the desert standing next to a medium-sized rock formation. On it, just within reach, there was a lever. And a sign which read "IN CASE OF EMERGENCY, PULL".

The quotation marks around it were superfluous. Or so I thought. So I took a handkerchief from my pocket and wiped them away. With that, the sign became ominous. A command I could not refuse. There was no one to either refute or consult about it.

Of course, there was no apparent emergency either.

I pulled the lever. A subtle steady woooosh ensued. The rock formation was being sucked into a black hole. And so was I, along with everything else. I could tell, for although I was being stretched by the force of the suction, I went in feet first. I saw cacti, rocks, startled lizards, a snake, and all the desert sand follow me in slow motion. Earth was turning inside out and other planets were following it.

The black hole polished off the sun for dessert. But that evidently wasn't enough to satisfy its appetite. Other galaxies followed. The universe was in reverse. The Big Bang was consolidating.

By this time, I had gone from being billions of miles in length (thin as a nano-zing) to being smooshed, packed, compressed, condensed into a mere nothing.

I wish I could say I, and everything else, became a marble in a game being played by giants beyond imagination. But no. We were so small it made the period at the end of this sentence comparable to a world so great it would take eons to explore.

I had been admonished before for meddling with the universe. I should have…

8/12/2024

NIBS INTRO TO
STRONG TASTE

This previously unpublished section
is included for artistic merit.
After serious consideration,
we believe it's a shame not to share it.

If it's too highly seasoned, I as this book,
have two other sections at which you can look.
And, of course, by perusing that two-section act.
you'll ensure that your taste buds remain well intact.

I do think, however, with well-opened mind,
you may savor the flavor of new tastes you find.

Nibs

Strong Taste   marc frederic

WHILE BARBECUING A STEAK

He is very large…a giant of a man.

Whether or not he purposefully stepped on my tiny daughter's foot, I'm not sure. I'm not even sure exactly how he did it. We were standing in line, waiting to enter the school, when it happened.

He seems to neither notice nor care. I ask him to apologize. He will have none of it. My daughter is crying.

I'm insistent! I now have him on the ground. I've got him by the ears. His ears disappear along with the rest of his body, as I stare angrily into his face. His face is round. It has taken the form of a concave dish.

I'm lying on the ground, my face over his, yelling into it. I'm threatening to tell the authorities he stepped on my daughter's foot. But how can I prove such a thing? The man has no feet…no legs…no body. He is just a face in a smooth, round, porcelain dish.

What a short, strange dream! It's one that would upset my wife.

It took place last night. I just remembered and thought I'd capture it while I have the time.

                                             8/25/2008

DUSTY WHITE SPONGE

My only hunt took place on an island of emerald mountains that ran down to be lapped by the sea. The ram I hunted is still magnificent, although its grass-munching days are now someone else's memories. Its surreal death plays my mind like a one-reel, Technicolor, silent movie in slow motion.

From below the top of a grassy knoll, I'm looking upward at the ram through the telescopic sight of a borrowed rifle. The ram's chest is in front of me; its face staring in my direction. Although the creature is thirty yards away, I can feel its curly coat through the lens.

There, before a blue sky laced by occasional strips of cloud, the ram stands, calmly watching me touch it with my eye.

Slowly, the silent movie continues…finger squeezing… *poof*! Finger squeezing… *poof*! Again…again…

Death takes a while to recognize itself. The beast's heavy chest wool simply absorbs bullets as if it were a huge dusty white sponge. It assimilates four invisible metal missiles while the snail-paced action lulls me from adrenaline rush into indifferent observation.

The grassy knoll sits solidly atop the emerald hill smelling lightly of summer. The sponge stands on that knoll displaying an extremely casual attitude. It remains dry and seemingly unconcerned.

Such prolonged nonchalance shocks clouds out of the sky, leaving an expanse of pure azure. But the sponge continues to look at me as if it has nothing to do other than soak up bullets.

Then, it slowly turns, takes four tentative steps, and tumbles heels over head into a deep ravine.

"Cut off its balls!" I shout to my guide who is picking his way down to retrieve the head.

Strong Taste NIBBLETS

The sponge's head now hangs over our bedroom fireplace. Its eyes tell nothing of what took place.

Its balls I devoured a short time after I shot it. Boiled, sliced, and sautéed in butter, they tasted like a chicken gizzard slow-dancing with an abalone. I ate them side by side with a peanut butter and jelly sandwich. They were delicious.

9/6/1987

Reading this vignette 36 years after writing it, I am satisfied by capturing the experience and pleased it was my only hunt. That handsome animal would have been killed regardless of my activity. The herd was being culled to prevent it from overrunning the island. I suppose it beats starving to death.

SCREAMER

Last night in a rustic, island hotel complex, I was startled awake by the screams of a passionate woman being made love to in a nearby cottage.

Seemingly coming out of nowhere, they yanked me into consciousness.

Possibly they were born of moans and heavy breathing but, if so, their parents were nowhere to be heard. The screams seemed to be on their own.

I listened...and listened some more. My breathing quickened as they went on...and on, grew louder...and louder. They mesmerized my ears, raced a few laps around my heart, ran down my stomach, and skidded into my groin where they continued to run in place.

I've never heard anyone scream like that before, let alone made love to someone who does. It definitely added juice to my libido. And from what I'm told, my libido is already awash in a sea of delight.

Today, as I temporarily sit alone at an outdoor café on this small island watching the diners and passersby, I wonder which, if any of them, is the screamer. Is she large or petite, plump or thin, blond, brunette or redheaded, black or white? She must have been somewhat young...but maybe not.

Does she know she screams like that? How could she help but know? Is she an exhibitionist or does she simply lose herself in passion? And how about the man making love to her? I assume it was a man...it could have been another woman... then again, maybe she was by herself...

I imagine making love to a woman who screams with such volume might scare me, at least the first time...not from being the spark that ignites such flaming resonance, but by its proximity. I mean her

Strong Taste NIBBLETS

ululation was not only hot but shrill and loud! It would be stimulating, though…if ever I got used to it.

Just who *was* that screamer I listened to last night? Actually, it's exciting not knowing. Every woman I see harbors the potential.

The fact of the matter is I want my lover to hear her tonight. Last night, after a long and beautiful session of our own, she fell asleep, cuddled against me, her head on my chest.

She says she heard nothing but my heartbeat. I'm not sure of that…when she awoke a bit later, it was all our libidos could do to keep from drowning.

9/10/1988

marc frederic   **Strong Taste**

GOBBLING GARY

Gobbling Gary eats his fill
at each and every sitting.
His bros and sisters soon fall ill
from Gary's lack of quitting.
He snatches rolls, inhales the soup.
And when he grabs for meat,
exuberance combined with greed
oft make him leave his feet!
A shambles he makes of the dining room.
He ruins many a table,
depriving his starving relatives
of all that he is able.

His parents finally chain him back
securely in his chair,
enabling siblings and themselves
to calmly eat their share.
Gary rants and Gary raves.
Gary drools and slobbers.
He pulls and strains against the links.
He then breaks loose and clobbers
his brothers, sisters, cousins, aunts,
even his mother and dad,
till there are none to tell the sum
of all that he has had.

A roast he tosses in the air
and catches in his mouth.
It is but three short seconds till
that meat is headed south!
He funnels carrots, corn and peas
with such apparent skill and ease
into the tunnel called his throat.
He then looks 'round and seems to gloat.
The bread and jams are next to go,

Strong Taste NIBBLETS

      then cakes and pies that he loves so.
      He bothers not with spoons or forks.
      He swallows bottles with their corks.
      He downs a candle with its moth.
      And now he eats the table cloth!

      A pause to burp…but he can't stop,
      so next he eats the table top!
      Then legs and chairs (they taste so grand).
      With nothing left, he eats his hand,
      which seems to cause him no alarm,
      so he continues up his arm
      and down his chest and waist and legs.
      By now he's down to the very last dregs.
      He smiles and, with his one arm left,
      wipes his mouth with stroke quite deft.
      His last appendage he then eats…
      the hand and fingers taste like sweets.
      He thinks, "Before I go to bed,
      just one more bite…and eats his head.

MORAL—It's OK to be messy as long as you clean up afterward.

I believe this poem was inspired by having read during childhood,
SLOVENLY PETER, a graphic book of harsh, rhyming fables.
I believe the same about my poem entitled Swampmoss Mose
(printed in *Who Put the "P" in Pneumonia*).

late 1970's

HER MOTHER'S *ILLNESS*

The woman's mother is quite ill. *The illness* has grown over the years. The mother wears her *illness* like a body mask—disguising, concealing the twisted psychopath inside. *The Illness* is rather talented. It can portray many forms—Diabetes... Osteoporosis... Congestive Heart Failure... Abusive Behavior.

Her Mother's Illness has played a major role in the woman's life. Over the years *The Illness* has worked its way up from minor stagehand to extra to supporting actor to the lead. *Her-Mother's-Illness* now looms large as a major star. Its billboards are plastered on the walls of everyday conversations. Clips of accidental falls and minor strokes are intermittently shown throughout the family members' dreams.

Being a "loyal daughter," the woman continues to serve *The Illness* as an attentive audience. She could, like her brother, ignore *The Illness* and leave the theater. A number of dimly lit *EXIT* signs clearly mark the way. Yet, such a thought is, to her, but a fleeting wish. Even if her thoughts were more tangible, they would most likely be squelched as a rude and raucous heckler, an interloper to be shouted down and snubbed by others in the audience. For, as we all know, *the show must go on.*

If, however, enough people recognize *The Illness* for what it is and silently leave the theater, there will no longer be an audience. And what good is a star performer without an audience to admire it?

The family has, indeed, arranged to skip out on some future performances. They have, in essence, scalped their season tickets by hiring a full-time nurse. The nurse has lived with the woman's mother for months.

Still, her mother's emotional exactions on her daughter are relentless, debilitating, and intentionally demoralizing. They turn life's many normal obligations into a surreal concoction being swirled in an

Strong Taste

electric blender. Ingredients: daily phone calls…subtle worry…bill paying… subtle worry…food & prescription pick-ups…subtle worry…cancelled insurance policy… major worry…ambulance trips…heavy duty concern laced with anger at her mother's continual physical carelessness and help-rejecting-complaints! There is no lid on the blender. Life keeps adding to the mixture. The blender is overflowing, spilling bilious green burps onto already rancid carpet! The blender has no switch to turn it off! How will this mess ever come to an end?

The daughter lies 'neath her bed covers in the dark, her emotions shrunken and frazzled like over-fried strips of bacon. The bacon is in dire need of a vacation. Luckily, long-awaited "tropic plans" are about to come to fruition…

Five hours of wings over water and forty-eight hours of rejuvenation later (*Ahhhhh*), the daughter now lies in warm shade 'neath a swaying palm at the edge of rhythmic, turquoise, liquid bliss. Relaxed and plumped up like a papaya on the breakfast table of a breezy lanai, she's now ripe and open…deliciously juicy…looking forward to being tasted.

6/23/2002

marc frederic **Strong Taste**

SIGHTS & SMELLS

Thirty-five years ago, the tour of a Texas slaughterhouse left its indelible impression on my mind. The images still hang in a bizarre collection on the walls of my memory. They begin outside the building with cattle moving single file through a chute to a literal dead end. Confronted by a cement wall, the lead steer halts, as a barred gate closes behind it. A man with an air-powered, captive bolt pistol leans over the chute and fires against the animal's skull.

As the unconscious steer collapses heavily on the floor, the side wall rotates vertically, scooping it out of the chute onto a cement slab. A sharp, metal hook is jammed through its back leg between hoof and tendon. Up it is hoisted, a huge hunk of stretching meat, hanging head down on the start of its ghoulish journey through the plant. The animal maintains its place in line as it pushes through the two large, black rubber, flap-like doors that swallow it with ease. Before us, the scooping-hooking-hoisting process continues.

It is now our turn, as visitors, to enter the building. We do so by climbing a flight of metal, grated stairs to a small door far above us. It is obvious from our climb that we will be looking down at the cattle from our vantage point inside the building. But, as we enter, the visual image temporarily loses consciousness. It has been smacked hard by an overwhelmingly strong odor.

The steers' throats have been slit. Blood, which minutes ago coursed through their large, bovine bodies, now pours onto a powerfully heated floor. All sides of this horizontal griddle tilt to the center. The crimson blood flows strongly, splashes brightly; then, cooked and coagulated, rolls darkly downward in tiny balls that will become chicken feed. The floor serves as a mammoth funnel, collecting the fried blood somewhere below its center; but not before its pungent odor permeates our clothes, body tissue, and souls. It is all we can do to keep from gagging. Luckily, our olfactory nerves are soon overwhelmed by the intense smell and lose their ability to pass it on to our brains.

Strong Taste

As the nerves become ineffective, intrigue takes over. I follow along the catwalk over the cooking blood until descending stairs usher me to ground level. I am now looking up, fascinated by the methodical dissection of these beasts. Moving along the disassembly line, their hides are vertically sliced, hooked along the edges, and automatically peeled from their slowly turning bodies, exposing mountains of raw flesh. Knives are wielded, organs removed. No parts go to waste.

The strangest, most surreal image is an endless line of hanging, horned skulls. Stripped of skin and flesh, eyeballs still filling their sockets, the bloody, white skulls glisten under bright light. Each is separated by its giant, hanging tongue. The odor of the frying blood river wafts casually in the distance.

Recognition of that blood smell deserted my mind a day or two after my visit. But not soon enough. Within the plush steak house where we dined following the slaughterhouse tour, the stench was a nightly guest. To this day, that same smell must emanate mildly from every steak I barbecue, but I can no longer recognize the odor that originally caused my stomach to roil.

It's more difficult to hold on to a smell than a picture...harder to hang it on a wall...even the wall of one's mind. I dated a beautiful, young lady in college. She wore Tigress perfume. Although I recall the dramatic effect it had on me, I cannot remember the aroma. But her nipples...to this day I can see her lovely erect nipples. And her delicate facial features I will never forget.

Sights and smells. How delightful it is that we need not separate them...that we can so easily combine them with touches, tastes and sounds. But what's more, is our ability to stir into that magnificent mix, "memory"—the miraculous preservative, which enables us to embrace past experiences at our leisure, and rob time of any fabricated importance we may have given it.

5/23/2009

MELLOW MUSES

Never before, have I realized how intensely my life has been driven by testosterone. Not that it has been unpleasant, but I have ceaselessly experienced a nagging compulsion…a constant state of sexual anticipation…one step away from actual arousal.

Over years I have learned to appreciate and control this muleteer of emotion.

I'm now "on hormones." Designed to chemically castrate, their job is to reduce the malignant tumors in my prostate gland. These imported hormones are expected to eliminate the testosterone on which the cancer feeds. Evidently, they are working. For the first time in my memory, other than immediately following orgasm, I am sexually mellow…not indifferent, as yet, but no longer "driven."

I now wonder if this new situation will affect my creativity. I've often corralled and harnessed that wild "push factor," guiding it toward the paper where it has quickly taken root and portrayed itself in blossoming colorful gardens of unexpected thoughts. What pleasure I have derived from its many expressions!

I somehow doubt my creativity will cease. I believe I will now simply be abetted by leisurely muses who stroke me with a subtle touch as opposed to prompting me with pricking darts or launching their stimuli in the form of inspirational arrows.

And with that, I suddenly feel it…a gentle nudge in the form of words that tickle my fancy… "My libido is incognito."

Just as I expected…very *amusing*.

So far, so good! And my wife now likes the way I "talk to her even more." She wants to "do lunch!"

2/1/2012

Strong Taste

"Don't answer that!"

"Don't answer that!"

The phrase reverberated in my mind.

My lawyer had been adamant about my remaining silent not only at the scene, but on my way to the police station.

I had called her as soon as I realized the circumstances might incriminate me. I wanted advice. Needed it desperately. There were still guns pointed at me from when I was allowed to gingerly remove my cell phone from my coat pocket.

The police had read me my rights. I had asked to make one call.

Thank God Phyllis had been available. Well, at 3:00 a.m. that was to be expected. I told her I wasn't sure where I was and the police wanted to know what I was doing there. That's when I received her advice.

I told her I was in the "great room" of a home. Men and women in various stages of dress, some nude, were everywhere – on couches, chairs, countertops, the floor. One lady sat in an oddly structured basket that hung from the ceiling just above a sofa upon which a man was lying on his back.

They were all dead. Not shot. Not beaten or stabbed. Maybe drugged. It was surreal. Disgusting. Sick.

I didn't want to be there. Couldn't understand why I was. I might have been in shock.

Phyllis said she'd meet me at the station.

The police asked me a few questions on the way. I couldn't seem to remember much except my home address, which turned out to be next door to the house with the strange scene.

All I could remember clearly was Phyllis's adamant advice—Don't answer that! Don't answer anything!

2/22/2018

marc frederic **Strong Taste**

JOYS OF SEX IN WRITTEN FORM

Unchecked passion is a world of vowel sounds.

Passion with perimeters is longer-lasting, more fulfilling and complete—

Both lust and love-making can be creative, break rules, take you places you've never been. In writing that's called poetic license. In life it's simply marvelous.

Enjoy the contrast…

>I don't want to fall in love
>just into bed.
>I want to suck your
>toes
>from the earlobes down;
>trade facial expressions
>and throaty sounds;
>slip and slide,
>buck and ride,
>'cause
>Damn it, woman, you sizzle!
>   (1975)

versus…

>Your drinks and subtle touches
>stir my passion; but you,
>not wishing to be hurried,
>read poetry to me
>and revel in the playground of romance.

>It's your lips that amaze me now.
>Through their soft shapeliness
>float soothing southern tones
>that caress my impatience
>and bring joy to my heart.

Strong Taste
NIBBLETS

I listen.
And, in turn,
I read to you—
my understanding enhanced a thousand-fold.

With ears bathed in tenderness,
senses relaxed, yet ripe,
we turn to other pleasures—
from delightful dalliance
                      to selfless giving
                to passionate taking!
Together we soar 'round spiraling peaks
and glide through lapping valleys
until,
emotions melding with one another,
we are overtaken by Contentment
who catches us in her net of love
and gently returns us
to the palm of your bed.

As we lie here in oneness
I know not
where you stop and I begin.

After a bit
you leave me for your bath;
time and space
blend with multicolored stars.

Later
as I slip softly
to and from my dreams,
you gently lift my arm
and snuggle kitten-like to my side.
Your perfume is my bedsheet;
my strength becomes yours.
                          (1975)

4/13/2017

marc frederic **Strong Taste**

MOMENT OF EMPATHY

Driving slowly through the afternoon on a residential desert street, I've just passed a cotton-tail rabbit that refuses to move from the center of the asphalt.

It's as if it is hypnotized or in a daze.

Suddenly, ten yards farther down the street, I see its flattened partner.

How very sad.

5/27/2018

THE DUMBEST THING I'VE EVER DONE

I hate recalling this event. Its possible consequences make me cringe, feel hollow, as if I have been disemboweled by a large, striated hunting knife.

Our family is vacationing in Kawaii. My four-year-old daughter faces forward on my lap as we slide down a smooth volcanic lava path covered with fast-flowing water. We're being swiftly propelled toward a ten-foot natural waterfall.

I've explained to her that, just before we hit the dark pool below, I'm going to raise her above my head so she won't dip too far underwater. I'll then resurface and she can hold on to my neck while I swim to the black lava shore.

Little do I realize, by extending my arms upward I will morph into a spear and plunge much deeper than anticipated. I recognize this fact too late to slow my descent through the never-ending depth. In a time-eating struggle, I break the surface to see my precious child's raised arm slowly sinking. Six feet away. Just out of reach!

Gripped by panic, I lunge toward her, sucking water into my windpipe just before my hand closes around her tiny wrist. I can't breathe! I'm choking! But I pull my daughter up so that her head is above water. She clings to my neck. Coughing furiously, I tread water. My daughter becomes a vice-like, living collar.

Help!

Finally gaining control of mind and body, I barely manage to dog-paddle my way to the jagged shore, my daughter safely in tow.

Even today, while describing that potential loss, I can feel the knife eviscerating me. Never have I set a more foolish plan in motion.

12/1/2016

SURPRISE!

***SURPRISE**!*

That's what the metal sign said in large, golden script. Above that, in slightly smaller letters, was WELCOME TO. And below everything, in small lowercase print, was "population 53".

The sign was located just beyond the end of a dirt road that twisted through the swamp like a huge water moccasin. A patch of damp sand, roughly the size of three melted elephants, lay between the road's end and the sign.

"What's it all mean?" she asked, looking out through the windshield of the bright red jeep after it slid to a halt.

"I'm not sure," he answered, "but I'm glad we came to a stop when we did. That looks like quicksand."

"What do we do now?"

"Darned if I know."

"I don't like surprises," she told him.

"Well, it doesn't look like much can surprise us here."

Just then the ground behind them began to silently lift, tilting toward the damp sand.

They scrambled out as the jeep rolled forward and began to sink. The road tilted more steeply.

"What's happening?" she screamed.

Neither of them could find a thing to hold to prevent their following the now submerged jeep. At first, they slid on their backs, trying to

Strong Taste   NIBBLETS

stop their descent by digging the heels of their feet and palms into the slanted road. Next, they turned over to try clawing their way upward.

That failing, they slid. into the quicksand where they flailed.in desperation.

As the sand slowly choked their screaming mouths, then covered their bulging eyes, the small print number on the sign smoothly changed from 53 to 55.

3/12/2020

MONEY, BOOK, END, PUNCTUATION, HAPPINESS

The **end** is simply another beginning.

It's the continuing evolution of our souls. That's what it's about. Not **money**. Not just **happiness**. It's a never-ending **book**—the story of this life and the transition to another. And another. And another.

My latest beginning took place in our retirement community's 25-meter, indoor pool. I was swimming my daily half hour of laps. I've always enjoyed swimming. It improves my physical and mental state. I use the time to memorize or silently quote verse I've written. It's fun. Time flies.

I thought it unusual no one else was in the pool, then realized it was almost dinner time. Something bothered me about being alone.

Our community is located directly over the San Andreas fault. Earthquake territory. I thought about the glass sections in the ceiling of the building. Would they survive a mammoth jolt? Would they shatter in a spray of chards? Or would large plates splash into the water? I've considered it before, but always dismissed the thought.

Until now.

As my right arm extends in mid-stroke, I hear a loud cracking sound. The water roils as if a giant has jumped into the pool. I see the tiles in the pool's floor ripple and break. As I watch objectively, a sheet of glass painlessly slices through my shoulder joint, separating my arm from my body. It reminds me of satisfaction I derive from slicing a roasted chicken's drumstick from its thigh with a single, surgeon-like swipe of the blade.

My arm slowly sinks through crimson water. It wears the silver identification bracelet that will tell anyone who finds it I'm on a blood thinner.

A rather dramatic end to this life. But I've had a ball.

And so my lives continue—an ever-lasting series of wonders interspersed with assorted **punctuation** marks.

4/29/2023

REQUEST FOR REVIEW

Thank you for nibbling the contents of this book. If you've enjoyed the experience, I'd appreciate your writing a short review on amazon.com books. Enter *Nibblets by marc frederic* in the search area, click on the book cover, scroll to the bottom of the page – to the Customer Review area. Click the *Write a customer review* button under the rating chart to open the Create Review page.

If you favor the GENERAL PIECES section, you will enjoy my book LOOKING AT LIFE THROUGH MY LEFT EAR.

If you found CREATIVE WRITING ASSIGNMENTS to be tastier, my book entitled A TOUCH OF CLASS is comprised completely of such pieces.

You may also wish to visit my website, www.worldofwhimsy.com, where you will find descriptions of my other books and information about the World of Whimsy and me.

marc frederic

NIBBLETS

INDEX

ACKNOWLEDGEMENT iv
WELCOME FROM MARC v
HELLO from Nibs vi
NIBS INTRO TO GENERAL PIECES 1
NIBS INTRO TO CREATIVE WRITING ASSIGNMENTS 180
NIBS INTRO TO STRONG TASTE 284
CREATIVE WRITING ASSIGNMENTS
   A Most Exciting Thing 190
   A Penny For Your Thoughts 229
   And, Just Like That… 236
   Art, Asparagus, Circus, Eagle, Spain 187
   Balloons, Random, Suitcase, Reunion, Cowboy 238
   Beauty, Indestructible, Oops, Shadow, Success 270
   Black And White 280
   Blame It On The Ice 223
   Blank Page Possibilities 222
   Consolidated, Bubble, Definitely, Cascading, Mesmerized 244
   Curmudgeon, The 265
   Decision 248
   Dog, Cat, Child, Woman, Man 200
   Don't Answer That! 297
   Dusk 279
   Five Memories 258
   From The Giant's Point Of View 261
   He Ended The Conversation 182
   Honey, I'm Home. 204
   How Would I Like To Be Remembered? 253
   I Can Hardly Wait For Tomorrow To Come 215
   I Don't Understand What Happened 225
   I Expected It To Be Hot 208
   I Had No Idea What It Meant 252
   I Made An Interesting Discovery Today (Claudette) 232
   I Made An Interesting Discovery Today (Salamanders) 234
   I Remember (Roscoe) 226
   I Saw What You Did 181
   I Stopped Dead In My Tracks 188

marc frederic

I Told Myself Not To Panic	192
Impulsbot	254
Inspiration	268
It Was A Night I'll Never Forget	202
It Was The Last Thing I Expected	239
It's A Miracle	207
Knots	228
Last Thing I Wanted To Do Was To Open That Door, The	273
Magic…	266
Missing It	260
Mysteries	198
Mystery Solved	240
New Year Resolutions	191
Obsession, Creative, Suave, Geometry, Bucket	274
Popsicle, Relationship, Safari, Oysters, Serendipitous	230
Prepare For An Emergency Landing	212
Prized Possession	237
Profound	272
Proposal	209
Reflection	278
Remembering	197
Seasons Of Life	216
Secret Love	264
Shared Adventure	184
She Turned Her Back On Me	220
Shut Up!	210
Stargazing	276
Suggestion, Sexy, Deadline, Mandatory, Metaphysical	218
The Last Time I…	282
There's A First Time For Everything	242
Things Have Changed	206
Things I Will Never Forget	194
Tragedy	214
Unintended, Champagne, Candles, Celebration, Hangover	249
Well, What Do Ya Know!	262
What Would I Do Without…?	256
What?	251
What's Important To Me?	186
Who Said That?	250

NIBBLETS

Whose Bright Idea Was This? 224
Wind Blew Out Our Last Match, The 243
You're Not Going To Drink That, Are You? 246

GENERAL PIECES

90 Minutes 3
A Laughing Matter 144
A Matter Of Timing 22
Amazed 52
Appreciation 44
Beauty And The Beach 91
Becoming A Turtle 174
Believe It Or Not 116
Beyond Conversation 165
Beyond The Five 152
Black Cylindrical Beauty 157
Bored 5
Brickle 4
Bush Cave 14
Buzz, The 94
Caller 167
Carnivalesque Charisma 80
Cat Tail 150
Coffee Mating 17
Complicated Banking 137
Confusion In Paradise 32
Crashed 54
Creating A Flower 43
Curious 178
Demise Of Cursive, The 170
Denali, The 146
Desert In July 100
Dhargo 110
Doodleberry Tree, The 154
Door Dash Dummy 6
Dream Time 2
Elusive Thought 153
Eyes Have It, The 58
Feeling Dusty 59
Filing 169

Filling Out Forms	12
First Reading	86
Focal Point	46
For This, I Am Thankful	136
Garbage Collector	81
Gathering Memories	161
Gaylan – Celebration Of Life	148
Half A Glass Of Water	85
Hangerville	27
Having Just Read A Poem	173
High-Definition Living Room	78
Hollywood Book Festival 2007	74
I Feel Like Writing	158
I Like It When The Ocean Winks At Me	84
I Never Knew You Were An Angel	149
I Used To Think I Know Myself	45
I've Melded With The Universe	10
Idea, The	1
Impressions During A South African Safari	89
Incongruity	92
Inkwell Productions	164
Istanbul, The Lady In Gray	98
Istanbul's "Egyptian" Bazaar (Market)	99
It Keeps The Polar Bears Away	132
It's Pleasant On The Patio	122
Little Boy At The Park	118
Living Here	104
Lost	126
Love Mirrors	70
Lovely Gift	141
Magic Nurse	124
Massage	38
Mental Exercise	130
Missing	140
Mistaken Identity	171
My Bed Misses You	21
My Favorite Gift	135
Night Before Africa, The	88
Not Enough Time To Forget	56

NIBBLETS

Old Address Book, An	156
Old Skin	139
Painting At Lake Como	42
Perfect	72
Phenomenon	69
Plant	114
Plenty To Go Around	64
Power Walk	66
Pre-Autographing Benny's, Jenny's, And Denny's Pets	172
Question Of Wonder	166
Radio Wave	37
Recognized	96
Relishing Words	138
Reminder	8
Return Of The Mallards	160
Rosebush	13
Sandy Dreams	82
Scuba Diving In Cozumel	29
Sea, The	28
Seascape	176
Sharing	162
She's Back	168
Sheets Aren't All That's New, The	79
Small Reassuring Story	102
Soft Shots	60
Somehow In Her Misty Mind	7
Something Really Important	18
Sporting Intangible Wings	155
Summer Camp	16
Sunsational	47
Switzer Learning Center	26
Take A Bite	20
This Time Around	30
Tomorrow's The Day	121
Toni Canucci's Time Machine	48
Two More Beautiful Leaves	101
Unbalanced	120
View, The	34
Wading While Waiting	83

Warm And Cozy Places 125
Where Are You? 109
Whizzing My Way Through Korea 40
You Grace Me With Emotional Milk And Honey 142
REQUEST FOR REVIEW 305
STRONG TASTE
    Dumbest Thing I've Ever Done, The 301
    Dusty White Sponge 286
    Gobbling Gary 290
    Her Mother's *Illness* 292
    Joys Of Sex In Written Form 298
    Mellow Muses 296
    Moment Of Empathy 300
    Money, Book, End, Punctuation, Happiness 304
    Screamer 288
    Sights & Smells 294
    Surprise! 302
    While Barbecuing A Steak 285

Made in the USA
Columbia, SC
31 August 2024